WARLORD'S OATH

LEGENDS OF KILRHINN BOOK 1

MIRA GRACEN

To G.J.—
Four years later and you still inspire me.
Thank you.

CHAPTER 1

*G*etting caught wasn't in Freya's plans.

All she wanted was to buy some starbread, a delicious chocolate-layered pastry that had fast become her favorite in this city, and now she'd been spotted.

"Look who I found," the Kilrhian sneered, his dark purple eyes fixed on her. "A *Lhianne.*" They found out what she was. She had worked to remain inconspicuous for far too long, but it looked like her luck had finally ran out.

Behind him were the imposing faces of his comrades, and on their breastbones, an insignia of a lion, two daggers, and a deep forest-green jewel. Freya didn't recognize which Family it belonged to.

She thought she hid her tracks well. It turned out there was a second enemy she hadn't accounted for—the one that had once sought to annihilate her people, in a battle for land and power. He raised his hand, trying to grab her.

She ran.

Instinct screamed at her to move—she'd learned never to question it. She pushed herself, pumping her legs faster than she could ever remember doing. She sucked in more air to fill her lungs.

Oh God.

Kilrhinns were deadly. They had the strength, agility, and keen eyesight that made them exceptional warriors. Large, powerfully built statures hadn't affected their speed at all. They were dangerous enemies to make.

If it were a test of speed alone, they had her beat, but Freya had committed the layout of the streets to memory. When you needed an escape plan, you had to. Even more so in enemy territory, where you had to be familiar in navigating it to survive.

And memorize, she did. She had done so in every spare moment for the past three months. Because knowing every little nook and cranny gave you every advantage.

She saw it clearly in her mind—turn left and it was where Klein, her new friend, sold large pots outside his house. Big pots could be good for cover. Then beyond that, further ahead, were the markets. It was a good area to get lost in the crowds and make her escape. *If* she could escape. Her feet caught on something on the ground, nearly tripping her—small moonstones the kids outside used to play, along with the chalk they'd drawn on the ground.

She turned left, finding Klein's house, and slipped into the small space in between two stone houses. She would have to leave soon, and she couldn't even say goodbye to her new friends. Her heart sank to the pit of her stomach, despair turning into a deep ache. Where would she go?

She heard a loud yell from behind her, the unmistakable voice of the Kilrhinn who had first found her.

No matter. She slipped into a small opening in the bottom of a wall where the bricks had come loose and crumbled. She had tested it before, and it was perfect for someone her size.

When she saw him run past, she waited. She poked her head out, seeing him disappear at the end of the alley. She slowly stepped out of her hiding place, patting away dust and debris. Careful to check that he hadn't hung around, she ran in the same direction. She eyed the vibrant markets as she drew closer. Here, everything was loud. People screamed for low prices, bargain deals. She smelled the alluring fragrance of flowers and ripe fruit. Peaches, sweet nectarines—they were all lined up, filling the boxes to the brim. One time, she caught a scuffle between two shop owners over "stealing" a customer. She found it all oddly entertaining.

"Rav! Other side!" she heard a Kilrhinn yell.

She nearly tripped over a box of peaches.

Run. Don't look back.

But she had to know how far of a lead she had. She spared a look behind her. Her eyes widened in surprise. An arm's reach away, a dark-haired tattooed man grinned at her, the dark slash of his brows menacing.

"Caught—" His grip slipped when she ducked down, twisting away from his clutches.

She kicked his legs. He swore.

She wasn't as strong as them, but her father made sure she wasn't helpless, either.

She rounded the corner, nearly slipping on the wet floor. A blond-haired man came at her, a little over six-feet tall and deadly calm. She saw an empty tub of water and flung it at her blond pursuer. He stared at her in shock just as she took that opportunity to make her escape. She ran over some boxes, and red apples toppled over. Guilt crept in, but she continued to run.

A hand grabbed her clothes, pulling her back. She thought she heard something rip from behind her. Unfortunately for her, her tactic to slip away only worked once. Surprise unhanding only worked so far. The apples had slowed her down.

Freya tried to pull herself free, accidentally kicking over a barrel of red liquid. Grape juice.

A cart barreled towards the aisle adjacent to her, someone pushing it fast. A woman screamed from afar. A child stood in the middle of the aisle, a small boy of around four. Freya didn't think. Her heart leapt in her chest, but she jerked herself from her captor's grip. She was lucky the cart distracted him, too. She ran, pushing the boy out of the way, as she narrowly escaped getting hit. The cart zoomed past them. Beside her, the boy started crying. Freya sighed in relief. He was safe.

The next thing she knew, strong arms gripped her biceps, locking her hands behind her back. She cried out, unable to twist herself free. She struggled against his vicelike grip. God, he was strong. A quick glance showed that he was the tattooed, dark-haired man. He released a triumphant cry, his voice booming. "I caught her!"

She should've known she could never outrun a Kilrhinn.

And again, she wondered where she would go now. She couldn't go back home. No, she couldn't even call it home anymore. And with those thoughts, where did she belong?

To think all she wanted was to buy some starbread.

* * *

"WILL YOU STOP MOVING?" her captor growled. He was getting annoyed at her. Good. She didn't like being tied much either. Freya stopped struggling momentarily, assessing the situation. *Calm. Stay calm.*

"Rav, I think you're bleeding," the blond guy said, clearly amused. Somehow, her captor, apparently named Rav, had a small cut that ran across his forehead. She winced. She didn't even know how he got that. It couldn't have been her fault.

Rav glared at him. If looks could kill, the blond Kilrhinn would've been dead twice over. "Yeah? You looked at yourself yet?" He stepped closer to take a sniff, and his expression scrunched up in disgust. "What the hell did she throw at you?" Now that Rav mentioned it, he did smell a little fishy —literally.

The blond guy's smile turned into a scowl. Well, she had soaked him in a bucket of... something. She was lucky she was still alive.

He only flashed his teeth at her dangerously. "I'm looking forward to interrogation."

Oh hell. Not interrogation. She went pale, fighting against the ropes they tied her in. It had started to chafe her wrists, but panic made her stop thinking.

"You act as if the world is ending if we'd caught you." It was the guy who had initially found her that had spoken. With his tanned skin and watchful eyes, he crouched down to meet her panicked gaze. His large boot kicked the side of her thigh. She gasped in pain. "Do you speak, Lhianne?" he asked her. She didn't answer in stubborn protest. "Do you have a voice? Or is all you know to run?" he continued to taunt her.

"Enough, Galen," the blond said. He eyed her with great interest. His eyes flickered to a curious pale yellow color. *He isn't pure Kilrhinn,* Freya thought. "She isn't going anywhere. Soon enough, she'll speak."

* * *

FROM THE INFORMATION Freya caught from the three Kilrhinns earlier, she knew she was going to be taken captive to travel with them. They spoke to her in Universal, but amongst themselves, they spoke in Kilrhinn. She could both speak and understand their language—but they didn't need to know that.

Her father taught her to speak in Kilrhinn. She was taught their language. Their customs.

"Why do I need to know this?" she remembered asking him.

"There may come a time you need to understand our kind. Perhaps you'd live among other Kilrhinns."

He had been teasing at the time, but for the past few months, she'd lived among them in secret.

She understood now. The more she knew, the more equipped she became at dealing with the Kilrhinns. At learning about herself. And she was grateful for the knowledge.

She wasn't sure what she could say to them that wouldn't dig her a deeper hole. She had gotten the job here in Maranthe because of sheer luck. Mr. Jenkins and his wife at the tailor shop were kind enough to take her in when she needed a job, and they didn't ask questions. She didn't know what fate awaited her. She only knew that it wouldn't be a good one.

Her train of thought drew to a halt—the horses had finally stopped.

* * *

"KANE? What happened to you? You're soaked." A slim woman addressed the blond Kilrhinn. Freya studied him. His hair was tousled, with high cheekbones, and eyes that were far too sharp and observant. Right now his lips were upturned in displeasure. The woman's confusion would have made Freya laugh, if Freya wasn't tied up. The woman's hair was braided all the way down her back, and she observed Freya curiously. She made no secret of it, either. Then she sniffed, looked at the blond apparently named Kane, and wrinkled her nose. "You stink."

"Shut up," he muttered. He walked past, dragging Freya, who followed along reluctantly. He pointed to a large tan-colored tent. "You'll stay here."

He pushed her a little roughly inside the flap of the tent. He left her then, but she was too busy gawking at what she saw inside. A makeshift table with some small glass bottles. Stacks of paper. Boxes. Lots of boxes. She wondered what were inside those. But then her eyes were drawn to the log, sitting near the center. She made her way there clumsily.

Someone cleared his throat from behind her. Freya froze. She thought she was alone. Of course she wouldn't go unsupervised. She was dragged to sit at the log, and she almost wept at how the ropes chafed her wrists even more.

And not for the first time, she wondered if her day could get any worse.

* * *

"You were working on Vhenn Bradis land. Did you know that, Lhianne?" The man who had dragged her to the log wore a stern look as he questioned her. Forehead wrinkled in disapproval, he had beady eyes and dark spiked hair. She thought he wore that style to make him look taller and seem more intimidating. He didn't seem as tall as the three who had caught her.

The name rang a bell, and it had to be one of the seven Kilrhinn Families, judging from the way they were dressed. Boots made of fine leather, armor that glinted in the sun.

She met his gaze evenly, defiant. It had been Lhianne this, Lhianne that. It was growing tiresome. "I have a name."

"And what is your name, Lhianne?"

"Freya."

"You don't have permit to work here," he continued gruffly.

"No," she admitted.

His eyes narrowed, suspicious. "And what would you be doing here, without a permit? Aren't you aware Lhiannes need one?"

"I was making some clothes." She didn't need a permit, because she wasn't using magic. In any other case, it wouldn't be much of an issue—but this land was apparently considered the Vhenn Bradis Family's. Maybe they were stricter.

He blinked. "I—I beg your pardon?" he sputtered.

Someone pulled the tent's flap open. Her three pursuers walked in. Her captor, Rav, glared at her. Kane looked curious, but he remained quiet. Galen was a mask of calm. It was terrifying to see their tall, imposing figures, entering one after the other, as if they were about to inflict some sort of grim judgement. Was she going to die?

"We'll take over from here, Ignas." Galen dismissed her interrogator with a flick of his hand.

Ignas opened his mouth as if to argue further, but seeing the look on Galen's face, he left swiftly without another word.

Galen nodded at her. "So you finally speak."

"Is he okay?" Freya asked, remembering the boy who had nearly been hit by the cart.

Galen raised a brow. "Who?"

"The boy. From the markets."

He frowned. "He's fine."

Okay. He wasn't going to reveal anything more. She met their gazes evenly. "I wasn't using magic. I was making clothes for people."

"You expect us to believe you were making clothes for people," Kane said.

She didn't know how to make them understand, and her

frustration grew. She couldn't knit. She learned to. She couldn't do embroideries. She learned that, too.

"Yes," she simply said. Would they believe her?

Rav shook his head, at a loss for words. "A Lhianne, working at the tailor's," he spat. "Ridiculous."

Galen went silent, crossing his arms and watching her like a hawk.

Why? Why was it ridiculous not to use any magic? And if she had, why had they always expected the worst? Her nails bit into her palm. The sins of other Lhiannes were not her own.

"You'll tell us what you're doing here," he demanded.

She shook her head. "Would it matter?" Her voice turned hoarse. They didn't seem to want to believe her. They would simply cast her out anyway, and she didn't want to give them the satisfaction of begging. Kilrhinns were known to be ruthless.

Rav pulled her hair in his hand and she gasped in pain. "You're right. It wouldn't." He narrowed his eyes. "Who are you working for?"

"No one," she snapped. He tugged a bit harder, gauging her honesty. When she didn't relent, he abruptly released her. He started to pace. She could tell he wasn't satisfied with her answer.

"You caused a ruckus at the marketplace," Galen stated.

Freya hung her head low, embarrassed. Those were people's livelihoods. Her survival instinct had kicked in and she had been so focused on running free. Now she had to face the consequences.

He smiled grimly. "The cost for repair... Two thousand silvers."

Her face lost all blood. *Two thousand?* There was no way she could pay them that much.

"But you don't have the money to pay for that, do you?"

Rav said. "Should have thought of that before you ran from us." What she thought he meant was—*you should have thought of that before you kicked my legs.*

"What will you do to me?" she breathed out, almost afraid to ask. Fear made her tremble, but she was determined not to let it rule her.

"I'm glad you asked," Kane said, his smile growing wider. His purple eyes frosted over like ice, glinting from the light. "You'll stay with us, until you give us some *real* answers." His words, softly and casually delivered, sounded ominous, sealing her fate. And that was how Freya, daughter of Kilrhinn and Lhianne, became their prisoner.

CHAPTER 2

*G*arrett Bradis knew what he had to do, even though many might not like it. He stood in front of his fireplace, hands behind his back. Many would say he was heartless and demanding for being Head of Vhenn Bradis. They would probably be right. But when it came to making tough decisions, he implemented them—even though the result would be something many would find hard to swallow.

"You've talked to Serafina," Xander, his trusted second, had surmised. The warrior, with the gold-dusted skin of the Kasa Altea family, turned to him. "Welcoming the Lhiannes here... Do you suppose it could work?"

"They could be a valuable ally," Garrett said. "The storms are growing this year." Storms had swept all over Arqand, causing devastation. Lethal winds, lightning and hail had sprung from nowhere in mere seconds, and sometimes, disappeared almost as quickly. Sometimes it felt as if it had a life of its own, devastating in the way it spread.

Though some Lhiannes had worked for them in the past,

their last one had just left, and many were afraid to settle where Kilrhinns were. Lhiannes typically banded together, preferring to keep to themselves. It was equally mysterious the way their magic worked, but they could control elements of the earth and even bring change to the weather, to an extent. Kilrhinns were naturally suspicious of the secrets they held. But the Lhiannes could keep the land fertile and had a measure of control over the storms, tempering their effect. He supposed that was why the Lhiannes were feared— they had magic, but so little was known about them. Lhiannes had sided with their enemy, the Scourge, during the last war forty years ago. Foul creatures with blackened skin, the Scourge hide so thick, only the fierce strength of a Kilrhinn could cut through. They couldn't allow the past to happen again. He was determined to change that.

"Where are Galen and the others?" Garrett asked. They were supposed to have been here an hour ago to discuss his plans.

Xander frowned, thinking. "They brought a prisoner with them. I suppose they're doing interrogation now."

"Find them."

He dipped his head once. "Yes, my liege."

* * *

FREYA LIGHTLY TOUCHED the marks on her wrists. She winced. They were an angry red from the ropes that had restrained her all day.

After the Kilrhinns didn't get any answers from her, they locked her behind the bars of the cold, damp prison cell, and left her. She supposed she was grateful for that. Maybe they expected her will to crumple after spending time alone. She had to escape soon. If word spread about a Lhianne prisoner in Vhenn Bradis land, Terrence would find her. There was nothing she could do about that. She didn't want to be caught in a prison cell.

Terrence was son to two of the richest Rose Tempest village elders, the village she had run from in the Far East. There, the soil was richer, and storms mild and infrequent. She missed it deeply. But their village life wasn't meant for her anymore.

Freya had loved Terrence at one point. He was one of her dearest childhood friends. That love had withered dry the moment he'd struck her. Greed for power had overtaken him, and about a year ago, in his anger, he had nearly taken her against her will. The memory of it terrified her. Her hand shook, and she closed it into a fist. He was determined to marry her, wanting the Kilrhinn blood in her. She told him to marry a Kilrhinn if he wanted to so badly, and she stuck a fork in his hand. She ran after that.

She could never go back to Rose Tempest. He had followed her to several different villages after, but by some miracle, she managed to escape. But here, in unknown territory, in Kilrhinn land no less, she had lasted the longest. She had started to breathe a little easier, and even made friends. But even though she knew she wasn't supposed to build close ties, she did. She thought hiding here was the last place Terrence would expect to find her. She'd even taken a job at the tailor shop as the perfect cover. She thought she'd hidden so well. And now it would all be for nothing.

Freya eyed the metal bars that caged her. She rubbed her arms at the chill that seemed to permeate the place, but she tried to ignore it. She'd endured worse.

The metal bars were thick, but even steel wasn't impervious to heat. Could she do it? She closed her fingers around the bars. They were cool to the touch, but slowly, she tried to draw the heat from the earth to bend it to shape. As her mother had taught her, she imagined the bars taking shape in her mind, curving a little. Sweat dripped down her forehead. Her breathing turned uneven. It had been so long since she'd last used significant magic. She just had to count on the reserves that she still had.

What felt like ten minutes later, when she opened her eyes, she saw that she managed to bend it slightly. She huffed out a breath, eyeing the bars like an interesting specimen. Would it be enough?

It had to be.

She would be here all day. With a sigh, she began to work on making them take shape.

* * *

XANDER SLIPPED BACK inside the hall, his expression grim. Garrett had just finished a meeting with the council about the implications of his alliance with the Lhiannes. They had agreed it would be beneficial, but advised him to tread cautiously. They were still wary of the Lhiannes, but they couldn't afford to lose more time. The storms shouldn't be let loose any longer and wreak more havoc.

"Well?" Garrett asked, impatience cutting into his voice. Where the hell were the three of his enforcers?

"We have a complication," Xander answered, his expression hard. The news wouldn't be good. Garrett waited, lifting a glass of fine red wine to his lips.

"There is a Lhianne prisoner."

Garrett's head jerked up in surprise. He lowered his glass, afraid that he would break it. He had broken things too many a time inadvertently. It was something Xander was only too aware of and sometimes, even made fun of. "Repeat that again. I think I've misheard." His voice, dangerously light, dripped with warning.

Xander cleared his throat, trying again. "The prisoner they brought in is a Lhianne."

Fuck. He pinched the bridge of his nose. "And where is the Lhianne now?" he asked sharply, his intuition all but ringing in his head.

Xander hesitated for a moment. Why did Garrett have a feeling he wouldn't like the answer?

But Xander held his gaze, and uttering the word like a curse, he answered, "Underground."

* * *

WRATH WALKED towards them in purposeful strides.

Galen and Kane stood by the entrance to the prison cells, leaning against the wall with arms crossed. Rav was completely absorbed, scanning the headlines on the paper. Kane and Galen didn't notice at first, until they heard the footsteps and looked up. Kane nudged Rav with his elbow. Rav was about to snap at them, but seeing who was coming over, he stood up almost immediately. The paper dropped down the ground, all but forgotten. They promptly realized the foul mood Garrett was in and stood straighter.

"My liege." Kane dipped his head in acknowledgement.

"Explain to me what's going on." Garrett reined in his temper, but his patience stretched thin after learning what they'd done.

They didn't speak, taken aback, as they watched him bristle in anger. "Galen?" he asked. "Tell me, what is a Lhianne doing in prison?"

"She was caught without a permit," Kane answered for him.

The Lhianne was a *woman*? Fucking hell. It was only getting better, wasn't it?

"And that's grounds for being kept underground, where our enemies have bled?" Warning rasped from his voice, and they were starting to catch on to the reason for his temper. Galen slowly took a step back. Garrett's eyes jumped to him. He wanted to strangle the idiot.

"She ran," Rav snarled. "She caused a commotion in the markets and couldn't pay for them. And we think she's hiding something." As always, Rav was the first to lose his temper. Kane placed a hand on Rav's shoulder, tempering his friend's mood. That was what made the three of them an efficient squad—they'd been through hell together and balanced each other out.

"A Lhianne was working here. Without a permit. Did you not hear what Kane just said?" Rav tried again.

Garrett's eyes narrowed to slits. "I heard him fine the first time." He passed each one of them a long look. "How much damage?"

"A lot," Rav replied, miffed.

"How. Much. Damage," he bit out, not liking the answers he was getting.

"Two thousand silvers." It was Galen who answered this time, his forehead creased in deep thought.

Garrett's eyes slid towards him. "I see." Not a whole lot then. What kind of woman gave his men chase in the markets, trying so hard to avoid them? She should've given up from the start to avoid the chaos and fines. There was no chance of escape. The men who worked for him were the very best. Making his decision, he nodded his head. He would very much like to meet her.

"Bring me to her," he commanded.

* * *

GARRETT ONLY CAUGHT a quick glimpse of her before she saw him. Immediately, she scrambled away from him in surprise. He caught a flash of golden brown hair and slightly tanned skin. She had retreated far back into the cell, until the shadows concealed her features. A part of him was irritated that she hid from him.

Garrett stepped in front of her cell. Now that he was closer, he saw her more clearly. He gave her a long look and she frowned at his scrutiny.

She had a slight figure. Her hair was a mass of waves that she had pulled into a ponytail, but no amount of containing it into a thin piece of cloth had tamed it. Her eyes were so deep a green that it startled him. Her nose was thin and delicate, her lips full and pink. To his surprise, she scooted closer to him. And strangely, no longer scared, she got on her feet. She studied him back with the same intensity. It made him grin. Well, this was interesting.

Only then did he notice the red circles around her wrists. And that the bottom of her dress was ripped, and it was stained with some red liquid. His body tensed. Blood?

No, he realized a moment later. It was more washed out. If it had been blood, he would have to return it to whoever had inflicted it in kind.

"Lhianne," he started. Her brows drew closer at what he called her. No, that wasn't right. He wanted to work with them as equals. He had to, or an alliance would never work. "Do you have a name?" he asked, as if talking to a scared cat that could bolt any minute.

"Freya." Her voice rang clear, but he thought it sounded like music. "And you're…?"

She didn't recognize him—not surprising if she hadn't lived here for long. "Garrett," he replied.

She only grew wary.

"So, Freya," he tested the name on his lips. He leaned back on the wall opposite the cell. "You gave my men quite the chase."

"Yep."

If he wasn't mistaken, she looked damn proud of it, too. It made him curious. "Why run away?" he asked plainly. "You had to have known there's no escape."

"I don't like being caught very much."

Her reply was so unexpected, it made him chuckle. She blinked, his reaction appearing to puzzle her.

"I heard you worked at the tailor's." He'd been briefed on the way. He found it interesting that someone with her kind of magic would work there. Why didn't she apply for a permit?

"I don't anymore, from the looks of it," she muttered.

"I find it hard to believe you stumbled upon the profession and decided it was for you. Why work there?"

She looked almost defensive, placing a hand on her hip. "They gave good benefits."

Benefits? She worked there for the benefits? Perplexed, he almost laughed. This Lhianne surprised him. His brows lifted up. "And what would those be?"

"I can take a day off when I wish. Everyone's nice there. And I get to read during my breaks."

So she liked reading. He wondered what kind of books she liked to read. They had a whole library in the upper floors, and—he stopped there, annoyed at the direction his thoughts were heading. "I'm sure they've told you why you're here."

Frustration flickered in her eyes. "Look, if you just let me work at Mr. Jenkins' again, I can eventually pay my debt. I mean, look at me." She held her arms out. "Do you think I have anywhere to run?"

She was trying to bargain with *him*? She wasn't stupid, but clearly, she didn't know who she was talking to. "I can think of another way you can pay your debt."

She went pale as a ghost, taking a few steps backwards instinctively.

"Not in that way," he growled, guessing where her thoughts went. She released a ragged sigh, her relief almost instantaneous. And he didn't know why, but her reaction bothered him.

"You owe the shop owners two thousand silvers. Have they told you how much you're fined for having no permit?"

Her green eyes went round, her lips parting in surprise. She hadn't considered that. This made Garrett smile. "Ten thousand silvers."

He took a few steps forward, closing his fingers over the bars as they stood mere inches apart. "There's no escaping this, unless someone lets you out," he stated plainly. "I can help you."

"No, thank you," the response immediately came from her lips.

What the fuck? "You'd rather be locked here?" He couldn't comprehend her decision. She would come around, he thought. He just had to give her time to understand that they wouldn't harm her.

This was a woman who was tested beyond her limit, but still her back stood straight, her eyes brimming with pluck and defiance. He couldn't comprehend such a state. Here she was, weakened, imprisoned, and at their mercy. And yet... She didn't look it. Was it a Lhianne oddity?

No, he decided. It was just her. The corner of his lip lifted up at her demeanor. He'd been so very bored. He had never met someone who could match him head on, and here she was, in a prison cell no less.

There was a saying in Kilrhinn folktale that when a Kilrhinn found their true match, it was as if their hearts were being pulled by a thread, an awareness spreading to every inch of their being. Like a draw that would gravitate them towards each other, as if the planets themselves conspired to keep it so. Most days Garrett wondered if he even had a heart. So much of his life had been ruled by hard decisions that had shaped his very being. He had to be ruthless. He had to be cold.

He didn't believe in old fairytales and folktales. No, they were all a lie—to keep false hope, to feed irrational fancies. But when his eyes found her, although they'd never met, it felt as if he recognized her. And almost as if a fist had grabbed hold of his heart, he knew—he would have her.

* * *

WHILE HE WAS SPEAKING to Galen, Kane and Rav, Freya took the time to observe Garrett. Compared to her captors, this man's features were sharp, as if cut from stone. He was taller than the three, his russet hair a little longer than theirs. A scar ran along one side of his cheek to his nose. Without it, Freya thought he would've been what most called handsome. But with it, many would stop and take heed—it was a reminder that he wasn't an easy target. Clearly, the three took orders from him. When he'd laughed, it startled her. It came out rough, as if it had been ripped from him than freely given, and she had a feeling it was a sound that hadn't often left his lips. He'd moved with deadly precision, and at first, she couldn't move from her spot, entranced.

This was someone who had power and knew it. Not just the kind of power borne from his position, like the village elders, but power that coiled in his muscle. Power that soaked his every move. Where other Kilrhinns' eyes were a violet that burnt like the center of a flame, his were a deep indigo that saw right through her. There was cunning there. Somehow, she knew in her gut he was a force to be reckoned with, maybe even almost as fierce as the storms that had ravaged across their lands. And her fate was completely at his mercy. She had to be careful with someone like him. She had no idea who he was.

She'd fought to keep herself upright, but she started to sway, her knees like jelly. She took hold of the bars to keep herself steady. Her adrenaline had kept her going earlier, the only reason she was able to stand up to him after expending so much of her magic. But now she was struggling to hold herself up.

She couldn't afford to go so easily. Not right here. It couldn't all be for nothing.

She was lucky he hadn't seen her work on the bottom left of her cell, where a child might've been able to pass through. Trying to gulp in a few deep breaths, she knew she was fighting a losing battle. Slowly, she lost her grip on the bars, her strength seeped from her. Spots began to fill her vision, and then darkness pulled her under.

* * *

GARRETT HELD Galen by the collar. "Release her."

They looked at him like he'd gone insane. He had no patience for this. She should never have been imprisoned. If the Lhiannes heard of it, it would kill their chances of sealing an alliance before it even began.

"But she's—" Kane began.

Galen laid a hand on his shoulder. "Garrett, as your friend —she's a Lhianne. You're not thinking straight."

"That wasn't a request," Garrett said, his voice dangerously light, but his meaning no less clear.

Their faces lost color at the impending threat in his voice. Galen nodded. He hurried past the entrance and scrambled towards her cell, fumbling with the keys. Garrett followed behind him. But what greeted him instead made his heart stop, his body going cold. The Lhianne had fallen unconscious.

CHAPTER 3

*H*ad she fallen from hunger? Thirst?

A feeling surged up to Garrett's throat. Galen unlocked the door with the keys. But it was Garrett who jerked the door open. What the hell?

Still breathing.

Earlier, she had talked to him and she didn't seem to be suffering any ailment. If she had, she'd fought to conceal it. Had they treated her so badly it weakened her so much? He thought his men knew better than to hurt a woman, Lhianne or not.

Galen threw his hands up at the dark look on Garrett's face. "Don't look at me that way. I didn't do a fucking thing."

"All we did was question her and bring her here," Rav supported Galen. "We didn't hurt her, God's honest truth."

"She was fine earlier." This time it was Kane who had spoken.

"I'll get Jess," Galen offered after a moment's pause.

Jess was their best medic. She would find out what the hell happened.

It was then that Garrett noticed what he'd missed while talking to Freya.

"Xander!" he barked out. "Have you seen this?" Garrett stared at the prison bars incredulously. He didn't know how he missed it. He was so focused on Freya, on trying to figure her out, that he'd been unaware of what she'd done.

The bars, made of reinforced steel that held even the toughest of Kilrhinn traitors, had been bent out of shape, giving space where a smaller human might've been able to slip through. She was no human—he had to remind himself of that. He touched the bars, realizing that there were ridges there. Her fingers had made an indented shape on the steel, and he'd laugh if he wasn't so damn impressed. She'd bent them herself.

No, she wasn't helpless. If she had enough time, she would have escaped.

Xander bent down next to him. Stunned, he gave his head a shake. "I guess we can add manipulation of steel to her talents."

"What the fuck?" Rav blurted out behind them, realizing what she'd done.

Kane whistled. "She did this?"

No one answered. But they knew. She had more tricks up her sleeve than any of them gave her credit for.

Jess didn't waste any time—she dashed to the cell when she saw Freya. If the Lhiannes were good with controlling elements of the earth, Jess was the daughter of Brions. Brions were gifted at being able to identify what people's sickness or pain were, and at dampening those effects considerably. She saw the body's sickness like a visual heat map in her mind. An ability of their kind that many Kilrhinns had thought long lost—until she punched Kane once in the gut for stubbornly doubting her when she claimed he needed to drink a concoction she made if he wanted to survive. It turned out it was an antidote, as he'd drank a poisoned bottle of sweet wine. He never doubted her after that.

Jess was also highly adept with a needle. So good she'd often threatened people with it, for the next time they needed stitches. No one wanted to face her wrath.

"What's wrong with her?" Garrett asked. "Is she hurt?"

Her brows drew together as she carefully rested a hand on Freya's forehead. She shook her head. "She's unhurt, my liege." Seeing the question in his eyes, she explained, "She needs to rest. She exhausted her magic."

* * *

"Bring her to the clinic. See to it whatever fines she has are paid."

He could tell Galen wanted to protest, but instead, Galen kept his mouth sealed and nodded.

Garrett stopped, looking back. "And Galen? You better hope to the gods she survives." He thought he saw Galen's ashen face before he whirled away. It was clear what it meant —trying to escape prison had taken a toll on Freya. Had she feared them that much? And even more pressing—just what had her exerting so much effort that she'd risk her life?

* * *

Someone was singing.

Oh. Freya was back home, her mother singing her a lullaby. The sweet voice sent a wave of calm through her, although Freya caught a hint of sadness in it. Her mother still looked the same, before her sickness had claimed her. She was sitting in their living room, the golden sunset spilling through the window, and the sun had lit her face with joy as she lightly adjusted the clouds for warmth. She always did that when the weather seemed a little gloomy. Freya tried to lift an arm to touch the ends of her mother's chestnut hair, making sure she was real. But her arm wouldn't move, as if bound in place. Just like that, her mother was gone. Freya let out a cry, lashing out against whatever force held her.

"Be still." A soothing hand brushed her forehead, and the man's voice held so much authority, so much reason, daring her to go against it, that all fight left her.

She was parched. She begged for water, only her lips didn't seem to move right. But then like magic, cool water hit her tongue and she swallowed. Who was it who cupped the back of her head, held the precious liquid to her lips? She could kiss that person.

She smiled, sighing deeply. There was so much tenderness in that touch. That person must be so kind.

"Drink," the voice ordered, rough. How bossy. It wasn't like she could help herself, anyway. She opened her mouth until she drank more of it. When she was done, her body felt cooler. The bossy but kind person was leaving, but she reached out and felt the edge of his sleeve. She tugged it closer to her. She didn't know why it was important that he stayed, only that his presence made her feel safe.

"How long will she be like this?" she thought she heard him murmur. There was a muffled response.

"Be careful not to leave her alone," someone said in warning. "She's flighty." How rude. They made sure she suffered, and they enjoyed it, too. She said as much.

She thought she heard someone roar with laughter, and she wanted to open her eyes to see who that was, but her lids felt too heavy. But the kind person didn't leave. She sank into the darkness once again.

* * *

FREYA BLINKED, her eyes adjusting to the light. She lifted a hand up, blocking the rays of the morning sun. Slowly, she sat up, taking in her surroundings. Where was she? This didn't look like prison. Her cell was dark and cramped, while this room was miles away from that—with painted white walls, it was light and airy, the wind hugging her, as if the room itself had welcomed her. Its way of making known that here, she was embraced by the earth. The curtains were drawn, a pale pink color that reminded her of the carnations she'd often seen in the markets. She'd never bought them. She'd passed by countless times, but she couldn't afford them, and there was a fear that the vendors would remember her face. The fear had gradually diminished over time, but it still remained. At the end of the room was a house-shaped clock that told her it was ten-thirty in the morning.

Freya rubbed at her forehead trying to recall how on earth she got here. What happened?

Then it came back to her, the memories murky—exhausted, she'd passed out after Garrett had talked to her. She groaned out loud, mortified. God forbid they'd think she was some delicate flower that fainted at the slightest thing that alarmed her.

She wasn't accustomed to drawing out so much of her magic. And even more than that, their magic wasn't meant to bend metal bars to their will. It was too sturdy, made of strong compounds that were hard to manipulate. If she had managed to fit herself in the gap, by that point, she would've already been drained. Desperate, she didn't think that far ahead, aided by the adrenaline that had pumped in her veins.

The doorknob twisted, the sound making her jerk in surprise. A tall woman pushed the door open with her back first, looking like she was carrying something. Her long, dark hair met silvery wisps at the end. The woman balanced a tray of food on one hand and pushed the door closed with the other. Freya realized the woman wasn't Kilrhinn—she was perhaps a little shorter than Freya herself, which surprised her. The woman's eyes had a remarkable pale green color that made her look ethereal.

Her eyes lit up when she saw Freya, a grin on her lips. "Good! You're up. Hungry yet?" she asked excitedly.

The thought of food sounded appetizing. "Yes, please." If she could guess, it was this woman that had helped nurse her back to health. "Thank you," Freya said, grateful. When entering a deep sleep such as she did when she exhausted her magic, she was as helpless as a baby.

"It's no trouble. My name's Jess." She set down the tray on a small board on top of the bed. A smile played on her lips. "And I'm not the only one you should be thanking."

What did that mean?

"I'm Freya," Freya replied. She hesitated for a moment. "Can you tell me what happened?" She didn't know what happened since the big scary Kilrhinn came to visit her in the cell, or how long she'd been unconscious for.

"You don't remember?" Concern had Jess' brows knitting. "You were in bed for two whole days."

Two days? She didn't expect that using that much magic made her lose two whole *days*.

"They brought you here so you could rest," Jess explained. She grinned. "Garrett was so mad."

Why would he be mad? Freya picked up her fork. She uncovered the foil that covered her plate. Poached eggs and crispy bacon, with a perfectly golden brown toast. She gasped in delight. "Wow! Thank you. This looks amazing."

"Elara works her magic in the kitchen," Jess said, with what Freya detected was a hint of pride. "I'll leave you to eat. Just let me know if you need anything."

Freya dug into her breakfast slowly, thinking of what she would do. She had to keep moving, or Terrence would find her. But she couldn't be obvious about it, or they would catch on to her plan. She would get up and move around, maybe get some fresh air…

* * *

TEN MINUTES PASSED, and Jess still hadn't returned to the room. Freya pushed her covers aside. It was time to make her move. Any longer and she'd lose her window of opportunity.

Freya got on her feet and steadied herself. She stretched her arms and rolled her neck. She should be fine to move around now. Carefully twisting the knob, she pulled the door open, and her smile dropped, seeing what awaited her outside.

Rav stood outside the door, leaning against the wall. Seeing her, he pushed himself from the wall immediately. "You're up." He didn't look too happy about it, if his scowl was any indication.

Thanks, Captain Obvious. "Well, good morning to you, too." Wonderful. Garrett sent someone to keep watch. It added a wrench to her plans. She forced a smile and hoped it was convincing enough. "I just needed to go… for a walk."

At some point, she would shake him off. She just had to find that one narrow window where he was distracted…

She looked longingly outside as they walked past the long hallway that led to the gardens. She caught a glimpse of the edge of the gate.

"Should you be going for a walk so soon?" he asked, pulling her away from her thoughts.

"I was holed up in the room for two days. So yep."

As they walked past the kitchen, the smell of freshly baked bread wafted over, and it almost made her weep.

"Mmm. Starbread," Freya murmured absently.

He snorted out loud. "That chocolate pastry? Are you seven?"

She wrinkled her nose. "How dare you..." Wait a second. She remembered that voice in her half-sleep state, and it dawned on her why it sounded so familiar. "I am *not* flighty."

Not that she wasn't trying to escape, but that wasn't the point. She hadn't always been a flighty person. Damn Terrence and everything she'd lost because of him.

He surprised her by bursting into laughter. "You remember that, huh?" Nope, not an ounce of guilt on his face. But somehow, he didn't look quite as menacing as before.

"Anyway, if you three hadn't caught me, I would've had some already. If I get my hands on one, I will *not* be sharing," she vowed.

"The keyword is *if*, Lhianne." It sounded like a threat, withholding starbread, and she took it as one.

Why wouldn't they call her by her name? It bothered her, but she bit her tongue. This was someone who would've had her locked up until she could pay her debt in some way. Of course they didn't care about her name. *But Garrett did.*

She wasn't naive enough not to consider how far they could take it to collect their payment. Her fists clenched by her side. Soon enough, they would lock her up again. She couldn't let that happen.

She just had to time things right. She prayed the winds would help her. This place was a fortress, but even a fortress wasn't completely impenetrable. She remembered the roads they took on the way here. She just had to follow the map in her mind.

A Kilrhinn wearing plain clothes approached them, carrying thick pieces of paper. "Rav. I've got the updated maps."

A gust of wind blew, the maps slipping from his hand.

There it is. She found an opening.

A crowd of Kilrhinns gathered, probably having finished training. Rav's attention focused away from her, Freya slid in with the crowd, mustered whatever speed she had in her, and ran.

* * *

FREYA HID WITHIN THE TREES. From the distance, she spied that the iron gates were closed. How to escape? She had to avoid the Kilrhinns who were guarding it heavily. She looked up the stone wall, stretching up to the sky. Well, it didn't look *that* high. Her heart sped.

Cautiously, she made her way to the edge, until she stood before the giant wall. Her palm laid flat against the stone, rough to the touch. Her hand swept over the surface and felt ridges in between. Slowly, she placed her toe in the groove of the stacked stones, to test if it would hold.

This was crazy... But it could work. She spun around and observed the tall trees around her. That should shield her from view, delaying them from noticing her plan. They would expect her to leave through the gate or some other entrance. She smiled. Before they'd realize it, she would be gone.

Freya looked up again. If they barred her escape, she would forge her own route—she would climb.

* * *

"SHE'S GONE," Rav snarled.

Galen had just finished a round of sparring with Kane. "Who?" Galen asked, wiping the sweat off his brow. They were both breathing hard, having gone a whole round.

They did this every week, needing to keep their reflexes sharp.

"Freya." Rav ran a hand over his jaw, irritated. "Chester gave me the maps and she escaped."

For someone who seemed so vulnerable in that bed when she was unconscious, she had evaded them. Again. They made sure she was comfortable, that she was treated well for a swift recovery, because Garrett wished it, and she repaid them by escaping.

"You've sent people out to look for her?" Kane asked.

Rav scowled. "No one's reported back."

"We'll split and look for her," Galen said immediately. They weren't going to make it easy for her. Anything that happens now, she'll have had it coming.

"She could be gone by now." Frustration tore through Rav's face as he dragged a hand across his hair.

"And where would she go? We'd find her easily," Kane reminded him. Ever so calm as always. It was his tactical mind that remained calm under pressure that kept them all alive. Kane sharpened his knives carefully.

"Garrett will have our fucking heads," Rav muttered.

They agreed with him. Knowing Garrett, they immediately sobered.

"When we find her, she'll pay," Rav declared grimly.

"No, she won't. You know very well Garrett won't let that happen."

Rav frowned at Galen. "How can you accept that so easily?" he grumbled.

"Haven't you seen the way he acted around her?" Galen found it hard to believe at first, but he could tell. Garrett was attracted to her. Trust him to go after someone so unusual.

Rav gave it some thought. "He waived her fines. He let her go, too."

"He likes her," Kane remarked, agreeing with Galen. "I think he means to keep her."

Rav's jaw dropped, his eyes nearly bulging. "Garrett Bradis? Who defeated hundreds in our battles?"

Kane shook his head. "Pick up your jaw."

"Why would he keep a woman? He can have anyone he wants." Rav's genuine confusion was clearly shared by all, and the two nodded their heads in acknowledgement.

"And he wants her," Kane stated plainly.

"He has strange taste," Rav voiced out, still stupefied.

"You don't say." The corner of Kane's lip twitched in amusement.

It looked like it would rain today. Galen wondered if another storm was coming. He wondered, too, if the Lhianne had something to do with that.

He glanced outside, his senses honed by years of following his intuition. Galen's eyes wandered, until they were drawn to the walls. He froze at the sight, so remarkably absurd, he could scarcely believe it. He cleared his throat. "Well, I can't say I expected this." A chuckle escaped him, unbidden. Who would have thought anyone would be insane enough to pull it off? This Lhianne was different, that was for sure. "Look behind you," Galen continued. Kane and Rav turned their heads to follow his gaze. And right at the wall was a small figure, slowly inching towards the top.

CHAPTER 4

*F*reya had the distinct feeling that she was being watched. The hair on her arms stood up in warning. Through the years, she prided herself on following the whims of the earth and the wind—they never steered her wrong. Had the Kilrhinns already found her?

She didn't have the luxury to look around to see who was watching—she was nearly to the top.

She *did* have Kilrhinn blood, and she had spent the past couple of months preparing herself physically and mentally for times such as these. She *would* climb a wall, if that was the only thing standing between her and freedom. Determination drove her forward. She pushed her body up, and flinging her leg to the other side of the wall, she used the spare moment to look at the view before her.

Big mistake. She might have been able to climb the wall, but she was still perched on the very edge in a balancing act. *Please cooperate with me*, she whispered to the wind.

When she was climbing, she didn't worry too much about the details—that she had scraped her arms and elbows during the climb, whether anyone had caught on to her plan yet, and how many feet laid between her body and the ground. She didn't realize she was so high up. Or that the fortress they had kept her in was *this* tall. And it was magnificent. The clouds cast the impressive stone structure in a gloomy light, and yet there it stood, dark and imposing. She could even see the top of the stronghold from here.

The harsh wind that whirled against her didn't let her get any rest. As if saying, *hurry.*

I'm hurrying, she thought. She inhaled a deep breath, mustering the nerve to look down at the other side of the wall.

Oh God. Bad idea. The ground was so far down, it was dizzying.

She told herself it would be much easier than climbing. She just had to not slip and fall to her death. *Easier said than done.* The plan seemed so simple before.

She wanted to rest, but she felt a prickle at the back of her neck that told her to keep going. Even though she hadn't seen anyone, she made herself move. She took a deep breath and slowly made her descent.

Minutes felt like hours. She nearly slipped a few times, but still she pushed herself to keep going. Her hands shook, but she held on as she ate up more space between her and the ground.

Three more steps.

She was so close, she could kiss the ground in her happiness.

"You know, they said you'd woken up, but I didn't imagine I'd find you scaling our walls."

In her surprise, Freya's grip slipped, and she landed on her ass. *Ow.*

She saw black boots first, slowly looking up. There stood Garrett, towering over her, displeasure plain on his face. He held out a hand.

Shit. She was caught. She only stared at his hand. How did he figure it out? She stood up on her own, patting away dust and dirt from her clothes.

"I have to wonder how you got the idea," his voice rumbled. It started to dawn on her that her chance of escape had been blown to pieces. "Did you wake up and think, 'I think I'll climb that wall today?'" His brows furrowed.

He was angry. When men got angry, sometimes, they forgot themselves and raised a hand. She took a step back, beginning to tremble. Only now had her muscles started to ache. She broke a few nails from the climb too, and she bit her lip. She'd thought of growing them again. Just a week ago, she thought she might've even been able to paint them again. Now she would have to wait for them to grow back. It seemed so petty, compared to the consequences that laid before her, but she fiercely hung onto the hope of freedom. It seemed like the price for her escape from Terrence was another, much more terrifying cage.

She was in trouble. Possibly in more trouble than before, when she'd simply been their captive who owed them some silvers. Now she'd played an active part in trying to deceive them. She braced herself, wondering what he'd do to her now.

"You could have died," he growled.

Why did it sound like it mattered to him? "I didn't." Yes, it was dangerous. But she learnt that if you were predictable, you were caught. That was how she evaded Terrence for so long. Too bad it didn't work with them.

He narrowed his eyes. "Not the point. Have you forgotten the fines you owe?" Garrett's voice rose.

She had. For a moment, she had been so focused on escaping. Imagining being locked up there again made her feel slightly queasy. "Am I going back to that cell?"

His jaw was hard. "No." He studied her, his purple eyes unnerving. "We've seen the bent bars."

She froze, deathly still. Of course they'd seen it by now.

"Tell me," he said conversationally, "how would you have dealt with the locked door?"

"Door?" she echoed, confused.

"The entrance to the prison requires another key."

She hadn't thought of that.

He snorted. "I see you didn't plan that far ahead."

"I would've thought of something," she muttered. Anything was better than being stuck there. She could hide among their people. She'd done it before.

"I have no doubt." He stalked towards her. She moved away, until her back hit the wall.

He'd been kinder to her than the others had. Maybe she could appeal to his compassionate side. "Can't you just let me go?" she tried. "I'll leave Maranthe. I promise you won't see me again."

* * *

FREYA DROVE HIM INSANE.

For any single woman to do that was an accomplishment in itself. When Garrett came to visit her after wrapping up another council meeting, she was gone, leaving a distraught Jess who explained to him that she didn't know where Freya went. Freya had somehow managed to give them the slip— someone who had been in bed for two days, helpless and weak. Restless unless he sat by her, as if his presence was vital to her well-being. He didn't understand it, but at the time, he indulged her.

When he went to see his enforcers, Galen had told him they found Freya. Then Galen had promptly pointed at the wall and told him she was going up.

What a puzzle she was. There were scratches on her arms, even small cuts on her cheeks, the dried blood coating her skin. Her clear green eyes stared back at him as if raring for a fight. Ridiculous. He would never hit her.

Just what kind of life had she lived? Was escape all she thought about? She acted like they would kill her if they caught her. He didn't miss the way she stepped away from him when she thought he was angry at her. She thought he would raise a hand on *her*.

The truth was he was furious she'd done something so fucking reckless, that again, he'd felt helpless. That he might've lost her before he even got the chance to discover her secrets.

"I'm afraid I can't do that," he replied smoothly. Disappointment made her shoulders slump. "You remember what I told you before?"

After a blank stare, recognition sparked in her eyes. She gave a slow, hesitant nod.

"I can help you, Freya."

Her lips parted in surprised wonder. He frowned, thinking back on what he'd said. Then immediately, it clicked. *A name.* All he said was a name, but it meant something to her.

"I have an offer."

Her lips lifted up, but the smile didn't quite reach her eyes. "Am I allowed to refuse this offer?" she said, resignation coloring her voice.

"I won't force you," he vowed fiercely. But he didn't think she'd refuse. In her position, he would accept.

Still, her expression was guarded. "What is this offer?"

"A week from now, a group of Lhiannes are coming." She jerked in surprise at his words. "You know what your kind is like towards ours. Secretive. Cautious. Terse."

"Your kind hasn't exactly made any effort to improve the situation," she couldn't help but add.

"The prejudice is still strong. But I understand how valuable Lhiannes are to us. Others don't understand it now, but they will." His eyes met hers, all steely determination and resolve pressing him on. "I'll be blunt—we want to secure an alliance with them," he revealed. "And we want you to help us."

* * *

KILRHINNS AND LHIANNES WORKING TOGETHER? Would that even work? Freya couldn't wrap her head around it. There was too much distrust and suspicion still.

"You're aware of how devastating the storms are. Their unpredictable nature puts us in a precarious position."

"And you want me to... do what, exactly?"

"Work for us during their stay. Help them feel at home. Help them trust us. And help us understand them."

Were Kilrhinns even trustworthy? But... he wanted to understand *them*. He wanted to see past that prejudice, too. It was madness, but from their actions so far, she felt like they had more honor than the village elders ever did. She felt the wind urge her to step forward. Her hair went flying, the wind letting its desire known. *Yes, yes. Calm down, please.*

"If I accept, will you let me go?" This point was non-negotiable.

"Yes."

She considered him for a moment. "How good is your word, Garrett?" she asked quietly.

His eyes narrowed. "I've never gone back on mine."

"Good enough for a blood oath?" she pressed.

He stared at her for a moment. Blood oaths were binding.

39

It was sworn with the very thing that flowed in their veins and made up their being.

"Why would you—" Seeing the uncompromising, stubborn stare she fixed at him, he sighed in capitulation. "Fuck. Yes, I'll swear a blood oath, if it's what you need."

She grinned wide, what felt like the first genuine smile in weeks. A heavy weight eased from her chest. "Then I accept." She'd have her freedom. She'd just have to work for it in a much different way. Terrence hadn't found her yet. Maybe the Kilrhinns could be discreet.

"And Freya?"

She stopped, turning to face him. "Don't even think about running. If you do, I'll catch you," he purred. She had no doubt—his eyes all but promised it.

* * *

ON A DECREPIT STONE BUILDING, a man stood, wearing a hooded black coat. The shadows the hood cast hid his features. "Where is the woman?" he asked. His voice held a musical quality, controlling the beast that laid at his feet. The beast left, only to come back, dragging a woman with him.

"Let me go!" The woman fought against the creature that held her. Half-beast, half-man, features so grotesque, its short black fur glimmered from the moonlight. People thought the Scourge had been purged from existence after the war forty years ago. They would soon learn that they were wrong.

The woman was pushed forward, and her ringed curls bounced as she slammed down to the ground, her hands tied behind her back.

"Katherine Rowes," he said, his voice hoarse. "I know about you. Born to a Kilrhinn and Brion."

"I'm not going to heal you, if you want me for that," she spat angrily.

"I need a simple favor."

She shook her head fiercely, trying to struggle against the creature that held her. "No."

Ah. Mulish, this one. "Today I passed by a Kilrhinn's house. Her name was Kendall—I believe you were friends? I came for the girl she was with. She was screaming so loudly when we took her, but now your sister's life is in our hands."

A pause, then—"You sonofabitch!" Her Kilrhinn blood lent her speed and she wrenched herself free. It didn't last long. The vile beast pulled her back, driving its claws from behind her until they pierced through her belly. She looked down at the claws that stuck out. Blood gurgled from her lips and she stared at him in shock. "You're... gonna... pay," she managed to choke out. Her breathing slowed. The beast pulled its claws out. He might've been wrong...

The wound was gone, as if sealing itself from the inside. She started breathing again, fury twisting her expression. Oh yes, he liked that look on her. She would do nicely.

He smiled, his fangs peeking out. It was rare, but some with Brion blood regenerated their own wounds. He heard about her and he wanted to see for himself. He was not disappointed.

"Even I know you're not invulnerable. You can't keep this up, Brion. Sooner or later, your magic will be exhausted, and you won't be able to save your sister."

Blood drained from her face. "W-what do you want?" she asked.

Excellent. She was ready to talk. From his spy, he heard rumors of the potential emerging alliance between the Kilrhinns and the Lhiannes. That couldn't happen. He needed the Lhiannes. "Infiltrate Vhenn Bradis land to the East... And kill the woman named Freya."

CHAPTER 5

"*I* heard he was so angry, the bars of the cell rattled," a woman spoke in Kilrhinn. Freya heard it a table across.

Nonsense.

"I heard he even tore down the prison bars. Eileen says she saw the bars were bent out of shape!" another woman from the table agreed heartily.

Freya's heart raced, and she nearly choked on her drink. That was *her*, not Garrett. But she couldn't expose the fact that she was fluent in Kilrhinn. In this place, knowledge was power, and she was already at a disadvantage as it was.

The poor guy was being blamed for something she did. They made him sound like some sort of monster. It didn't matter what race—people loved to gossip. Since she agreed to work for Garrett, she heard people talk about her. Apart from the few friends she made while she worked at Mr. Jenkins', Freya was used to being alone. Reaching out to others felt like a struggle. She didn't want to involve them and risk putting their lives in danger, too, as it seemed to happen around Terrence.

"I've heard that when he's mad, if he wanted to, he could grab out and eat your heart," the first woman said. This was getting ridiculous. Why would he even do that?

The woman across from her only gasped. "Wasn't there a bloody prisoner that one time?"

As if on cue, Garrett walked in the hall, and stopped when he found Kane. Immediately, all chatter about him died off. Freya bit into her peach. She slid a glance towards him once more. She slowly considered him. Yes, he looked fearsome. A force to be reckoned with. The scar on his face didn't help. If only he smiled, he wouldn't look so intimidating.

But she couldn't imagine him doing what they mentioned, with all the fanciful rumors of him tearing down the prison bars. Just what did they think he did in his spare time? Eat rocks?

Garrett caught her staring. Heat spread over Freya's cheeks. He smirked, and just like that, he was striding towards her.

She edged away from him. She glanced behind her. Nope, he was still heading here. She wanted to slap a hand down her face. Now *she* would be the topic of their conversation. Great.

He stopped by her table.

"Are you ready?" he asked.

She didn't know why, but nerves filled her. Tonight, he was going to swear a blood oath that he would let her go after her job was done. Then she'd find out if Garrett was a man of his word.

* * *

FREYA WAS LED to a small room that looked like an office. A fire burned at the hearth. The room was warm, and a large rug sat at the center, like fine silk. There was a large shelf of books, too.

Her eyes swept over the room. Galen, Rav and Kane were all here, as well as Jess, and another person Freya didn't recognize. She tried not to stare. He was as tall as Garrett, his skin as if dusted with gold. His dark brows were a stark contrast against his skin, casting his features in a harsher light. She thought he looked like a fallen angel, if the tales on Earth were to be believed. His expression was shuttered.

Blood oaths required witnesses. She just didn't expect there to be so many.

"I trust each person here with my life," Garrett said quietly at her inspection.

Jess smiled at her encouragingly. Freya returned it with her own shaky one.

Someone cleared their throat. Galen passed Freya a dagger. It looked old and scratched, but it still looked sharp.

She accepted it, balancing its weight on her hand. It was a good weight. It felt solid and sturdy, too. She slashed it across her palm, lightning-fast. Better to get this over with.

"I'll work for you, Garrett, um…" She stumbled over his name and looked up at him in question.

"Bradis," he answered smoothly.

Her jaw dropped. He was a *Bradis*. How had she missed that?

Quickly masking her surprise, she continued, "And—and I'll help you secure a treaty with the Lhiannes. This I swear on my blood." Her skin prickled as she spoke the words.

He did the same with his own dagger. "While you work for me, Freya de Rayne, you'll be under my protection. Anyone who harms you will answer to me."

His promise stunned her. Not only did he know her full name, but she honestly hadn't considered what else he could offer her.

His expression darkened. "After it runs its course, you'll be free to leave, if it's your wish. This I swear on my blood." He made it sound like she wouldn't want to leave. As if that would ever happen.

"So witnessed," the fallen angel Kilrhinn said solemnly. The rest of them answered the same.

That sealed the deal. If you broke a blood oath, it was punishable by death.

Freya breathed a sigh of relief. It was finally done. She wouldn't be trapped here when it was over. Still, she eyed Garrett warily. She had questions for him.

Everyone left one by one, until only the two of them remained. Freya looked down at the cut on her palm. What fate awaited her now?

"Freya." The way her name curled on his tongue made a shiver of awareness run through her. "Satisfied now?" he asked.

"I've never told you my last name."

He raised a brow. "We did a background check. Did you think us lax with screening?" *No.* Someone like him would be thorough. And it wasn't fair, because he had the advantage in that regard.

"There wasn't much we found, as if someone made the effort to bury all the information. But I think you already know that."

He found out about that, too. How long until he uncovered the truth?

"Your job is important, but it also makes you a target. Did you honestly think I wouldn't consider your safety?" His temper sparked—but not at *her*.

No one had ever gone to such lengths before—not even her former best friend. Garrett certainly didn't have to. She always had to look out for danger, because at the end of the day, the only one she could count on was herself.

Garrett drew his own conclusion. "You didn't," he murmured. "A blood oath works both ways. I swear to uphold my promise as you do yours." She met his steady gaze, his dark eyes pulling her in like a deep ocean. Warmth suffused her at his words.

"You work for me now," he said, the meaning of his words starting to sink in. "And I take care of my own."

* * *

"YOU WOULD'VE BEEN BETTER off by staying in the fort," Rav grumbled for the third time.

Freya examined a flaire closely before she dropped it in her basket. A sweet and slightly tart fruit that grew progressively bitter towards the center, flaires glowed a pale yellow at night, but in the morning, it was the color of persimmons. "I'm not a prisoner anymore. Besides, you didn't have to come." She missed walking freely outside. She was thrilled when Garrett told her she could buy what she needed for the Lhiannes' arrival, to make them feel at home.

He snorted. "And risk you leaving again?"

"I swore an oath to do my job." She added more flaires to her basket.

"You're a flight risk. Oath or not, I don't trust you to wander Maranthe's streets and not try to find a way to escape."

If she knew better, he was trying to get back at her for being able to slip away last time. "Suit yourself," she muttered in reply.

Rav took a flaire from the pile in the stall, tossed it in the air, and caught it with a hand, bored. "How many flaires are you going to need?"

She snatched the flaire from him. "Careful with that. If

you drop it, we may have to pay for an extra one." Flaires were more expensive than most fruits in the markets.

Rav was prickly, but she learned he often spoke his thoughts aloud, sometimes with less tact than the situation warranted. But even his tattoos now seemed less intimidating. His honesty, she found, was refreshing.

"Flaire pie is Lhianne comfort food. It's practically mandatory for a welcome party."

"But it's bitter."

This made her smile. He teased her about starbread, but he had a sweet tooth too, she just knew it. "Have you ever had flaire pie outside at night?"

Rav considered her question. He shook his head. "Can't say I have."

"When you cut them into pieces, they glow, like little boats. Stories tell us that long ago, our planet had a moon twice the size of the Earth's. Lhianne children have flaire pie as a treat when they're little, for birthday celebrations and such. But more than that, holding one feels like holding a piece of home."

"Huh. How much bigger is it than our moon?" The curious Kilrhinn looked up at the sky. The moon couldn't be seen this time of day, but he still squinted against the light.

"The moon here is maybe three-quarters of the Earth's."

He whistled, absorbing what she'd said.

There was a commotion by the peaches, where a woman with caramel-brown curls, tinged with silver, tried to remove her arm from the grasp of a wiry man. Her eyes glowed purple in her struggle. *She was half-Kilrhinn.*

"What seems to be the problem here?" Rav asked, his voice commanding.

The man, seeming to recognize Rav, let her go immediately. The woman's eyes widened, seeing them, as if she recognized them. But that couldn't be. Freya had never seen her before in her life.

"This Brion woman wouldn't help me find out what's wrong with my daughter. She is capable of it, but she refuses to."

"Aurelio, your daughter is dead," the woman said, the tremors in her voice only lending more strength to her words. The people in the markets gasped. It surprised Freya how the woman kept herself calm.

The man named Aurelio slapped her face with his palm. She let out a cry in shock, covering her cheek with a hand. Her hand shook.

Rav immediately grabbed the man by the collar. "Is this true?" Rav growled. "Lead me to your daughter."

Freya's heart ached, and she found herself walking towards the woman. Gently, she helped her up.

"Are you okay?" Freya asked.

"Thank you," the woman whispered, still shaken.

"My name's Freya. You are...?"

A small smile touched the woman's lips. Strangely, she thought there was something wistful about it. "Katherine," she answered. "My name is Katherine."

* * *

THE MAN'S daughter was dead. He refused to acknowledge it and was all but in tears. He didn't calm down immediately, but a woman from the marketplace gave him a good scolding, whacking a spoon down his head, which promptly shut him up. It was then they decided to leave.

Freya thought she saw Katherine's shoulders sag in relief when they did. "Do you need a ride home?" Freya offered.

"Oh, it's okay, I don't live far from here."

"We'll walk you home, then," Rav said, apparently making it his duty that she came home safe.

"I don't think that's a good idea," she said carefully.

"Why not?" Freya's brows drew together. It didn't seem safe that she'd walk home alone.

She pulled in a deep breath. "I live in the slums."

The simple confession made Freya's heart squeeze in her chest.

Rav looked at a loss for words. "You are a daughter of Brion. Our liege can speak to you. I'm sure you can—"

Katherine seemed to be terrified by the very thought. "Oh, no thank you," she cut across him.

Why was everyone so terrified of Garrett?

"Thanks for helping me today. Really."

"Are you sure you'll be okay?" Freya took Katherine's hand into her own. Katherine's eyes softened, but she didn't say a word, until their horse made a whining sound.

"Yes. Thanks again for your help." Slowly, Katherine pulled her hand away, giving them a big wave. Then she was gone.

* * *

THE CLOUDS WERE HEAVY TODAY, Garrett thought, as if an omen sent straight from the heavens. They hadn't had a storm in over a week. They'd all been tense, ready for the havoc it would wreak, due any moment now.

"They're coming tomorrow," Xander spoke, just as restless as Garrett. "Do you think she's ready?"

"She bought a basketful of flaires today," Garrett said, thoughtful.

"Flaires? What the hell for?" Xander asked, his body turning towards him.

Garrett grimaced. "She said Lhiannes love them. The

cooks wanted to make it, but Freya insisted. She said, as Elara described it, *it has to be done by a Lhianne.*"

Xander's face turned pale. "Elara may never feed her anything good again. She may be human, but she doesn't take kindly to any slight to her craft."

No, any Kilrhinn knew never to insult the ones who prepared their meals. Garrett wondered who would win between them in a battle of wills.

"You have something on your mind," Garrett said, noting the way Xander's body had tensed. He knew him well enough to tell he stewed on something.

Xander hesitated for only a heartbeat. "Don't you find it odd that the moment we're poised for an alliance, a Lhianne falls right into our laps?"

This made Garrett smile wide, all teeth and grim resolve. "Good thing I'm a gambling man."

CHAPTER 6

*F*reya felt jittery, the nerves making it hard to eat. Not to mention, someone had peppered her breakfast with some chili.

She had to remind herself that among those here, she understood Lhiannes the most. Not only could she speak their language, but she understood the importance of culture and tradition—her parents made sure of that. People talked about her, especially when they didn't know that she understood them. Some were afraid of her. It had always been this way—two halves, both Kilrhinn and Lhianne, that belonged nowhere.

She had finished making the pies in the kitchen, and she was a nervous wreck. By late afternoon, she waited outside, where others also gathered, intrigued by the news of the Lhiannes visiting. They were due to arrive any moment now.

She spotted Jess among the group of people. She felt guilty seeing Jess again, knowing she caused a fuss when she attempted to escape before.

"People are curious," Jess said when Freya caught two people whispering behind her. Guilty, they moved away.

"They want to know more about the Lhianne who made our liege swear a blood oath."

She didn't think of it that way. And because Freya couldn't help it, "Jess... About the other day, when I left... I'm sorry."

"It's done. I get it," Jess said sympathetically. "I just wish you rested for longer. You've barely been out of recovery."

"I feel fine now," Freya reassured her. "I think I've slept long enough." But still, her stomach was in knots, not knowing what to expect from the Lhiannes.

Jess studied her for a moment. "Are you scared that they're coming? Don't worry, the Lhiannes won't get to try anything funny."

It came from nowhere—a gust of wind. The horses began to react at the sudden change. The trees shook, and Freya got knocked on her butt. Jess managed to hold on to a lamp post. She swore.

Oh God. Why now?

Suddenly, the sky had darkened. A droplet of rain hit Freya's cheek. Another. More clouds had gathered, thickening against the sky. Not good. It was escalating fast. Lightning struck, a fierce roar that pierced their ears.

What would follow would be devastation, if she didn't hurry to stop it. Fear always gripped her whenever there were storms. Nature was wild and untamed, and the vast energy of the earth meant it was difficult to contain. Just because she was a Lhianne, capable of stopping them, didn't mean she didn't feel it. It had still claimed the lives of those close to her, as well as her father.

Freya bounded to where the storm gathered.

"Freya, no!" Jess yelled. But she didn't understand. Freya had to reach the eye of the storm, before it got progressively worse.

She nearly made it, when, a heavy weight knocking her

breath out, she skidded against the ground. "No!" She struggled against the grip of the person who held her there.

"I know you don't like it here, but it doesn't mean I'll let you run to your death." It was Galen who spoke.

She couldn't believe this was happening. "Galen, I can stop the storm!"

"You'll die if you get any closer."

"No, I won't!" At least, she didn't think she would, while it had only just started. She couldn't say the same if he continued to keep her here. "Please, let me stop it! The longer it takes, the harder it will be to contain."

Galen was quiet for a moment. She could feel him thinking. Then, without warning, he loosened his grip on her, and then she was free. His expression, fierce, "Do it fast, or I'll take you back," he snapped.

Freya didn't waste time. The storm was growing stronger by the minute. She bolted, heading towards the center, where it all gathered. She met resistance as she tried to go against the wind. She held out her arms.

Please, she thought. *Please leave us.*

The wind tried to rebel against her, challenging her.

I don't want anyone else to die. She let that thought power her through, trying to get the winds to listen. The dirt under her feet rose, too, slashing small cuts on her skin. She needed to stand her ground, or they would all die.

Lightning struck an area to her left. Something exploded behind her.

She didn't let that deter her. She closed her eyes and took one step. Another.

Please stop.

In a flash, the wind eased, scattering away. A violent wave of wind spread outwards. Just as quickly, the clouds moved away, and the sun peeked through. Freya fell to her knees. She released a breath she didn't know she was holding.

Crisis averted.

Within a minute, she saw that a group of people had emerged from the drawn gate—the Lhiannes were here. An older woman rode in front, her hair a silvery white. With prominent cheekbones and intelligent deep green eyes, she rode with authority. Behind her, a young woman with short, jet-black hair eyed Freya with great interest. Next to her, a young man with copper hair and olive green eyes looked around, scanning for any signs of danger.

It wasn't exactly the first meeting she'd imagined. Still, Freya mustered a smile.

"My name's Freya," she said. "So glad to have you."

* * *

DISMOUNTING FROM THEIR HORSES, a tendril of wind leapt forward and tested Freya, checking for any signs of danger.

The older woman smiled back, crinkles forming around her eyes. She extended a hand. "That was quite a storm," she remarked. "I must say, I'm surprised they sent someone like you. I'm Serafina."

Serafina? Where did she hear that name from?

"I'm Lily," the younger woman said, her voice clear as a bell. "This is Jon." She gestured to the young man next to her. They were both around the same age—sixteen, Freya would guess.

"So nice to meet you," Freya replied warmly. But Freya's eyes returned to Serafina, and recognition struck. Her mouth hung open as she realized who she'd spoken to. Just what kind of pull did the Kilrhinns have that they'd managed to invite one of the oldest elders of the Lhiannes? Their connection with the earth was the deepest—they were the most knowledgeable in the villages, and they could help control the weather with great ease.

Freya fell down on a knee. "By the earth. My lady, how can I—"

"Oh, no need to be so formal." Serafina waved a hand at her.

"But—" It flustered Freya. Respecting the elders had been so deeply ingrained in her.

Serafina pulled a pot from one of the straw bags they brought with them. "A gift. Celes flowers," Serafina said, passing it on to her. The Lhiannes' native flowers from their former planet, Lhyris. Pure white flowers that unfurled at sunset. They were delicate and precious. Freya held it close. Remnants of their history that she was able to hold in her hands. "Thank you." She couldn't keep the wonder from her voice.

"They're resilient plants. You shouldn't have a hard time keeping them alive. They only need to be watered twice a week."

Freya thanked her again, and entrusted care of the flowers to one of the men she'd seen at the gardens. They were escorted inside the fort, and Freya followed behind them.

When they pushed the doors to the banquet hall open, the sight that greeted them inside frustrated Freya. They sat the Lhiannes at the far west of the hall. The Kilrhinns didn't understand it, but the small change was important. At a banquet meant for *them*, that was highly unusual, and not to mention, inappropriate.

"I'm really sorry. There must have been some misunderstanding," Freya apologized on their behalf. She was embarrassed that the simple request she asked for earlier was ignored. "Excuse me." Freya knew just who she needed to see.

* * *

GARRETT WANTED to throttle the two people who were taking up his valuable time, arguing their point about which one was more suited for overseeing guard duty tonight. Considering that ensuring tonight went smoothly was important, he didn't have time for this. "Enough," Garrett snapped. "You," he pointed at Chester, the one he trusted more with always being alert on the job. "You will do tonight. You," he pointed at the other guard, "will do tomorrow. Understood?"

They nodded their heads.

There were two quick raps on the door.

"The Lhiannes have arrived," Xander informed Garrett. He hesitated. "There was a storm earlier, before they came. It's all under control now."

He had a feeling he knew who helped with that. "Freya?"

Xander nodded.

"Then I should go meet them."

* * *

GARRETT FOUND Freya bickering with Elara, whose face was now flushed in visible frustration.

Freya's lavender dress hugged her body, emphasizing her curves. He had never seen the pattern of her dress before. It had flowers and golden lines at the edges. He frowned, eyes drawn to the cuts on Freya's arms. It must've been from the storm. She was almost as fierce as it, too, as he watched her with mild amusement, judging from the way she gestured with her arms.

Time to figure out what was wrong.

"Is there a problem?" Garrett asked, his voice smooth.

"My liege," Elara greeted him. "The Lhianne requested a change for the banquet table. I tried to explain to her that the tables have already been set, and it would really mess up the seating by having her rearrange them again, for her pleasure."

"Only two tables will need to be rearranged, and I can help. The table is on the west. I specifically requested to have one on the east. When you put them on the west, you're telling them they don't matter."

Elara spread her arms out, clearly at the end of her patience. "It's a *table*."

Freya's shoulders stiffened, fists clenched beside her. "There's hierarchy to it. The table on the west is furthest from the moon."

"What does it matter if it's close to the damn moon?" she shrieked. "It's the same table!"

Freya would fight this tooth and nail, and he'd expect the same for Elara. He needed to nip this in the bud before it got any worse.

"As it happens, the Lhiannes are valued guests for the duration of their stay. See to it that it's changed," he commanded, his voice brooking no argument.

"B-but she just—" Elara stammered for a moment. She took a deep breath, pulling herself together. "Yes, my liege," she replied through gritted teeth. She spun on her heel and headed towards the swinging doors of the kitchen.

"Thank you," Freya said when their eyes met, her cheeks turning a slight pink. "I told her many times, and she was so determined not to change anything."

He watched her, fascinated by the way she reacted around him. "You should be careful in angering our cook. She has a penchant for creating truly horrifying meals when upset."

"I'll keep that in mind," she muttered. Then, "I didn't do it on purpose, just so you know."

This made him grin. "I know," he replied. He saw his guests, now being escorted to the new table, and decided to head there. He took Freya's hand and linked her arm against his. He told himself it was important they give a united front. Truthfully, he enjoyed her scent—like those white flowers Jess had in her clinic, and the sweet scent of vanilla. Freya baked the whole morning, he was told. That was probably it.

"How are you feeling?" he asked. His question seemed to surprise her. He gave her a pointed look, his eyes dragging to the cuts on her arms. And also, he was noticing, one on her cheek.

"I'm—I'm fine. The storm was a quick one."

She downplayed her efforts, he thought grimly. Even storms that ended quick were almost never completely harmless. "Thank you, all the same," he said solemnly. "You've helped us in more ways than you know."

She dipped her head, conscious of his attention.

"It's that important?" he asked. "The seating arrangements."

"Yep. They're very fussy about things like that. We're very superstitious. Hierarchy gives order to our chaotic lives," she revealed lightly. "You... You guys are so practical, choosing to analyze what only you can see, it's hard to adjust to that kind of thinking, so I get it."

Her eyes focused on the distance, deep in thought, as if it reminded her of something. She tried to understand them, even while it frustrated her. The combination was oddly endearing.

They were lucky they caught Freya from the start, even though he wished they hadn't started out on the wrong foot. Even when they reached the table, he didn't let her go just yet. He wanted them, and everyone else in the hall, to understand that no harm would come to her. But it was more.

Freya cleared her throat, sliding him a questioning glance. He let her go then, but he held out a seat, a hand resting on her back.

"Serafina," he greeted respectfully in a small bow.

"Garrett." Sharp green eyes met his. From their discussion on the phone, she was receptive to the idea of being invited. But still, he wanted to know what their reasons were for accepting the invitation he extended. That was what he planned to figure out during the rest of their stay in Maranthe.

"Hi," Lily said, beaming at him. "I'm Lily."

Jon gave a small nod of acknowledgement. "Jon."

"Welcome to our home." They took Garrett's outstretched hand. "I hope you forgive my people for their transgressions. They're unfamiliar with Lhianne customs, and as you might imagine, a little reluctant to accept help."

They regarded him curiously, just as he observed them back.

"Freya isn't," Lily voiced out.

"What?"

"Freya isn't unfamiliar with our customs," Lily explained.

"That she isn't. Her presence here is a treasure."

"On that, we can agree," Serafina concurred. She smiled— the first real one she flashed at him. It was gone almost as quickly.

* * *

"I HOPE the food's to your liking," Freya said as the food was delivered.

Each large plate came, vibrant with the red of the toma-toes, the white of the grain, and thin strips of meat at the center, marinated and lightly spiced. She couldn't fault Elara —the cook had insisted on doing the presentation, and it was impeccable. She had to remember to give her compliments when she saw her again. Elara had listened to what she said were important in terms of placement.

Elara had chosen the wine carefully, too. It was the color

of rubies, and Freya swirled it in her glass. She gave it a small sip, and she wasn't that knowledgeable when it came to drinks, but she thought it had a rich, complex flavor that didn't burn. It made her feel warm and relaxed. After a long day, it loosened the anxiety that had tied her in knots since last night.

Lhiannes didn't enjoy too much conversation during their meals—they preferred to savor it and give it their full attention. Love went into creating the dish, and so love went into consuming it. It only seemed fair to devote to it the time it deserved.

Dessert was a different matter. Flaire pies were eaten outside, as per tradition. Had she been back home, they would have moved the clouds a little, making the moon a little brighter on a night such as this. But she understood why they were reluctant to do it, especially in unfamiliar territory.

Garrett caught them looking at the milky deep blue sky, and his eyes turned alert. "Do you think another storm's coming?" he asked, watching the sky intently.

Freya shook her head. "One shouldn't come so soon on the heels of another."

Tension visibly left his body.

But still, one couldn't be certain when it came to storms. She understood his concern. She found herself taking his hand. "It's okay. There are four of us, we can help put one away if it does come," she reassured him, lifting her lips up in a smile. He looked down at where their hands met, his thumb sweeping over the back of her hand. A jolt passed through her where he touched her and she gasped at the sensation. Freya tore her gaze away. "Ready for dessert?" she asked distractedly. She felt his gaze on her. Still, he didn't let go, until he walked her to the large oak table out in the open, where the flaire pies waited.

Pride filled her at her creation. A rich golden brown crust, the edges dented with small crescent moons that circled the pie.

She baked the crust three times, to give it the crispy, flaky texture. The flaires were then cooked and combined with heavy cream and sugar, giving it a creamy texture. The buttery crust combined with the sweet and light filling worked well together. It offset the bitterness of the flaires. She added a touch of salted caramel, brushing it on top before baking—the one ingredient her mother swore by that Freya noticed made a difference. She made it as her mother had. She just hoped she'd done it justice.

She was heartened by their approving looks.

"Do the honors, please," Freya said, her nerves starting to get the best of her. Hilt first, she offered the cutting knife to them.

Serafina accepted it. Slowly, she cut the pie in a V-shape, and did the same for the other pieces.

She heard the Kilrhinns' murmurs when it glowed against the dark.

Freya waited, her heart in her throat. They examined the pie and took a cautious bite. Their concern melted away immediately, delighted at the pie.

They liked it. Freya released the breath she held.

She glanced surreptitiously at Garrett, curious about what he thought of it. He frowned, studying his portion. He took a bite of the pie, and his scowl vanished. He looked at it with great interest, fascinated by its appearance. Freya hid a smile.

"Where did you learn to make it?" Serafina asked.

"My mother taught me."

"She must be a talented cook," she said, her voice softening.

"She was," Freya replied, wistful. It had been years already since her mother passed away, but she felt the loss keenly.

Serafina dipped her head. "I'm sorry, Freya. May the earth bless her soul."

A lump in her throat, Freya felt the ground vibrate beneath her feet. A slight tremble, but she felt it to her soul.

It was a gift from Serafina. Reminding her that even those long lost returned back to the earth, and still, they remained. The earth remembered, just as she did also.

She touched her cheeks, wet from the memory of her mother. "Thank you, Serafina." With a quick glance, she knew everyone else felt it, too. The Kilrhinns around them seemed deeply unnerved, their faces reflecting unease. She felt a spark of irritation that something done out of kindness could be taken negatively, just because they didn't understand it.

"Don't worry about them," Jon said, speaking to her for the first time. "They don't understand us. How can they?"

"I know they try," Freya replied gently. She needed to remember that. Considering Lhiannes had always stuck with their kind, she knew it would take time. She was determined to help bridge that gap between them.

"What did you do?" a Kilrhinn suddenly burst out, his face twisted in outrage. Freya recognized him as the one who had questioned her in interrogation before, the one with spiked hair. Freya tried to recall his name—Ignas.

"Was it you?" He crossed the distance quickly and grabbed Serafina's shoulders roughly. It happened in a flash —Ignas got knocked down by the wind, landing flat on his ass. He looked up at Serafina in surprise. *Didn't expect that, huh?*

Around them, several Kilrhinns' hands went to their sheaths, guarded.

Freya stood directly front of Serafina while Lily and Jon joined her, too.

"We should head inside," Freya said loudly, hoping it would break the tension brewing between them. Either side was a trigger away from attacking.

God, these idiots. The Kilrhinns didn't know they were a hair away from being knocked on their asses. This wasn't going well at all. Slowly, they moved their hands away from their sheaths.

But Garrett stepped forward, fury radiating from him. Now Freya understood why there were rumors believing him to be ripping people's hearts out, in the literal sense. Largely unfounded, maybe, but he had an air about him that demanded they listen.

She knew this wasn't over. If she survived this day without them ending up killing each other, she would consider it a success.

* * *

"The Lhiannes are here as our guests," Garrett said, his voice soft. Still, the threat was there, and everyone knew it. "If anyone sees that as a problem, they're welcome to come forward now."

No one came forward. Considering the matter settled, he strode towards Xander.

"If there are any further problems with the Lhiannes, refer to Freya," he told him in a low voice.

Xander's eyes flicked to her. "Noted."

* * *

"I must say, I thought we'd have to suffer through these pompous, condescending Kilrhinns who don't have the decency to ask for a name, but I'm glad that isn't the case," Serafina said over her glass of wine.

Freya blinked. Did Serafina actually just say that?

"They aren't stupid," Lily agreed. "They kept you."

"The Kilrhinn likes you," Jon added, cutting another piece of flaire pie. Now that he had dessert, he seemed more inclined to talk.

Freya snorted out loud. "Garrett?" The idea was so ludicrous. "Why would you think so? He's only been polite."

"*Polite*?" Serafina laughed out loud, the sound rich and throaty. "Oh yes, he certainly can be. And charming, if he wishes it. But if so, one would think he'd do it for a very good reason. But he doesn't need one when it comes to you, does he?"

"They need my help," Freya tried to explain.

Serafina narrowed her eyes. "Threats can achieve their goal, too. Kindness isn't necessary."

The Kilrhinns hadn't been cruel. They could've been, so easily, but they weren't. That counted for something. But Serafina was wrong. It was all business for him, for their alliance. In any case, Freya didn't want to dwell on it too deeply.

* * *

SHE SURVIVED THE DAY. Somehow, it seemed that Garrett's warning dampened the tension between the other Kilrhinns and the Lhiannes. Freya dropped down on bed, facedown, arms spread. She was so tired...

There was a knock on her quarters. Freya thought she imagined it at first, until the knock came again. Freya frowned, not wanting to move an inch. But after a groan, she made herself move. She had to see what they wanted.

She pulled the door open, wondering when she'd get her

sleep, and stared at the face of the familiar warrior. Well, this was unexpected.

"Freya. We need your help," the gold-custed skin Kilrhinn said. He was one of the witnesses during her blood oath with Garrett, and she'd seen him around a lot, too.

"Hi. Your name is…" She struggled to remember but came up blank.

"Xander."

"Hi, Xander." She was glad to put a name to the face.

But right now he didn't look pleased. "They've gone insane, the Lhiannes. They said they want to leave."

CHAPTER 7

S tairs. There were lots of stairs that stretched high up in a spiral. Xander was brooding the entire way.

"Did something happen?" Freya asked, trying to fill in the silence. The Lhiannes were just fine before they retired to bed. She wondered what someone did to upset them. Remembering what had happened early tonight, "Did someone try to attack them?" she asked.

"No one attacked them." He sounded almost insulted at her question. "They would probably blast that person with the wind, anyway."

Freya's brows knitted in confusion as they climbed more stairs. "Then why are they angry?"

"I don't. Fucking. Know. They went in the room, and they were angry, threatening to leave." His lips curled. "If they didn't want to stay here, they should've said something from the start."

And then he'd gone straight to her. "Something about the room, then," Freya concluded.

"Tell me, should we have thrown rose petals in their

bath?" he uttered dryly. "Should we have lit dozens of candles in a precise pattern to spell the name of a god?"

Ha. Sarcasm dripped from his voice, and she rolled her eyes. "Nothing so drastic. We'll understand soon, anyway."

They finally reached their door. Well, the room was high up. A point for them, at least. She noted there was a walkway that led to an open garden on the balcony.

Freya knocked on the door twice and waited. Serafina threw the door open seconds later. She was incensed. Lily looked embarrassed, while Jon met them with a hard, unyielding stare.

"Is this some kind of insult?" Serafina burst out. "I had no idea the Kilrhinns were that eager to send us home so early."

"Please, what's wrong with your room?" Freya pleaded, wanting to understand.

"See for yourself and tell me this room is inhabitable," she hissed. "Lily's and Jon's are much the same."

Serafina moved aside, tapping her foot on the ground, her impatience felt by everyone.

The room was immaculate. A large bed that took up nearly half a wall, with white sheets that Freya imagined would be as soft as a feather. A large rosewood table that looked solid, topped with a vase of fresh yellow flowers. Was it their bathrooms that they found issue with?

"What seems to be the problem?" Xander asked smoothly, not revealing an ounce of his frustration from earlier.

"The problem? *The problem?*" Serafina's voice rang, shrill, her temper mounting. Not good.

Freya's eyes roamed around the room again. Her eyes snagged on something fairly innocuous.

It was easy to miss it at first glance. The room itself was spacious and luxurious. It was far bigger than her room. Everything seemed perfect, except one thing—the window. It was a small rectangle, about the size of those leatherbound volumes she used to read. To an ordinary Kilrhinn, it didn't matter. But Lhiannes needed larger windows.

"The windows," Freya whispered. "We need windows."

"There are windows."

"They're tiny," Freya revealed. She drew the curtains aside more fully. The thick, flowing, royal blue curtains made the windows seem huge, but they were much smaller.

"So you're claustrophobic," Xander surmised.

"No. That's not it." Freya started to pace. "We need to connect to the earth and the wind. To nature itself. It's not fear, exactly. For us, it's essential, like our need for fresh air. The sun."

He grimaced. "I don't really understand, but we'll look for other rooms nonetheless."

"Thanks," she told him, grateful for his help.

He looked hesitant for a moment. "Will you let me know if anything's wrong with the new rooms?"

Freya nodded. He was out the door in seconds, and just as Freya was about to follow, someone tugged at her sleeve.

"Thanks, Freya," Lily said, relieved.

"Can't believe they put us in these rooms," Jon muttered.

"No problem at all," Freya replied. "I'm sorry about that, too." She didn't even consider the rooms. She assumed it would look similar to her own. She counted herself lucky her windows were much larger.

Appeased, a thoughtful look crossed Serafina's face. "You may be right. They're trying."

* * *

"You're falling asleep," Elara said, voice as sharp as a whip.

Freya's head bobbed up in surprise. She snapped to attention, embarrassed. The cook sighed. Elara was pretty, she thought. She had her dark hair always tied up, and the barest hint of makeup, but she had hazel eyes—brown that changed to flecks of green against the light. Freya stifled a yawn. By the time she returned to her quarters last night, it was late. It had taken Xander a while to find suitable rooms. When her alarm rang at six in the morning, she felt like she barely slept a wink. She had to prepare the food for today, since Elara was still unfamiliar, but not unwilling to learn, about their way of cooking.

"Sorry." Freya rubbed at her eyes and slapped both hands down her cheeks, in an effort to wake herself up.

"If you fall asleep on your feet, ice water can help with that," Elara offered.

Freya couldn't tell if Elara was joking or not. She decided it was best not to even test it. She slapped her cheeks again for good measure. "I've got this." Freya cracked four eggs open, mixing in a set of herbs she prepared.

"You mix it fast," Elara observed.

"It has to be, to make it fluffier."

Elara was quiet for a moment. "Yesterday, you lifted two sacks of rice grain when it needed to be moved."

Oh, crap. Freya didn't think anyone was watching. "It was on the way."

Elara tilted her head to the side, frowning. "You're fast for a Lhianne, too."

"I lift," Freya quickly tried to cover her misstep.

Elara threw her hands out. "Oh, please. You have tiny arms. Barely any muscle."

For a human, she was the first to figure it out. Their reflexes may be weaker, but their instincts were sharp.

A cryptic smile touched Elara's lips. "You're not pure Lhianne are you?"

Freya froze.

"You're half-something, and if I'm gonna guess, it's Kilrhinn," she added.

Freya quickly covered Elara's mouth, glancing around the kitchen. She hoped no one was within earshot.

Elara removed her hand, looking at her strangely. "It's early. No one's up this time yet," she said. She patted Freya's back soothingly. "Why are you so worried? Is it a secret?"

Freya's hands trembled. She set the batter aside. "I don't need to attract the wrong kind of people. I'm already odd enough to them as it is. The less they know about me, the better."

Elara nodded. "Knowledge is a weapon."

Freya took Elara's hands into her own, a new kind of fear sitting in her throat. "Please don't tell anyone."

It felt like she held her breath for a while as Elara studied her.

"Not my secret to tell," Elara finally said quietly. She took over with beating the batter.

"Thank you," Freya breathed out. She was a little surprised, but also more than relieved.

"Is this fine?" Elara asked. Apparently, the matter was settled.

Freya nodded. "We use a square pan, typically."

"Why square?"

"We will roll it up and the cheese might spill over."

Elara continued to shoot her own questions, and Freya answered what she could. Elara hadn't probed, and she was grateful. They sampled their own meal in tiny plates, and even as more people came to help, they stood next to each other in silent company.

A little while later, Galen found her. Seeing his face, she immediately knew something happened. "Is something wrong?"

"There's been a fight."

* * *

FREYA FOUND Lily and Jon huddled next to each other outside. Jon had a scratch at the top of his cheek, and what looked like the beginning of a bruise. Lily had scrapes around her knees. It looked painful.

They looked up warily at her approach, like they were expecting this.

"Are you okay?" Freya asked, concern making her rush towards them. "Where's Serafina?"

"She's meeting up with some people today," Lily replied quietly. She noted that they hadn't answered her first question.

Freya bent down, sitting next to them in the patch of grass beside a circular pond. "Will you tell me what happened?" Jon tossed a pebble to the small pond. It bounced, creating ripples. "Jon?"

"They wouldn't leave us alone. I blew them away," he said bitterly.

"I told you you didn't have to do that—we can't control it that well yet!" Lily burst out.

"They took it too far," Jon retorted. "I'm not gonna let them hurt you."

Freya was definitely missing something. "Who are 'they'?"

"I don't know their names. There were several of them," Lily replied, embarrassed.

"I remember their faces," Jon claimed.

"Tell me what happened from the start."

"They called me 'witch'," Lily revealed, her brows drawn together. Her lips pressed in a thin line. It was the Earth term people used for those who were able to practice magic, and for Lhiannes, it often came with the implication of dark magic. As if they were part of some sort of cult that taught or encouraged it. Freya had been called that before, too. "And we didn't want to stay inside and hear everyone talk about us over breakfast. So we went outside. But they followed us."

"They told us to *go back home, but wait, your planet exploded,*" Jon mimicked them, growing furious by the second. "Home" was Lhyris, their planet that no longer existed. The Kilrhinns weren't making this any easier for them. How cruel, reminding them of a place they could never return to. A place that was once their home.

"We tried to ignore them, but they put their hands on Lily, telling her to listen."

Ah. She can guess what happened next. "So what did you do?" Freya asked gently.

"I pushed them," Lily answered, straightening her back. "Just a small tap." She meant she used some of the force from the wind to compensate for the strength they lacked. Freya wished she could've been there so she could see their faces when Lily did that herself. "They got angry. Then Jon reacted and knocked them over with the wind." She slid a gaze at him, chiding.

"They struck back," Jon added defensively.

Freya sighed. Lily was right. "I know it's hard. But using your skills without full control of them is dangerous." With enough potential but lack of training, it could kill.

"The next thing they would've done is taken their weapons out," Jon tried to reason.

He had a point, but… "Did you see them do it?"

"They would've."

"Did they?" she asked again, her voice firmer.

"No," he replied grudgingly.

Suddenly, she knew what she had to do. "You're going to stay with me until Serafina's done. Got it?"

They started to protest, but she silenced them. "They won't try anything while you're with me."

"I thought Garrett said last night that anyone who came for us would be in trouble," Jon recalled.

"Yeah, well... Sometimes people are dumb."

Lily giggled.

"If they try it again..." Jon's fists curled.

"I'll talk about it with Garrett. Promise me you won't try anything dangerous."

Jon scowled. "If we're in danger, I can't promise."

"Promise me, short of your life in danger, you won't try it again." Seeing the stubborn tilt of his jaw, she added, "If you go get yourself locked up, you can't protect Lily."

This made him jerk in surprise, and she saw the moment he gave in. "Fine," he relented.

"I don't need protection," Lily muttered.

"It doesn't matter if you're talented or smart—if you stick out, you're going to be a target for those kinds of people. They do it because they're scared, even intimidated, but those kinds of people aren't worth your time." She made sure she met their eyes. "You know yourselves better than them."

Her heart squeezed in her chest. She knew what it was like to not fit in anywhere. She didn't fool herself and think the Kilrhinns would welcome her with open arms, even though she now worked for them.

They were good kids. She didn't know their family or their history, but right then, she decided she wanted to help them while they were here. Not out of a sense of obligation, but a sense of kinship, even though she didn't have much of a family left.

"Were you? A target?" Lily asked.

Freya looked at the pond as the water rippled from the wind, forming the shape of a smiling face. "Yes." Deciding it was best they move on from the topic, she announced, "Now let's see to your wounds."

* * *

THE FAMILIAR CLINIC greeted Freya once more.

It was amazing how it didn't have the chemical smell of a hospital. The windows were pushed open, fresh air ruffling the curtains, making them look like they danced on their own. White flowers sat in a vase, and Freya moved a flower that nearly fell out back inside. It looked a little dull, so she drew the water in to give it a little more life. The brown edges of the petals melted away.

Just in time, Jess found her.

"Freya?" she said in a manner that sounded much like, *you again?* She placed a hand on her hip. "I hope this isn't going to become a regular visit," she teased lightly.

Freya only smiled. "It's not me, it's these two." Lily and Jon emerged from behind her.

Her eyes sharpened on the scratches on them. "What happened?" she asked. Then, "Does *he* know?" She meant Garrett.

Freya shook her head. "Not yet."

Lily and Jon perched up on the white bed.

"Oh my God. Who did it? They'll be shitting bricks when they find out he knows."

Jess dipped her finger in a yellow salve. Lily drew back as Jess tried to apply them.

Frowning, Jess held out her hand. "It's just medicine, see?"

They sniffed at the yellow concoction. Lily dipped her own finger into it, examining it. She rubbed the mixture on the side of her skirt. "It makes my skin tingle."

"It stains, too. Don't just rub it on your clothes, sweetheart," Jess said mildly.

Lily had the grace to look abashed.

"Will it help the wounds heal faster?" Jon asked curiously.

"Yes. It'll help it become less inflamed."

"They got into a fight with the younger Kilrhinns," Freya explained.

"Wait. Was it Resty and Helos? Tall, wiry guy with big arms, and the one with a square face? They came crying here earlier and thought they'd broken a bone."

A rueful look passed over Jon's face. "I didn't mean to do it," he mumbled. They both knew he did, but Freya understood what he meant. They'd learn now, Freya thought, that their actions had consequences.

"They didn't, by the way," Jess added, biting the inside of her cheek. "Break their bones, I mean. Helos had a nasty bruise, though, the size of Maranthe. Resty just grazed his arm." Considering Maranthe was the biggest city in Arqand, that was saying something.

"Good," Jon decided, a satisfied grin touching his lips.

Freya rolled her eyes. *Teenagers.* "He thinks he's won."

"I did, though," he claimed proudly. Well, she couldn't argue with that.

When Jess finished with applying the salve on Lily's knees, Jon said, "I don't think that's needed. I'll keep this as a badge of honor."

"I'm sure you'd want that, but our liege wouldn't."

He immediately looked deflated. Freya wanted to laugh, but kept a straight face.

"I'll just add a little bit," Jess soothed him, her index finger and thumb nearly touching.

He considered it and slowly nodded.

She dabbed a bit of the salve over the scratch on his cheek and the bruise on his jaw.

"All good!" she chirped.

Jon touched his cheek and winced.

Footsteps echoed from the outside. A familiar face walked in the clinic, carrying a box. Katherine's curly hair was pulled back in a messy bun as she stared at the contents of the box. "Jess, I couldn't find the—Freya?"

"Katherine! You work here now?" Freya exclaimed, thrilled. A pair of startled eyes stared back at her.

Katherine lifted her shoulders up in a small shrug, smiling. "I've just started. I considered what your friend said before and thought I'd give it a shot."

"I'm glad for you," Freya congratulated her excitedly.

"Thanks!" As if remembering she was carrying a box, she said, "Jess, I couldn't find the green bottles you were talking about."

"Oh, that's right. There was a new delivery. They're right here," Jess said, pulling a box from the cabinets.

Katherine carried the new box, balancing it in her arms.

"Need help?" Freya asked.

Katherine shook her head. "Thanks, but I'll be all right, I just have to take these to the patient." She waved a hand as she left. "Hope we can talk more later."

* * *

"THERE WAS a storm that came just before you arrived, I heard," Garrett said as soon as he and Serafina walked into the gardens. The sun would be setting soon, an angry orange that cast the sky a light pink against blue.

"Dangerous things, these storms are. Awfully unpredictable, too," Serafina answered. Perceptiveness hid behind those eyes. He didn't know if he imagined it, but he thought the sun burned a little brighter now that they were outside.

"Were they as violent in your village?"

Her expression turned grim. "Not always. We're very careful—we have to be. We don't have it as frequently as you do here, but we've had some terrible storms too." So she understood. The storms weren't to be taken lightly.

"We could help each other out,' he stated plainly.

They walked further in the gardens.

"You're talking an alliance," she said carefully. She got it.

"Yes. Of course, it will be mutually beneficial."

"Mutually beneficial," she echoed. "You do have a way with words. I can see how you were able to convince Freya to work here." She paused, a knowing look on her face. "Will you have me watched, too?"

She was aware of that, was she? Serafina kept her eyes peeled. After Freya nearly escaped last time climbing their *walls* of all things, he didn't want a repeat of it.

"She's escaped from us before. It's simply a precaution." But also because it's true, he added, "It's for her protection, too."

"And you'll be trying to ensure we won't break an alliance. Protection?" Her lips curved up, but it didn't reach her eyes. "How very noble of you."

She sighed wearily. "I'm getting old, Garrett, but I'm not stupid to think the peace will last for long. The earth tells me change is coming."

An omen. He didn't like the sound of that.

"I'll think about it," she said quietly.

That was good enough, for now. He stopped when he saw the familiar figure of a woman pass through the flower archway—lithe and light on her feet, Freya disappeared with Lily and Jon in tow. What were they doing here?

He made a signal with his hand. From the shadows, Kane emerged.

"I can take over from here," Garrett told him.

Kane tossed him a candied apple. Garrett caught it easily. "From the kitchens. Thought I'd have a longer shift." Kane held another apple in his other hand and bit into it. He made a quick salute and jogged away.

Serafina didn't like having a guard. That didn't bode well. It seemed like the Lhiannes needed a leap of faith from him.

Clearly, Freya didn't react to having a guard well, either, judging from her previous attempt to escape. He thought it was a good idea he hid it from her for now.

"One of my dearest friends met your father," Serafina revealed, this new piece of information intriguing him. "She said he was a great leader. I trust Maranthe is in good hands."

"You pay us the highest compliments. He's retired, but he'd enjoy learning that." While they talked, they followed the path Freya and the other Lhiannes took.

* * *

THE GARDENS WERE Freya's favorite place outside the fort.

Freya waved at the ones who tended the gardens. Just yesterday, she saw them plant the celes flowers close to the heart of the gardens. She had answered some of their questions, too. There were some plants on the balconies of the fort, but those paled in comparison to the ones down here—a vast field of flowers, from white, to purple and pink. Some yellows planted in between added bright spots of color.

"Fina!" Lily exclaimed. Freya and Jon both turned to see Serafina from the distance, with Garrett behind her. Freya wondered why she was intensely aware of his presence. Her heart beat wildly in her chest. It was an odd feeling, especially when Garrett's eyes found hers—his gaze turned heated, and it felt heady, knowing that for a single moment, she had his complete attention.

Lily waved both hands up, calling their attention. When Garrett and Serafina stopped, Freya decided there was no harm if they all watched the celes together.

"We were going to watch the celes bloom, it should be really soon. Want to watch it with us?" Freya offered.

"Flowers that bloom during sunset?" Garrett asked, skeptical. He bent down to study the flower, still firmly coiled onto itself.

"Yes, celes flowers do," Freya said excitedly. "They're beautiful."

Jon swept over the grass with the wind, to blow the dirt away, and Lily proceeded to sit down before the flowers first. Freya's lips quirked up as she watched Jon get settled next to her. It was such a small thing, but it was thoughtful and sweet.

Serafina sat beside them on the grass. "They're quite a sight when they do."

Right on time, the white flowers slowly unfurled, the edges opening up. It happened one after the other, like a small wave. Inside each flower was a soft yellow center, like a crown. The flowers were larger than they appeared to be at full-bloom. It was a visual feast for the eyes.

Intrigued, Garrett plucked one celes bloom from the flowerbed. Freya's eyes widened. Immediately, the flower wilted. He frowned, puzzled. "Fuck."

His surprise made Freya laugh. "They're fragile." She slid him a look. "You know, it's bad luck to pick a celes as soon as it blooms."

She was so used to seeing him in control that throwing him off-guard was something she found she secretly took pleasure in.

Looking chastened, he uttered an apology.

"They say the bad luck lasts for a year," Jon added. Freya covered her mouth, stifling a laugh.

Garrett eyed the flower like it had grown another head. He scowled, seeing her reaction.

"Jon. Lily. We should have dinner," Serafina said. Lily and

Jon were both reluctant, but after she mentioned dessert, they eventually gave in. Serafina tipped her head towards Freya and Garrett. "We'll see you tomorrow."

Freya waved at them as they left. It was just the two of them now, Freya realized.

"Tell me, how many times did I offend them in the past ten minutes?" Garrett asked.

She bit her lip in thought. She couldn't tell him. What he didn't know... "You don't have to worry about that. They were minor ones," she tried to comfort him. How ridiculous, she thought. As if someone like him really needed comfort. But still, she didn't want him to feel bad all the same.

"If you say so," he replied, a corner of his lip tugging up. "Freya..." It looked as if he turned something over in his mind. "Are you free?"

Freya nodded. "Did you need something?" she asked, wondering what this could be about.

"I have something to show you."

* * *

FREYA DIDN'T KNOW where Garrett was taking her, but one idea began to crystallize in her mind as she noticed the distinct lack of people—here they were, both alone, going God knows where upstairs, where half the lights were out, and the chill had started to sink in. Here, in the long, seemingly endless corridor, the laughter and liveliness from downstairs were a distant memory. He told her he'd protect her from everyone else—she realized he never told her he'd protect her from *himself*.

Maybe he had failed in convincing Serafina, and now he was going to choke Freya to her death. No witnesses.

Kindness isn't necessary, Serafina said. Maybe she had a point—he had simply stopped the act.

"What are you doing?" Garrett snapped.

Startled, Freya missed a step, and before she knew it, she was falling. In the next moment, strong arms held her up, catching her in time.

She blinked, slow. This close, his eyes really *were* a nice indigo color, and, she noted, it reflected a hint of annoyance. Those same eyes roamed all over her.

That was close. She shouldn't be so reckless. She wondered why being this near to him scrambled her thoughts. She had to pay attention. He was most likely plotting her demise.

"You need to be more careful." He set her down with such surprising gentleness, it confused her. He must've been trying to lower her guard first, before he attacked her.

Garrett's intent gaze had her heart hammering in her chest. He leaned close just as she moved back. "You're doing something with the wind, I can tell."

Damn it. She couldn't get past his sharp senses. The wind was reacting to her fears, which may or may not be unfounded.

"I—I've changed my mind. I've remembered I have to help Elara after all," she suddenly blurted out.

Baffled, he considered her. "You don't even like each other. This won't take long."

She just bet it wouldn't. He'd have her quiet and dragging her somewhere no one would find her in no time. Why was he dragging it on, anyway?

She gulped, extracting her hand from his hold. To her surprise, he let her go. "I happen to like Elara," she replied defensively.

He scratched his chin, studying her. "Don't tell me..." He paused. Did he finally guess that she caught on to him? She moved a step backwards, prepared to bolt. "Don't tell me you're afraid of the dark?" His purple eyes glowed, but instead of anger, humor lit his eyes.

The statement was so ludicrous, it was bordering on offensive. Instead of running away, she closed the distance between them instead. "Excuse me? I—I can move around a dark room in my sleep!"

He roared in laughter, his deep voice rumbling against his chest. Why did she like the sound? His shoulders shook, clearly finding something funny, but she watched, annoyed. *Yeah, yeah. Laugh all you want.*

She narrowed her eyes, both hands planted on her hips. "I'd wager I can do it better than any Kilrhinn, even with your superior eyesight."

His eyes glinted at her dare. "I'll take you up on that challenge someday, Freya."

Great. Now she presented a challenge, and he seemed like someone intent on winning. Still, thrill coursed through her at being able to provoke him just a little.

When he sobered, "Then what is it?" he asked.

He sounded so sincere. She second-guessed herself for a moment, until his eyes searched for something behind her, his hand moving towards the hilt of his sword.

This was it. She was going to die. She began to tremble.

His forehead creased. "What's wrong?"

She wrapped her arms around herself. "It's cold." It wasn't exactly a lie, but it wasn't the entire truth either.

His hands wrapped over her shoulders, rubbing up and down. It was almost soothing—if not for the fact that he wanted to kill her. Abruptly, she decided she didn't want to die in the arms of her killer. She slipped free from his hold and walked faster, ahead of him.

She stopped short when she reached a large dark toffee-brown door. Maybe going through the door before her, in the place he'd led her to, was a bad idea. She turned around and found herself staring at a very muscled, broad chest. He was only a breath away.

She tilted her head up to meet his eyes. Deflated, she realized the only exit was behind him. Ahh.

"I realize I never told you where we're going, but it's a surprise. What's your hurry?"

If he was going to kill her, they may as well get it over with. "You should—you should just get on it with it! Just do it."

CHAPTER 8

They were here. They were... in his torture room?

Garrett's brows furrowed. "What the hell are you talking about?"

Before she could respond, Garrett impatiently pushed the door open. Light spilled from behind her, and rooted to the spot, she was unable to look. That would almost be like facing her death.

"Garrett, I—I don't think this is a good idea."

"It's an excellent idea," he drawled. "When you decide to look behind you, maybe you'll realize that."

He nudged her. She squeezed her eyes shut. He turned her around by her shoulders, making her face the room. She kept her eyes tightly closed. Still, she could tell warm light lit the room before her.

"You're not looking, are you?" he guessed.

She shook her head in answer. Why on earth would she want to know what her torture room looked like?

He chuckled. She heard his footsteps as he walked around her, heading inside.

The sound of his steps faded. She didn't sense any more movement. Was this a trick?

When she was convinced he was far enough, slowly, she opened her eyes. She blinked, the magnitude of what was before her assaulting her senses.

Books. There were lots and lots of books.

"Oh my God." This wasn't a torture room. It was a library. She never even considered that they had one. Rows and rows of shelves lined up, stretching up to the top. Not quite all the way to the ceiling, but close. Rows of red, green, blue, and more. This was the furthest thing from a torture room—it was paradise.

When she worked at Mr. Jenkins', his wife loved to read books so Freya always picked one up from their shelves when she had her break.

She found Garrett already with a book open at a table.

"I—I thought…" She trailed off, embarrassed about her line of thought.

He raised a brow. "Where did you think I was taking you?"

"This place is practically hidden. I didn't know what I was supposed to think," she blurted out. She decided to keep the fact that she thought he was going to kill her to herself.

Her fingers traced the spines of the books she passed reverently. She'd never seen so many books gathered in one place in her life. She slid one free from the shelf and opened it. This was about history.

"The Universal books are over there," he mentioned. She'd forgotten that they weren't supposed to know she could read Kilrhinn too.

"Thanks," she murmured her reply, hoping he didn't notice her slip.

"Long day?" he asked. The question surprised her. He

seemed genuinely curious about how it went for her, and she found that she wanted to tell him.

"You could say that. Lily and Jon... The younger Kilrhinns haven't exactly been kind to them," she admitted. "They're the odd ones out."

His expression went alert, catching her meaning. "Is it becoming a problem?"

"It might be. They've handled it for now. They're still young and learning the extent of their abilities, but they're not weak."

He gave it some thought. "You'll tell me if it gets worse. If they need to be put in their place."

He said it like he expected to be unquestioningly obeyed. She rolled her eyes at his tone. "Yes, *my liege*," she added extra emphasis on the title, laying it on thick.

Did he actually crack a smile at that? Yes, he did. Part of her perked up knowing that.

"You can read here when you have the time," he added. "You're welcome to."

She spun to face him. "Do you really mean that?" She was almost afraid he would deny it to her after showing her this incredible space on the upper floors.

Her question baffled him. "I wouldn't say it if I meant otherwise."

She hooked her finger on a random spine of a book from the Universal section and pulled it out carefully. She cradled the book close to her chest and walked to the table. She could almost kiss him for showing her this place. "Thanks, Garrett." He didn't know what he just gave her, but she treasured it with her heart.

"Did you really work at a tailor shop?"

"Yep."

"Why?"

She opened her mouth to answer, but immediately closed

it. Trying again, she said, "It seemed like a good idea at the time."

He hummed in reply. She could tell he didn't buy it. Why was he fishing for answers now?

"Sewing a couple of pieces of cloth must've been mind-numbingly tedious," he said conversationally.

She smiled at the memory of working at the tailor shop. If she closed her eyes, she could still remember the smell of leather and cigar in the shop, and the sound of the machines that worked their magic on the clothes. "Actually, I enjoyed it."

Was he scowling? "Mr. Jenkins doesn't have our coffee. Or Elara to make you food."

"True," she replied. She wasn't a coffee person, but she could appreciate the hit it gave when she needed it. But she couldn't deny that Elara's cooking was amazing. "Still, I learnt a lot from the experience." Such as the fact that hiding in the most mundane of places bought her some time. Working at Mr. Jenkins' meant it was the least likely place Terrence would expect. But more than that, she made some good friends, too.

"Why did you take common jobs? You could earn more on a job with your skills." He wasn't even pretending to be reading anymore. His book laid open on the table, some printed map of the Earth abandoned. He was trying to understand her, and it seemed like he was having a rough time with it. It made her own lips pull up in a small smile.

"I didn't want to do those jobs." Because Terrence would find out if she did. She never liked being put in a box, anyway.

"So it's not about the money. I can't imagine it was possibly stimulating for you. Necessity, then?"

The thing was, Garrett's senses and intuition were razor-sharp. She couldn't answer any more of his questions. "What is this, an interrogation?" she asked a question of her own. She'd spent all this time evading questions, and she wasn't going to stop now.

Dissatisfied with her answer, he rubbed his jaw. His keen gaze missed nothing, and she couldn't focus on a single word she was reading anymore.

"You know, you understand Lhianne culture, but you never once made a misstep with ours. Almost like you understand us perfectly."

"Kilrhinns don't have much of an obsession with hierarchy or order," she countered. She hoped he didn't catch the slight wavering of her voice, or how her pulse quickened...

"We have some of those, too," he answered smoothly. His wicked grin made her heart stop. Something glinted in his eyes, dark and hungry. "Power creates hierarchy in itself. And bonding puts our partner's lives above our own." He meant mates. Soul partners. Like her parents were. Her cheeks heated at the turn of conversation. "I look forward to teaching you about them," he said.

She had the strangest feeling that he enjoyed this—throwing her off and flustering her. "That—that won't be necessary. I don't imagine you'll have any trouble securing a deal with the Lhiannes, anyway."

He only smirked. "I hope so."

Then he dropped asking her questions, focusing his attention back on the book. But even throughout it, he kept her company. She found that she didn't mind it at all. If she could admit it to herself, she actually found comfort in the quiet, in the way he made her feel safe.

She had to be realistic—there were so many variables. It may be going well now with the Lhiannes, but if she couldn't fulfill her task, what then? Would they cast her aside?

No, she didn't have a choice.

She had to help them secure the deal. And then she would leave.

* * *

SHE HAD FALLEN fast asleep over a book on the origin of different herbs, her face resting on the crook of her arm. Garrett watched as her breathing turned slow and even, a peaceful look on her face. She was a small thing, but she was fierce—she had fire, and she had no trouble showing it. She also proved that she was not only both smart and attentive when it came to the Lhiannes, but she was equally capable of adapting to their world.

His hand lifted up to touch her face. To feel if it was as soft as it looked. He stopped himself in time. Damn if he wanted to kiss her.

He had a lot of questions when it came to her. Where did she come from, and how was it that she worked at a tailor shop when she didn't have to? And when her fingers had brushed over the words on a book she opened before, it was as if she could read Kilrhinn herself. Perhaps it was only a mistake. But with the way she'd looked so entranced as her eyes swept over the page, he wondered.

He was right in bringing her here, seeing how it pleased her—and the way she held each book, like it was a prized possession. He'd gathered she had no such means of accessing books in her village—at least, not to this extent. Satisfaction surged through him at the thought of giving her a piece of something she valued. Even if it was only to lessen the sense of isolation she had to feel being far from home.

He didn't know why he did it, but before he could help himself, his lips touched the top of her head. Just a quick brush, but it felt right. She didn't know it yet, but she was quickly becoming important to him.

Asleep, she was defenseless and vulnerable. He gave a quick word to Rav so he could guard her in his absence. Only then did he leave.

* * *

KATHERINE ROWES WAS a stranger to kindness.

In the slums, people looked after their own hide. She was only half-Kilrhinn, and she was often reminded of it. But in the days since she started working for the Vhenn Bradis Family, she hadn't felt an ounce of their judgement.

"The best way to sabotage the alliance is to work your way in," Yael, the hooded man, had told her. He had tossed her the notice that they were hiring for their clinic. She didn't think she'd get accepted. It felt like a fluke. She was torn between triumph and fear.

She didn't have to live in the slums anymore. She had enough food to fill her belly and wouldn't feel the gnawing hunger anymore. She might get a chance to save her sister... But she didn't want to have to kill to do it. The alliance would mean everything for the Kilrhinns. Not just now that the Scourge were back, but because the storms had taken her parents away from her. How many lives could the alliance save? How many families would they protect, with the Lhiannes at their side? And she had to sabotage it. The Brion blood in her had been nothing but a curse she had to live with.

Katherine hid behind a tall bush in the gardens. Freya frequented the place when she wasn't in the kitchens. She had a guard with her too, just like always. These weren't ordinary men. They were good at hiding their tracks.

She didn't think Freya was even aware of it. How must it feel to live like that, without fear that at every turn someone would take advantage of you?

Katherine only had a moment of warning before she felt the heat of the body behind her.

"You're quite far away from the clinic," the voice drawled. His breath tickled her ear.

She whipped her head around, looking up only to face the most gorgeous man she'd ever seen. Gold-dusted skin, full lips and clothes that hugged his sculpted body. She'd seen him before with Garrett Bradis, but this close, she only stared. He had never spoken to her before, but he had brought some men into the clinic several times. He never seemed to smile at her, not even in greeting. Always preoccupied with some task, and always in a hurry to leave. Xander, she seemed to recall, was what Jess called him.

"I—I needed some air. Jess told me to get a breather," she found herself admitting. She was still new to the job. Because Brions had the ability to sense pain and sickness, if one was especially sensitive, they felt that pain too, for a brief moment. And Katherine *felt*. She hadn't ever taken a job like this because it had taken a toll on her when she was younger.

"A Brion with little tolerance for pain. Imagine that." His lips curved up just slightly, but humor didn't touch his eyes.

"I'll get used to it," she said, not liking his words. He might've been gorgeous, but she wouldn't let him walk all over her.

"I'm sure you will. You don't adapt, you don't make it around here."

Oh, please. She wasn't that fragile. "I've been through worse," she replied, her voice coming out sharper than she'd intended.

He raised a brow, his curiosity piqued, but she kept her lips firmly sealed. She revealed more than she'd meant to. How did he do that?

"Not surgery work, surely? You nearly fainted that one

time." This time, a real, smug smile. She decided she rather preferred him not smiling.

She didn't answer him. She continued to head towards the Earth's flowers, gathering in one section. She kept Freya at the edge of her vision.

He followed behind her, steps as quiet as a whisper; if she didn't look, she wouldn't have thought he was there at all.

"Don't you have things to do? People to boss around." He was starting to irritate her. If he wanted to follow her around, how was she supposed to execute her plan?

She plucked a red flower, its petals so thin she was afraid they'd fall off.

"Brions are in charge of our lives. I figure it's important to get to know each one." Well, wasn't that wonderful?

"And it just so happens to be my lucky day?" she asked dryly.

"Something like that."

"Yay me," she murmured.

He snorted. "Your sharp tongue could get you in trouble."

It already had in the past, being involved in a couple brawls. She bit her tongue.

"Something tells me that isn't something new when it comes to you," he surmised.

Suddenly, he whirled his head around, something appearing to have caught his attention.

"What is it?" She saw a gardener tip his head at them and cut the edges of a bush.

"Know that guy?" he asked quietly, tension in his voice.

She squinted. He seemed just like another gardener, she wasn't too sure. "No. Why?"

Xander shook his head, carefully keeping his expression blank. His hands went to her shoulders, urging her to hurry. She shivered from the contact, warm hands easing down to her arms. "Felt him watching."

The back of her neck prickled. Although there was nothing particularly distinctive about the gardener's features, she committed it to memory. So it was true Yael had people everywhere. Any hope she had since meeting the Kilrhinns dissolved, leaving a pit of despair in her stomach. So much for thinking that here, she was safe.

CHAPTER 9

"*F*reya?"

Freya turned and saw Jess in the Kilrhinns' traditional flowing gown. Her hair was half-tied up, the edges curled, the silver ends glowing from the lanterns.

It was the Commemoration Feast day. The holiday was one of the reasons the Lhiannes were invited, since it coincided with one of the Kilrhinns' biggest festivals. The celebrations involved fireworks, getting drunk, and lots of dancing. She'd only heard about it, but never been to one before.

Earlier, she'd helped Elara with the preparation of some Lhianne dishes, but she was largely shooed away from the kitchen, saying they were making "Kilrhinn dishes, not Lhianne" for the feast.

"Where are the Lhiannes?" Jess asked, peering behind Freya. The Lhiannes were the guests tonight, at the front row.

"They're down at the celebrations."

Jess' brows shot up. "Well? Why aren't you there?"

There wasn't really a need for her there, with everyone

being so busy. The Lhiannes wouldn't be alone tonight. They wouldn't even notice that she wasn't there. Besides, this was the Kilrhinns' celebration, and she didn't feel right pretending to fit in. She'd be happy watching from the distance.

She had spent all these months running away, avoiding any kind of attention. She should've been used to it by now. But still, a feeling of longing gnawed at her.

"I'll be okay, Jess. I can still watch from here," Freya simply said, mustering a small smile.

Climbing up the stairs, someone was running, calling out an exuberant, "Jess!"

Jess checked who'd called her name over her shoulder. Then she looked back at Freya, biting her lip.

The woman reached the top of the staircase and hurried towards them, her energy boundless. She was a human, Freya realized. The woman was shorter than her, her sable hair reaching up to her shoulders. Her lips parted in surprise. "Wait a moment," Jess' friend said, recognition sparking in her eyes. "You're the Lhianne, right? Freya? Did he make you drink blood like a vampire, in his oath?" she burst out, eyes round.

What? It took Freya a moment to grasp who she meant— Garrett. "No."

"Izzy!" Jess chided.

"Sorry," Izzy mumbled. "Everyone was talking about it. I'm Izzy, by the way."

"I'm sorry, Freya," Jess said, abashed. "People talk."

"It's fine. Really. I've gotten used to it. And it's nice to meet you."

Izzy smiled back, scratching her cheek. "Likewise."

"You shouldn't have to," Jess said, a stern look casting over her face. "Are you sure you'll be fine staying here?"

"Positive."

"If you change your mind... Feast day is no good cele-brated alone. I think you'll love it. You should come and see the madness for yourself."

* * *

IT WAS odd to witness such an event, all the celebrations and laughter, feeling separate from it all. Freya was reminded that she was only a stranger in this new, strange place. She had to keep it this way, so that no roots kept her here. So that by the time she finished her job, she could leave.

Freya looked down, trying to make out the small heads below. She slipped her toes in the gaps of the balustrade and pushed herself up with her arms. That was better—it gave her an unimpeded view down below. She looked down at the lights and lanterns, like speckled jewels from the distance.

"Don't even think about it," a deep voice warned. Rav slipped beside her the next moment, his speed catching her off-guard.

"Rav!" Freya burst out. She beamed at him. She hadn't seen him in a while.

He pushed her further back in, putting more distance between her and the edge of the balcony.

She found herself rolling her eyes. "I'm not going to jump."

"You can climb down. Who the hell knows." He turned to look in the direction of her gaze, on the circular area where people had gathered around. His brows pulled together when the music started. "You should join."

"I—I don't dance." It was the first excuse that came to her, but it was also true.

He roared in laughter, hand clutching his stomach. "You think Chester can? Or Ignas?"

His laughter was infectious, and she found herself snickering, too. "Okay, you have a point."

She slid a glance at him. Well... "You're not dancing either," she commented.

He shrugged. "I'm working."

She snorted. Yeah, right.

Fireworks exploded in the sky. Red and orange, shooting up the inky vastness and fading fast, only to be replaced by a more splendid cascade of color.

She leaned forward again, climbing up the raised platform in the balustrade. She watched, enthralled, as sound erupted with the burst of color, and people cheered. Music started to play. Some danced along with it, bodies moving from the distance.

"Make a wish," Rav said.

Startled, she looked at him questioningly. He shrugged. "They say if you make a wish when the fireworks hit, the souls will work to make your wish come true."

"Do you believe that?" she asked curiously. And for whatever reason, something told her he did.

"Dunno. My mother did. She said unanswered wishes don't mean they won't come true." As if shaking off an unpleasant memory, his fingers curled. "Doesn't matter. Make a wish, it's tradition."

Her hunch was right. He *was* superstitious.

Her gaze was drawn back up to the sky.

A wish.

She never really allowed herself to dwell on something so fanciful. But sometimes, in the middle of the night, she wondered what her future would be like without Terrence hunting her. She closed her eyes for a moment. She just wanted to stop running. She was so tired of it.

Done making her wish, she gasped in surprise, seeing the blond Kilrhinn leaning on the rail beside her, opposite Rav, calmly observing the crowd below. How did they keep doing that so silently? "Kane?" And just how long had he been standing there?

"Freya," he acknowledged when she saw him, a corner of his lips quirking up. If she could guess, he probably enjoyed sneaking up on people. "Garrett was looking for you."

"Did something happen with the Lhiannes?" she asked, a surge of concern making her jump down from the raised platform and find her balance.

Rav cursed and helped steady her. "Acting like you're a damn Earth bunny," he muttered.

Kane looked at her oddly. "No. Why do you think so?"

"Why else would he want me there?" Perplexed, she wondered if another fight had erupted. "I'll go look for them, then. Thanks for watching the fireworks with me, Rav." She grinned at the grumpy Kilrhinn. She turned on her heel, only to find Kane a step ahead of her, light on his feet.

"Oh, you don't have to escort me," she offered him an out. She was sure he had better things to do than babysit her. "I can manage."

He was quiet, turning his head to study her, then he looked away. "You think so little of your value."

"Excuse me?"

She tried to keep up with him as he effortlessly evaded people and stalls. He moved quickly and efficiently. No movement was wasted. She thought he moved like a shadow.

"That's a dangerous line of thought," he went on as if she hadn't asked a question. "Make no mistake, right now you're probably a target, and you don't even know it."

His words chilled her. Did he know about Terrence? Her heart nearly stopped. What if he was here *now*?

"No one's after me," she denied flatly. She glanced behind her surreptitiously.

"Now I know you're lying."

She nearly stumbled over her own feet. How had he seen through it? She looked behind her again, trying to search for any signs that Terrence was following her, and bumped onto a hard back. "Ow."

"Around here," Kane said abruptly.

She rubbed the tip of her nose. "A little warning would've been nice." Her eyes swept over the area. The smell of vanilla and honey drifted over. Around her, there were some candied corn and rice crisps on a stick. Her eyes roamed over some more. Kids laughing and playing with chalk. Flower beds. She stopped when she saw a man wearing a smoky gray hat, walking with a familiar limp. Beside him was a man with light-brown hair and dark skin. She'd forgotten that they opened the gates to the public for today.

No way.

"Klein! Mr. Jenkins!" she called out.

"Freya—" Kane started, but she didn't listen, running to meet her friends.

They met her halfway. She noticed Klein was carrying some flowers in a plain black pot.

"Freya! Are they treating you well?" A stern look crossed over Mr. Jenkins' face. She hugged him, tight. "They took away my best knitter."

This made her smile. In the time she'd worked for him, both him and Mrs. Jenkins treated her like their own daughter. She was grateful for their kindness. It was one of the reasons she stuck with them for so long. She brushed away a tear that escaped.

"They are," she answered earnestly.

Klein had one of those pink carnations she liked, and she accepted them, moved by his thoughtfulness. She hugged him, too.

"I was hoping to see you," Klein revealed. "I heard you

worked here now. You just... disappeared." His eyes swept over her. "You're happy here?"

She thought of all the people she'd met in the short time she'd stayed here. "Yes. They've been good to me."

As if sensing the truth in her words, the worry that marked his face melted away. "Glad to hear it."

Friendly faces. She missed her little apartment on the corner of the street. The way the aroma of the freshly baked pastries flitted past as she'd made her way to work.

"Freya." The familiar deep voice cut through the night from behind her, curling over her, and she spun around.

"Garrett!" The large Kilrhinn strode towards them with single-minded purpose, his eyes flicking to Freya. Her stomach dipped. After he left the library last week, she hadn't seen him much. She occasionally snuck into the library, wanting to read, but also hoping to see him. He seemed to be busy lately. He nodded at Kane, as if an unspoken agreement had passed between them. Kane slipped through a small crowd, and then he was gone.

Klein and Mr. Jenkins went alert when they saw Garrett.

"These are my friends," she said brightly. Garrett's eyes dropped to her flowers. Was it her imagination that he glowered at them? She clutched the flowers tighter to her chest. The poor flowers didn't do anything to incur his wrath.

"Klein, Mr. Jenkins, this is Garrett Bradis," she introduced them. She could imagine what they were thinking—he was tall and intimidating. It didn't help that right now, he wasn't smiling at all. She nudged his shoulder a bit.

Garrett greeted Mr. Jenkins politely, but his expression turned stiff when his eyes met Klein's. Okay. Maybe it wasn't a good idea for them to talk after all.

He turned to Freya. "Where were you?" he asked brusquely.

"Upstairs," Freya replied, surprised at his question. She did a little shrug. "Just watching."

"Why?"

Why? "I wasn't needed down here," she answered.

His eyes softened, and he tugged her hand. "Lily and Jon are looking for you."

It hadn't occurred to her that they would ask where she was. She thought they would be pretty occupied tonight.

"They are?"

"Yes. You sound surprised."

Her cheeks flushed. She *was* surprised. She turned to wish Mr. Jenkins and his wife well, apologizing that she had to go, but promising to visit them, too. Freya gave Mr. Jenkins and Klein one last hug before she had to go. She thought she saw Garrett tense behind her, but paid him no mind. Klein told her he'd send her one of his newer pots that he made. She touched his cheek, thanking him, thrilled that he thought of giving her a gift.

She waved at them as they left. She wished she could talk to them more. She missed them.

"You were crying," Garrett muttered, displeased.

"I'm just happy to see them. They're good people. They made me feel welcome when I first came to Maranthe."

"And Klein?" he prompted.

She glanced at him, wondering at the bite in his words. "What about him?"

"Who is he?"

"A good friend. He makes great pots. They're beautiful," she revealed proudly. They made excellent hiding cover, too. But she didn't say that.

"He gave the flowers," he guessed.

"Yeah. I've always wanted to buy them, but—" She stopped, realizing she was about to reveal something personal. "Anyway, they're my favorite," she finished awkwardly.

Seeing her friends again made her heart full, lifting her spirits. As much as she tried to be kind to the people she met here in Maranthe, she knew the Kilrhinns didn't consider her one of them. Especially since she spent so much time around Serafina, Lily and Jon. That was just something that she had to deal with. Part of the job she accepted.

"You said you didn't think you were needed down here," Garrett said.

She wanted to ask him what he meant, when "Freya!" Lily called out. "You're here! Where were you?"

A hand resting lightly on the low of her back, Garrett led her to an area where the other Lhiannes sat, perched on a bench. Freya was intensely aware of where he touched her. It was highly distracting.

Lily waved both arms. Freya waved back, grinning.

Jon looked pleased to see her. "You missed the fireworks," he said.

"So he found you." Serafina fought a smile. "As I was saying, your Kilrhinn was about to rip someone's head off."

Her Kilrhinn? She slid him a look, but Garrett's face was inscrutable. "Why would he do that?"

"He couldn't find you."

Jon passed her a small paper plate. "Freya—Elara brought this over earlier. She insisted you try this."

"What is it?" Freya asked. It was a light yellow cake, with swirls of purple that decorated the top, giving it a patterned design, looking almost like flower petals. "Is it lemon-flavored?"

"It's berry bliss. You've never had it?" Garrett asked, surprised. "We have this every year for the feast. It's tradition to have some."

Freya never really went to any celebration like this before. "No, I've never had one." She cut off a small piece and took a bite. A burst of sweet flavor exploded on her tongue. It wasn't lemon. It was a yellow custard, the top with swirls of some berries, but it was only a little tart, balancing with the cream of the custard.

Watching her, "You like it?" he asked.

Freya had no other words except, "Elara is amazing."

Garrett chuckled. "It's why we keep her around."

And as she had dessert, she watched everyone. It was as if the boundaries between Lhiannes, Kilrhinns, and others melted away. The joy of the celebrations went way beyond that—up close, she could see that now.

And it struck her that she was wrong—they *had* felt her absence.

The music shifted to a slower beat. Most people had left the center, but a few couples, she noted, had also came in. To her surprise, Garrett held a hand out.

Her eyes widened. He couldn't possibly mean...? As odd as her circumstances were, she found she trusted him. Perhaps more than anyone else here. She placed her hand in his. Their eyes met, and a small grin pulled at his lips—he knew what her surrender meant. He led her to the heart of the celebration, right at the center, where the crowd parted. Oh hell. He really did want to dance. For a moment, she thought it might've been for another reason. He was going to hate her.

"Garrett, just so you know, I'm a terrible dancer," she warned him. It was better he learned this now.

He leaned close to her ear. "Do your worst."

He thought this was some sort of joke. "I'm serious. I've stepped on my partner's foot a time too many."

His lips quirked up. "I'll survive."

He *still* wasn't taking her seriously. "Garrett—"

His hand dropped lower, down to her waist. She forgot what she was about to say.

"Relax," he said.

She drew in a deep breath. Maybe all she needed to do was to stop thinking.

True enough, she never stepped on his foot. She figured it had to do with the Kilrhinn's great reflexes. Or maybe he was just great at leading the dance. *Because, maybe, he'd done it many times before.*

"You're really good at this..." He spun her around. "You must've had a lot of practice," she found herself saying.

"Hardly," he replied, drawing her back into him as they danced.

Someone who moved as good as him? She couldn't believe it.

She felt people's eyes on them. She rested her cheek on his chest. It felt warm. Like a wall of comfort. She could hear his heartbeat, and it seemed to settle her nerves.

"Too much?" he asked.

"People will talk," she murmured.

"Let them." He didn't even seem the least bit bothered about the fact. But he should've been. The rumors that circled around him couldn't be further from the truth.

"Did you know people think you made me drink blood in our oath?" she blurted out. She lifted her head up to see if he knew.

He looked so stunned by her question that she wasn't sure if he realized they stopped dancing.

"That's what people are saying," she continued. "And that you bent the bars in the prison cell, like you're some sort of madman. Then there's the one about how you eat people's hearts out..."

His head bent down, she saw his shoulders shake, and he burst out laughing.

She blinked. Coming from him, the sound wrapped all over her. Deep and rich, the rumble from his chest came out rough and unexpected. Now she was certain *everyone* was looking.

When the music ended, she couldn't look at everyone. Her cheeks heated, and she slapped both hands on them. *Calm. Stay calm.*

But without warning, a gust of wind had blown over.

* * *

KATHERINE PULLED the vial from her pocket. Inside was a light peach, pearlescent liquid. She closed her hand around it. Poison. A weak one, but potent enough. It would do its job, keeping whoever ingested it sick for days. An old friend had passed it to her when she had ventured outside the fort to buy some medicinal herbs. It cost her fifty silvers from her pay.

This was her only chance. She had hung around the kitchens all day waiting for an opportunity. They were sending out cocktails next. She only had to know which drinks the Lhiannes were having.

This way, she wouldn't have to kill Freya. There would be blame, and it would create a rift on the tenuous relationship between the Kilrhinns and the Lhiannes. It made her sick to her stomach, knowing what she was about to do, but she didn't have a choice—she had to do it.

Loud cheers burst from outside. Startled, the vial slipped from her gasp, and to her horror, it landed on the floor with a crack. Her heart stopped.

"No, no, no..." Desperately, she tried to gather the substance back into the vial, but it was pointless. Its contents had already spilled out.

A ball of panic gathered in her chest. How was she going

to replace it? What would she do now? Her hopes plummeted. For a while, she'd thought that maybe she could sabotage the mission in a different way instead. Now all of that was up in the ashes.

Katherine wasn't one to break down easily. The slums had toughened her and Rina, her sister. Not even when their food was stolen and they had to go without for days. Or when the kids cornered her and pummeled her until her ribs broke, when she was younger.

But now the walls were closing in around her, until she found it hard to breathe. She brushed a tear away, but another kept coming. She covered her mouth to keep the broken sound from escaping her lips.

"For a Brion, you're almost never at the clinic." Katherine jumped back in surprise. Xander.

Just her luck. She tried to gather the jagged pieces of glass and gasped when she cut herself. She heard him mutter a curse. She sniffed, wiping her tears. He helped her dispose of the shards. Then, at a loss at what to do, she started crying again.

"Shit," Xander muttered, pressing something on her finger. A cloth.

She had to be strong for Rina. Why did he have to catch her at her lowest?

His hands on her arms, rubbing soothingly, he asked, "Everything okay?"

His face was so fierce, like some sort of knight, that she could only stare at him, wide-eyed. Except she wasn't some princess, and she didn't need a knight. He wanted to help someone who didn't deserve his sympathy.

"I-I'm f-fine." She started to hiccup. God, she was pathetic.

"No. You're not," he bit out.

He led her outside. She started to breathe a little easier,

his presence like a balm to the fear battering at her senses. He hesitated for a moment, but then he pulled in a sigh. "They say when you say it out loud, you'll feel better."

She didn't know him. Not really. She'd only ever spoken to him that one time in the garden, and still, he was here for her.

"My sister's d-dying." Her voice came out brittle. Admitting it nearly broke her. She didn't know why she said it—it simply came out. It was the truth, even though it was only part of it. Except her sister wasn't dying from any sickness or injury—her sister's life was in the hands of the foulest creature that ever walked this planet.

His face was torn, grief overtaking it. And then she knew —he understood. Maybe he lost someone, too.

He met her gaze. "I'm sorry," he said grimly. He meant it, too, and she felt it with her heart.

"She's the only family I have left. I don't know what to do." Suddenly feeling vulnerable before him, she quickly added, "Sorry, I didn't mean to burden you with my problems."

"Katherine—"

In the blink of an eye, clouds started to gather, forming a black cloud. The winds, untamed, swept over them.

Fear slammed into her, rooting her to the spot. It was just like this, the day her parents died.

Xander stood up, alert. It was as if a switch had turned on, and the protector in him took over.

"Get inside," he ordered, his voice brooking no argument. "It's safer there. I have to go."

She watched his back as he left, disappearing into the crowd.

Katherine heard the screams of many, and her heart clenched in her chest. Out there, she was needed. She may be powerless when it came to her own fate, but in this at least, she knew she could do something.

I'm sorry, she thought. *I can't go back inside.*

* * *

THE STORM STARTED to gather like a monster.

It wasn't like the last storm. It was growing too fast, and it was already getting harder to contain by the second.

Behind her, Garrett sprang into action, helping people take cover.

Serafina pushed the clouds further away, making them scatter. Freya went to work in aiding her. The clouds drew back in, like an elastic band snapping into place. Lily and Jon helped with adjusting the clouds, but in the face of the storm's fury, their control was lacking. More clouds had gathered to the center, the tempestuous wind wrecking the decorations of the feast. People screamed behind them. Dread filled Freya. The mass of clouds continued to grow in size.

"I can put it away," Serafina hissed, "but someone needs to—"

"I'll do it," Freya volunteered. She didn't wait for a response. She dashed to where the tumultuous storm had reared its head, not looking back. Not pausing to stop. She needed to head to the eye of the storm.

The clouds had thinned a little—Serafina's work. Still, it was growing. Panic gripped Freya, almost paralyzing.

People were finding shelter, following the drill the Kilrhinns made for emergencies. Around her was chaos. *No.* She couldn't let it consume her.

Freya made it several yards, her eyes focused on the distance. She was close. A heavy body knocked her over, and they rolled on the rough ground. She tasted salt and chalk and coughed. Her pursuer moved fast, and before she knew it, he settled on her back. Someone had pinned her to the ground. "You want to die that bad?" Kane snarled.

She wanted to scream in frustration. Not this again. "Kane, let go! I've never seen anything like this!" she yelled. "I *need* to stop it. Let me do my job. Please!"

"I let you go, and it will shred you!"

He didn't understand. Everything lay on this crucial moment—even Serafina and the others couldn't hold off this storm for longer by themselves.

"We might be able to save everyone!" she screamed. Still, he didn't budge, like an iron weight pressing down on her.

"Please! I can help stop it." She turned her head and looked him in the eye, and she didn't know what he saw—maybe it was wild desperation, or maybe her words finally sank in. But to her amazement, he released her.

He pushed his hair back, his bottom lip curling. "Fuck. You need to survive," he told her, hands shaking her shoulders. "You don't, the storm may be gone, but Garrett will fucking kill us all. *Shit.*"

She doubted she mattered that much to anyone, least of all the scary Kilrhinn. But Garrett was kind to her. In his arms, tonight, she had forgotten who she was, and why she was here. She was simply Freya.

She didn't waste another second—she ran. She lifted her arms up, testing the wind for a response. It answered back, caressing her cheek. Serafina had done a tremendous job thinning the clouds. But if Freya didn't do her part, it would all be for nothing.

A sound grabbed her attention. Sobbing.

She squinted her eyes. A little girl was hugging a tree, terrified. Freya watched as a blast of wind whipped towards the child, like a snake hunting its prey. Freya deflected its course. She didn't get a chance to celebrate. In her miscalculation, it headed straight towards her instead. She didn't have enough time to react.

"Freya!" Serafina called out. At the last second, the gust of wind exploded upwards, narrowly avoiding Freya in time. The impact of the wind knocked Freya back on the ground, hard. She skidded against the dirt ground, its roughness digging into her skin. But still, she was close. She crawled towards the heart of the storm, on her knees, resisting the wind and its attempt to knock her down. She lifted a hand up, trying to grasp some control of it.

Please. With great effort, she pleaded, *let me in*.

From the distance, she thought she heard a loud roar tear out, as if the heavens were lashing out its fury.

Then the wind swallowed her whole.

CHAPTER 10

"Someone explain to me what the hell just happened." Garrett's voice swept over the room, piercing. Frost had settled in his eyes as he looked at each of his men.

No one spoke. Kane looked away, his jaw hard. Rav's face was stony.

Garrett narrowed his eyes. "You were all there." He had worn the carpet thin from the way he paced around the room when they first arrived. "What I don't understand, is why you let Freya run *into* the fucking storm."

He had to watch her run straight into the storm that everyone was trying their damn best to run away *from*. His best men, and for whatever reason, they couldn't stop a single woman from doing something so fucking reckless.

Galen stepped forward. "My liege, she's a Lhianne," he stated plainly. As if that should explain everything.

"I know what she is," Garrett growled. "I also know that just because she is, it doesn't make her invulnerable to it."

"She has better chances of stopping it than any of us here. Isn't that why you wanted an alliance with them?"

"And in letting her go, how certain were you that she wasn't running to her death?"

Galen wasn't, but then he remembered, "She survived before." As soon as the words slipped from his tongue, he knew he made a mistake.

"Before?" A cracking sound. Garrett looked down at his glass. Ah, shit. It was his third that he accidentally broke. Elara loved her crystal glasses. He'd have to get it replaced.

Galen winced. His mouth snapped shut.

It all became clear now—the first time the Lhiannes came. He was told there was a storm. Freya stopped it, then, too. Only then, the storm was much less violent. "How sure were you that if she stopped it, she'd survive?" he repeated the question.

"She said she could save everyone." It was Kane who had spoken this time. He sported a bruise on his cheek, now starting to darken.

Everyone's eyes shot to him. Kane was always the calm one, unbending, despite all the pressure. He weighed in all odds before acting. In the same way, he observed from the distance before he spoke, but he always did his job without fail. In place of his usual reserved demeanor was one of begrudging respect. "She seemed so damned determined, I took that chance." He rubbed at his cheek, deep in thought. "I won't promise that I can stop her next time, but I can promise I'll do my best to keep her alive." He met all their eyes evenly, so they'd all understand. "Even if I have to go with her to do it."

* * *

"Can't believe she just ran into the storm," Rav said irritably. "Going to give her hell when she wakes up. Never seen a storm like that, too." He looked down at his raw fist, now an angry red. He was the first to punch Kane when he let her run into the storm. It was too late to stop her then. Kane didn't return it—it was the only reason Rav's anger had dissipated. He picked up his glass of beer and tipped it to his mouth.

He didn't know how Freya survived all these years, because it seemed like she had no sense of self-preservation. She was small and fast on her feet, but while she always gave a good fight, she wasn't a warrior. She could've died—it was what weighed on their minds so heavily. And if she did, it would've been on their hands. His grip on the glass tightened.

If they needed a reminder that they needed the Lhiannes, the storm had just confirmed it.

Galen grimaced at his words. "Well, this *was* the woman who tried to climb our walls to escape. She just saved our asses, too."

"Damn straight," Rav muttered.

Kane had downed his own glass of beer, a dark look crossing over his face. "She's a handful. But we knew that coming in." He regretted letting her go. Good.

They'd seen her fight her way to the center, and she disappeared. Then almost immediately, the storm had spread outwards, rapidly dissolving, leaving an unconscious Freya on the ground. The other Lhiannes could help stop the storm too. But would they run straight into it without a thought to their safety, like Freya did?

Rav knew the answer.

* * *

"How is she?" Garrett asked. He'd met Jess at the entrance of the clinic.

They had never seen a storm of that magnitude before.

The last destructive storm that passed them, many had perished. The Commemoration Feast had turned into chaos in mere moments. Due to practice drills, they had survived, but many were injured. Still, the damage was done.

With a sigh, "See for yourself," Jess said. She pushed the door open wordlessly.

He found Freya, swinging her legs down from the bed, pushing the covers away. Was she trying to get out of here so soon? She froze when their gazes met, caught.

His eyes ran over her. She had grazes over her knees and arms. He gritted his teeth.

"I'm fine," Freya stated.

"She *needs* rest," Jess stressed. "She'll insist she won't need it, but she just doesn't feel it yet."

"I can move!" Freya protested. She jumped on her feet to prove them wrong and raised her arms up. "I'm not so fragile."

"I know you're not," Jess agreed gently. "But a little rest won't do you any harm. Your body's tired. You've nearly tested your limits."

Seeing how she couldn't convince them otherwise, she rolled her eyes, muttering something low under her breath. She hesitated, but decided she needed to know—"How is everyone?"

"Alive."

"Thank God." She exhaled a breath. He watched her shoulders slump in relief, her efforts earlier taking a toll on her.

Before he could stop himself, he ate the distance between them.

Nothing had prepared him for the cold fist that gripped his chest seeing her run into the storm. He hadn't felt fear for anyone in a long time, but watching her, it had nearly driven him mad. If he wasn't in charge of bringing the others to safety, he would've been there with her, and damn if the storm would've torn him apart.

He considered himself a rational man—tonight, because of a single woman, he realized he couldn't have been more wrong. For a little while tonight, he'd held her. And he nearly lost her.

"You won't do that again," he commanded.

He noticed the guarded expression in her eyes.

The complete authority in his voice made her stand straighter. She lifted her chin up. "I will, if it could save lives," she defied. "You can't order me around."

Fuck. She made him crazy. She had to be the obstinate one. "You can't keep running to your death," he snarled.

Her eyes were a wild green—fierce and bright, and right now, he couldn't help but be drawn to it. "I get it, you need me for your alliance and I'm no good dead. But I'm not going to stand by and watch people die if I can do something about it. I'm not that kind of person, and I don't think you are either." The gentle breeze in the room began to blow stronger in his direction. He suspected Freya didn't even notice she was doing it.

Jess concealed her laugh with a cough. "I, uh, have to check on the other patients." She quietly left them, and then they were alone in the room.

No one had challenged him this way before. She didn't know what it took to hold onto his control. She was a warrior of her own, choosing her own battles. He had to give it to her—she had the grit to make it out alive. Because he didn't want to admit it, but she was right. In her place, he would do the same.

Securing the alliance was crucial... But so was keeping her. He would let this slide for now. But if she thought she could do the same thing again and not expect them to help her with it, she'd be in for a hell of a surprise.

"I'll give you this," he conceded. "But you're not alone. An alliance means we also do our part."

She listened, her lips parted in wonder. As if his response was entirely unexpected. She turned a slight shade of pink.

Unable to help it, he lifted his hand to touch her cheek. She flinched, taking an involuntary step backwards.

He froze. He'd seen this reaction on a few people, and there was usually one main reason for them. "Who was it?" he asked, his voice deceptively light.

"W-what?"

Shock hit her, and then even more telling—fear. He thought of a man's hands on her, hurting her, and saw red. "Give me his name and he'll never hurt you again."

* * *

HOW DID HE KNOW? Panic pinned Freya to the spot. What was she supposed to do? Where could she go? Escape. She needed to—

"Breathe," Garrett's steady voice calmed her, like an anchor that gave her mind clarity. She didn't realize she was gulping in air. Her hand rested on his hard chest, warm to the touch. With conscious effort, she followed the rhythm of his breathing, feeling the beat of his heart.

Slowly, she began to realize he didn't know about Terrence.

So stupid. Her reaction earlier was instinctive, but she didn't realize she'd given a clue to what chased her in her nightmares.

She squeezed her eyes shut. Oh, it would be so easy for him to fix everything. But it would mean telling him the truth. She didn't want to put anyone in danger and she didn't want to involve him, of all people. "No one." He was perceptive. If she closed her eyes, he wouldn't see how difficult it was for her to hide.

It was only a matter of time now before Terrence found her.

Garrett's hand continued to roam over her back soothingly, distractingly pleasant and not at all unwelcome. As if touching her pleased him.

Yeah, right. She was starting to imagine things. Right now she needed to think. Flushed, she told him, "You can—you can let me go now."

She couldn't forget that he needed her for this job. But for a brief moment, she wondered what it was like to earn his trust, without the contracts or oaths that bound them. It was a shame she'd never find out.

Slowly, he released her, but not before a frown settled between his brows. He muttered something under his breath that she didn't quite catch, but his eyes burned hot. "You'll tell me one day."

So arrogant. But it made her smile. "We'll see."

He grinned wide, all teeth and resolve darkening his expression. Terrence better hope to God they never met—it was the look of a bloodthirsty Kilrhinn on the hunt.

* * *

FREYA ONLY MEANT TO have a look. She slowly pushed the curtains aside to check out how the others were doing. As soon as they saw her, all murmurs stopped.

She found Serafina first. Serafina seemed a little exhausted, but no worse for wear. Next to her, Jon held a piece of starbread, and he perked up when he saw her.

"Freya, you're okay!" Lily cried in relief. Her bottom lip trembled. "I'm sorry we couldn't be much help."

"I knew you'd be okay," Jon said. He rolled his eyes. "Lily thought you were dying."

She punched his arm lightly. "You were worried too—admit it. You saw her running into the heart and nearly ran for her. I had to stop you."

"It wasn't just me," he argued. "Garrett—he was so mad, the gold guy had to tackle him."

"Xander?" Freya asked, stunned.

"That's his name?" Jon considered the new piece of information. "Anyway, you heard Garrett roar, didn't you? Could've woken the Scourge from a mile away."

The Scourge?

"Jon," Serafina hissed.

His face turned pale. "Sorry."

"They're gone," Freya said. "The Scourge is gone." The Kilrhinns got rid of them all.

"Of course," he answered quickly, abashed.

Freya's mind ran over what Jon said about Garrett. She remembered hearing a loud thundering sound. She found it hard to believe it was Garrett—that she would have that effect on him.

"Lhianne," a Kilrhinn called out. With hair graying at the ends, he said, "You saved us."

"How do we know she didn't cause the storm herself?" one of them said. Freya recognized him as Ignas' friend, and she remembered seeing him during the banquet, when the Lhiannes first arrived. Dark hair and beady eyes, he eyed them with great suspicion. "It only got that worse when you all arrived."

The question stumped the first Kilrhinn. "That's—that's impossible." But even as he said the words, he eyed her with fear. Hushed whispers floated in the room.

Did they really just say she caused all that devastation?

The accusation hit deep, as if they'd struck her. She couldn't even speak.

With a pang, she remembered this was what she got herself into. She knew it would be hard for them to trust her. But for them to think she was capable of starting a storm and bring it onto them? Hadn't she been trying her best to help them? To do her job so that they could work together and stop the storms?

"Because then she wouldn't risk her life to save everyone's asses." It was Rav who answered. She hadn't even noticed when he entered the room. He glowered at Ignas' friend, threatening with his large frame. He shrank back.

Serafina started to laugh humorlessly. "I can't believe this." Her eyes glowed green. She was angry. This was bad. "You blame *her*? After *she* stopped the storm? After we decided to help?"

"How could you think that?" Lily burst out, affronted.

The room suddenly dropped in temperature. Freya sought out who was causing it. She laid a hand on Jon's shoulder. His eyes widened. Immediately, the icy wind dissipated. "Sorry," he murmured. He didn't even realize he was doing it.

Somehow, everyone grew more afraid, placing more distance between them. "You'd defend her—you worked together," the dark-haired Kilrhinn sneered. "Lhianne witches."

Another dig.

Serafina's own smile chilled Freya. "I'll remember your face, Kilrhinn. When you cry for help in a storm, with the wind slamming you into the ground and crushing your bones, I wouldn't lift a finger."

His mouth clicked shut. He scurried away, terrified.

"Don't listen to him," Rav said vehemently.

But Freya couldn't help it. Their words latched onto her,

reminding her of her place. Doubt had already been planted in their minds. And even though it wasn't fair, she wondered if they'd ever take her word. In their eyes, she wasn't one of them.

Without warning, a little girl bounded towards her, hugging her. Freya recognized her as the one she'd saved in the storm. She was just glad the girl was safe. Her hair was tied up now, her arms wrapping tight around Freya's waist. Instinctively, she hugged the little girl back.

Then Freya bent down so they were at eye level. "What's your name, sweetheart?"

"Leslie," she replied with a small, toothy smile. "Mama says I should say thank you. Thank you, Li-Ann."

Leslie's clumsy shyness tugged at her heart. Freya beamed at her. "Anytime. There's a storm next time, make sure to hide somewhere safe, okay? Stick with someone you know." That could mean the difference between survival and death.

Leslie nodded emphatically. To Freya's surprise, Leslie pulled her hand and placed a tiny pink flower on her palm. Freya accepted it, touched by the gesture.

Leslie grinned and then turned to run back to her mother. Somehow, the woman's face seemed familiar. With kind eyes, a square-shaped face, and hair pulled back, she carried Leslie in her arms.

Freya twirled the precious, fragile stem in her fingers. Such a small flower, but it made all the difference.

And as they left, Freya realized where she recognized the woman from—she worked in the gardens and helped with planting the celes flowers.

* * *

"WHY DO YOU WORK FOR THEM?" Serafina asked, seething, as they walked back to their rooms. "Half of them don't even trust you."

A direct hit. Freya took it in stride.

"If this is what working with them is like, I wonder if we'll have a future," she continued.

Freya's steps faltered. "Please, don't think that way."

Serafina scoffed. "They accuse you of things, but you still defend them. I don't understand it."

The Kilrhinns were suspicious by nature of those with magic, but they still welcomed Freya here. She'd still made friends. "It's in their nature to distrust us." And it hurt, Freya could admit that, but she couldn't change what they felt.

"Let me tell you what you perhaps don't see—the Kilrhinns are ruthless. Do you think in such a storm, they'd save *you*, if you were incapable of stopping it?"

She thought of Garrett, the way he tried to protect her. She thought of Rav, Jess, and even Elara. Her answer came easier than she thought—"Yes."

Serafina stared at her for a moment. She heaved a sigh. "You trust them."

"You think I'm stupid, and that they're using me," Freya surmised. Serafina was welcome to think that way, and maybe her faith was misplaced, but this time she learnt to follow her heart.

Serafina shook her head. "Not stupid. But I think you can be too soft, and they take advantage of that." Freya had heard that before. And maybe it was true. It made people think they could walk over her, just because she wanted to help.

"I've been around people who've wanted me for their own gain. They force—they hurt, to get what they want." She closed her eyes at the memory. "The Kilrhinns here... They aren't like that. They took me in. They gave me a job. They protected me."

They arrived at Serafina's room. Serafina wore a thoughtful look as she faced Freya. "We are not the same, Freya. They are Kilrhinns. Their fear can put a wedge between us, if they let it rule their actions. Never forget that."

* * *

"It's my understanding that you're supposed to kill the Lhianne," the man hissed.

Katherine tried to lift herself up from the ground, but a hard kick to her side sent her back down. Her mouth filled with blood. "I—I am."

He caught her outside during the storm, after she'd decided to help the others. She recognized him as the gardener from before, but now he was dressed up as kitchen help. So that was how he was able to get around the fort.

"Then why is she still alive? And why were you helping the Kilrhinns?" He pulled her hair until she cried out and tears stung her eyes. To her horror, his hand was blackened, like the Scourge. It was probably what lent him the strength.

His smirk made her blood run cold. "We thought of something to speed up the process."

No. He held out a familiar gold bracelet with a small heart attached at the end, dangling it in his hand. She tried to snatch it from his grasp. It was Rina's. "What did you do to her?" Her voice didn't sound like her own. She didn't know what she would do if he hurt her. But he didn't answer her question. Her nails dug into the ground.

"We'll start with the nails. Next the teeth."

Her stomach turned.

She'd tried. But there was no escaping this from the start.

"I—I'll kill Freya," she said desperately.

"Don't make us wait any longer," he ordered.

"I need to—I need to set things up." *She needed to buy some time.*

"How long?" he asked sharply.

"Three days," she pleaded.

Satisfied, he released her abruptly. "Those guards of hers are a problem. If you can get past them, this would be much easier." He paused, a calculating look on his face. "If an alliance is forged, your sister is dead. Remember that." His voice was soft, but the threat was clear. She heard his retreating footsteps, but she couldn't find the strength to move.

She emptied the contents of her stomach on the grass. Curled up on the ground, she sobbed. Broken. Bleeding.

She would heal in a few minutes—she could already feel her wounds starting to close up. No one would ever even know.

A Brion who was supposed to save others... But she couldn't even save herself.

CHAPTER 11

Freya watched intently as Elara worked the dough with both hands.

"First thing you need to know about starbread—dark chocolate spread wins."

Freya nodded obediently, taking the glass jar Elara mentioned.

"Try it," Elara said.

Freya dipped a spoon in the jar. She plopped the spoon in her mouth and watched as the dough became more elastic. Mmm. Dark chocolate really was the best.

"Feel the texture," Elara said, gesturing for Freya to test the dough.

Freya poked her finger into the dough and it bounced up, like magic.

Behind her, Galen poked his finger, too, examining the dough as if it were a foreign specimen.

Elara slapped his hand away. He scowled, rubbing at his hand. She narrowed her eyes. "Did you wash your hands?"

Freya didn't even notice he was here until he decided to poke the dough. Somehow, she wasn't surprised. Either him,

Kane, or Rav popped up at the oddest of times. She found she didn't mind the company.

Chastened, Galen proceeded to the sink to wash his hands. There was his answer. She thought she heard Elara growl and fought a smile. "Don't. Touch. The. Food. With those. Hands."

Galen dried his hands with a tea towel and held up both hands. "They're clean now."

"You already touched it!"

Elara slapped the dough against the counter once more, working off her frustration. Galen drew back a little at the force she was putting on the dough. She folded it to form several layers. Satisfied with her work, she announced, "This is fine. We put it aside for an hour, maybe an hour and a half."

Elara wet her hands in the sink. "Now we work on the chocolate filling," she explained, beaming at the job they'd done. Her smile froze. She saw Galen with a spoon in the half-empty chocolate jar, and in that moment, Freya feared for his life. If Elara could shoot flames from her hands, she would've.

Before she could watch Elara explode, Lily and Jon burst into the kitchen. Kane followed behind them silently, oddly enough, with a bruise on his cheek. Freya had a feeling not many who tried to hit him would even land a clean one. She wondered who did it.

"Hey," Freya said, giving them a small wave.

"Hi. They said you were here," Lily said, sheepish. Somehow, Freya suspected Kane didn't want them to come here at all.

"What are you making?" Jon asked, intrigued.

"Starbread," Elara answered.

Lily gasped. "Those chocolate things?"

"Yep."

Reluctantly, Galen handed the jar back to Elara, who guarded it as if it were a precious vault.

Jon hesitated. "Can we watch?"

"Of course," Elara said. "We were *supposed* to be further along with making the chocolate filling, if someone didn't eat them." She glared at Galen, who simply shrugged. "No matter. We'll make a new batch."

She glanced at Lily and Jon. They looked a little downcast today. Freya wondered if the other kids went to tease them again. Her protectiveness kicked into gear. "Why so glum?"

"The other main families are coming today. They're having a meeting with Serafina." That was news to her. No wonder Elara was making some starbread.

"She said it was for 'adults'," Lily added.

Ah. She was starting to understand their frustration.

"We're not involved in any of the decision-making, even though we came all the way here," Jon admitted.

Oh, but they were, Freya thought. They just weren't aware of it. Otherwise, Serafina wouldn't have brought them with her.

Elara melted squares of dark chocolate in a small saucepan.

"She invited you guys," Freya said lightly. "I think it's because your opinion matters to her."

Jon's expression brightened. "You think so?"

A wide smile hit Lily's cheeks. "I've never thought of it that way."

Lily helped with mixing the melted chocolate, her focus intense.

Freya gave them a sidelong glance. "So... Why are you really here?" she asked them. Somehow, she didn't think it was simply to vent about not being invited to the meetings. Lily faltered in stirring the ladle in the saucepan.

So Freya was right. They did come for a reason.

Lily and Jon exchanged a glance, unspoken thoughts passing between them. Lily nodded.

"We... We saw how you did with the storm," Jon started.

"We thought..." Lily bit her lip. "Can you teach us?"

They meant Lhianne magic. Freya had never taught anyone before. What she knew had simply been passed on by her mom, and through practice. A lot of practice.

She considered it for a moment. Seeing the eager, expectant looks on their faces, she had to tread through this carefully. "That will depend... Why do you want to learn?"

"We want to become stronger." Lily answered.

"That's not enough," Freya replied softly. "Can I ask—didn't your village teach you?"

"They tried," Lily admitted, but Freya didn't miss the misery in her voice. "They said... They said we were too wild. Our control just isn't as good as the others. They gave us to Serafina."

"She treats us like we're ticking bombs," Jon said. "We want to prove to her we can do it. We want to help, too." Freya understood after last night. That Jon could make the temperature drop considerably without realizing—he had the blood of a Lhianne elder, too. "We know we can trust you."

Freya understood feeling helpless. She'd been there too. For a moment, she considered them. They were still learning, but they had potential. Lily had more restraint, so she would learn faster, but Jon had the sheer connection with the earth without even realizing. More, they trusted her, even though they didn't know each other that well yet. She had to go with her gut.

Gently, she began, "I'll be honest—I can only teach so much. Control is difficult to master. That will depend on you."

They listened, rapt.

"We can work hard," Lily insisted.

"Work hard on stirring the pan," Elara said.

Lily stirred it quicker. Elara brought out a small carton from the fridge. Seeing Lily's work, she muttered her approval. "Good. Now we add some cream."

They would probably try to practice their magic even without her. Seeing their resolve, Freya decided to give them this. She sighed, relenting. "I'll help."

* * *

THE LHIANNES WERE STALLING. Garrett didn't know why, but considering Serafina hadn't given an outright rejection, he knew she wanted something—he just wasn't sure what. Not knowing grated. He'd sent Xander to keep a pulse on their movements. He hadn't reported anything unusual.

"Garrett," Serafina acknowledged once the others had left the room. "May I talk to you?"

He gestured for her to have a seat. He was curious what this was about. Perhaps she would finally tell him.

She sank into the chair, watching the flames crackle. From the fire, her hair reflected an orange glow, almost ethereal. She was silent for a while, as if something in the flames were divining some sort of mystical truth. But she wouldn't come to him if it wasn't important, and so he waited.

"Did you know the other Kilrhinns blame her?" she finally asked.

His brows drew together. "Who?"

"Freya."

The name stopped him, his attention drawn like a hawk's. "For what?"

"They think she caused the storm."

He will find them, and they will pay for even having that thought.

Displeasure made her lips purse. "Somehow, they think we're capable of creating one in a matter of seconds." Her lips lifted up only slightly, but it hadn't reached her eyes. "While I'm flattered they think we have that power, quite frankly, it's insulting."

"Serafina—"

"You invite us here, you welcome us, we risk our lives and you treat us like we're different. No, don't even try to deny it."

Fuck. He felt their chance for a partnership slipping from his fingers. "I won't deny what my people think. That much is clear to me." He knew they would have this reaction from the start. But to create change, someone had to instigate it. "I can't control what they think," he admitted. "But I can promise we'll do our best to shield you from any possible harm."

Serafina was worried about the tension and distrust. It was a valid concern, and in time, he hoped working together would soften people's opinions about them.

But he had no clue. If he could strangle people for their sheer idiocy, he would've already done so. The Lhiannes had protected them from a devastating monster of its own kind, and his people had the audacity to blame the *Lhiannes*. Freya, who had only sought to help, putting her own self at risk. He had the urge to see her now.

Serafina looked at the flames again, and this time, a genuine smile touched her lips. "I'm going to hold you to it."

* * *

ELARA'S FEET ACHED, but she was glad to be almost done in the kitchens. She wiped her hands dry. All day, they had been preparing and cooking the finest Kilrhinn dishes.

She loved working in the kitchens, but she needed a rest.

In times like these, she wished she had a Kilrhinn's fast reflexes and speed. She could sure use some of those neat skills.

From the corner of her eye, she caught movement to her left. Her heart sped. Everyone should've left. She whirled around.

Oh, their new help. A hand on her chest to calm herself, she realized she'd forgotten his name. "You are...?"

The man bowed his head upon seeing her. "Oliver," he answered. He wasn't as tall as most Kilrhinns, but he had a lanky figure, almost sickly pale color, and black, sunken eyes. Blacker than she'd seen in anyone. When she first met him, he unnerved her. It was the color of his skin—like he hadn't seen the sun in months. From their Earth tales, her kind would suspect him to be a vampire. She snorted. How ridiculous. Since when did she get so superstitious? She didn't like to pry into anyone's lives, but she wished she knew a little more about him.

"Why are you still here, Oliver?" she asked him.

He held up a tray of starbread. "I believe the Roark Family wanted more."

"Ah." She had a bone to pick with the Roark Family Head. She nodded stiffly. She couldn't stand the man, and she hadn't even met him. But her friend Anita told her he constantly asked for a refill of their finest red wine.

"You better bring this too," Elara said with a weary sigh. "I'm sure they'll ask for more." She popped open the cabinet, looking for the right bottle. "Where did you move from, Oliver?" she asked conversationally. No answer. When she turned her head around, he was gone.

* * *

THE DINING HALL WAS FULL. Freya, along with Lily and Jon, watched the flurry of people arrive. But it was the ones who occupied the table in front that snagged her curiosity. There, she was told, the Heads of the Main Families in Arqand sat.

The one on the left-most front table caught her eye. The Kilrhinn was charming and easy-going, a contrast to his features—rich, coffee-brown hair, a sharp jaw and almond-shaped eyes. But she noticed that his eyes swept over the room every now and then. She had a feeling he was constantly aware of his surroundings, even while holding a proper conversation. Beside him was an attractive woman who looked like she could be his sister, with lips painted red, and her dark hair pulled into a tight braid. She didn't speak much, Freya noticed, but she listened.

Opposite them was another man who was much older, white hair in a buzz-cut. He didn't smile much. Out of the three, he was the one who looked like he could kill even in his sleep. Freya felt a frisson of fear down her spine. His eyes met hers and she jerked in surprise. She looked away guiltily.

When she thought it was safe, avoiding looking at the older Kilrhinn, her eyes roamed a little further, and beside them was Xander, who talked to them with the ease of old friends. Garrett wasn't here. She found herself looking for him and stopped herself.

A woman with familiar ringed curls ran past in a hurry.

"Katherine!" Freya called out with a wave. Katherine didn't seem to hear her. In fact, she seemed distracted. That was odd. Katherine threaded past the people around her without looking back.

"You should be careful of her." It was Jon who'd spoken.

"What?" Freya glanced at him.

"The winds tell me to be on my guard," he said quietly.

"Of Katherine?" She liked Katherine. Freya didn't know why, but she felt a kindred spirit with her. Someone new, who was just trying to fit in. With all the suspicion and doubt around Freya after the storm, she felt that connection even more so.

Usually, she could tell if the winds were trying to send her a message, but she hadn't felt the winds warn her about anything.

One of the servers stopped by them. Freya snagged a piece of starbread. "Lucky last piece!"

"You and your starbread." It was Rav who spoke. Since when had he arrived? Beside her, he rolled his eyes. He was snacking on something round, like a small pie.

"Freya?" Lily said as Freya bit into her bread.

"Mmm?"

"Umm. Garrett's coming."

Freya coughed, nearly choking on her starbread. Rav clapped her back hard.

"He looks angry," Jon added helpfully.

Sure enough, he stalked towards her with long strides. He reminded her of a predator finding its prey.

Since she last saw him, she was afraid she'd reveal something again without meaning to, and that he'd piece everything together.

Garrett's eyes ran over her, almost like a physical touch. For some reason, she thought he felt relieved to see her. There was a slight easing of the tension on his shoulders and the tightness around his eyes.

"Freya." The sound of her name on his lips made a shiver course through her.

She always liked that he said her name. That from the very start, he was interested to learn it, and that he made an effort to use it. In a place where she could've so easily been cast as a "Lhianne", she appreciated it.

She thought he would head to the table in front with the

others, but he hadn't so much as spared a glance in their direction.

"How are you feeling?" he asked.

She mustered a small smile. "Better." It turned out Jess was right—a little rest had done her some good. "You?"

He held himself well, but she suspected he was tired. They had the meetings today, after all. He had the look of a man who had seen a lot and carried the weight of the world on his shoulders.

"Surviving," he answered.

"All right, you two, let's go," Rav said from behind her, a hand on Lily's and Jon's backs. He was ushering them towards the food now. She heard both ask a stubborn "why", but still they followed along.

Traitors. They were leaving her. She looked back at Garrett. Being alone with him made her the sole focus of his attention. Her heart thudded in her chest. "You—you aren't going to join the others at the table?" Freya blurted out, her curiosity unable to be contained. She gestured towards the table, towards Xander and the other Kilrhinns.

Garrett flicked a glance in their direction. His eyes went back to her, gentle amusement reflected in them. He shook his head once. "Not this time."

"Oh." She didn't know what else to say. She shifted on her feet awkwardly.

"You have dinner yet?" he asked gruffly.

"No. Well... I took some starbread." She held it up. "I was too nervous to eat," she admitted.

"Nervous?" he echoed. His forehead creased. "What for?"

"The outcome of the talks. I've... I've heard you had the meetings with Serafina." Freya wondered what they said. If she was going to be kicked out anytime soon.

His lips thinned. "Not good. She had some... misgivings.

But the discussions have only started. Airing them out now is good."

Her heart sank. That wasn't good. Still, she held out hope that it would get better. Now she had the chance to study him better. "Have you?" she asked back at him hesitantly. "Had dinner?"

"No," he replied. A slow, devastating grin made its way to his lips, and her heart stuttered in her chest. A man who seldom smiled, but now aimed it at her, was brutal in its intensity. "I was hoping I'd find you."

* * *

XANDER WATCHED as Katherine flitted past and disappeared through the exit that led to the gardens. It was dark outside. What would she be doing there? The talks hadn't gone well, but the Lhiannes were still here. That meant they had their own reasons. Possibly their own terms.

"Seems like a woman caught Xander's eye, V," Zeke, the Head of Roark Family said to the old man seated across from him. "He hasn't heard a word you've been saying."

Xander froze, caught. A smile played at Zeke's lips. As usual, the Kilrhinn noticed everything.

Xander wasn't sorry. He was tired of the same conversation about the Lhiannes. His eyes still on the exit, he excused himself from the table smoothly. He wondered why she stirred his interest so much. On the surface, she was a Brion. And yet she rarely seemed to be where one would expect her to be.

At first, he thought she was hiding something. He had the chance to observe her the other day, but she simply watched the flowers in the garden. When it began to drizzle with a light rain, she didn't even move from the spot. She simply closed her eyes and raised her head to the sky, as if each drop against her skin was a gift.

Her records revealed that she came from the slums with her sister. A record of theft once, but nothing else. But even that in itself wasn't uncommon. She had a job here now—he doubted she was here to steal.

He shadowed her from the distance for a minute. Right now, she wandered aimlessly. Perhaps walking to clear her head than for any real purpose.

He closed the distance between them in a heartbeat. She yelped in surprise when he appeared beside her. "Katherine."

She was crying. Fuck.

This close, he realized how fragile she was. Was she even eating much? The thought of it darkened his expression. He lifted a hand to wipe away the tears. She jerked away from him, like he'd hurt her. He dropped his hand. She tried to mask her surprise, but he caught it.

"What—what do you want?" she hissed.

She was different this time. He recognized her reaction—like a wounded animal's. The question was, what had caused it?

"It's not safe," he told her. A storm could break free at any time. Yesterday was a stark reminder of that.

Still, she muttered something under her breath, but continued to walk further in. "It's better here," she said, staring up at the sky. What did that ever mean?

"Out here, I can breathe... Out here, nothing's wrong."

"And what's wrong back there?"

"Everything," she breathed out, like the single word pained her.

He didn't understand her. As someone who often sought answers, he needed to know. "Your sister?"

He heard the sharp intake of her breath. That was answer

enough. Then, unable to help it, "Anything we can do to help?" he asked.

He watched as her eyes shuttered. "Nothing." There was finality in that word.

Her fire was gone, as if the embers had burnt out, leaving nothing but the shell of a person. What the hell happened to her?

CHAPTER 12

*G*arrett was brooding. Freya was almost scared to poke the lion. But he would never hurt her—she understood that now. From what she'd seen, everything he'd done was to protect.

They had more privacy now outside in the benches overlooking the gardens. They brought their plates outside too, piled with food.

She touched the tip of a yellow flower on the table's vase absentmindedly. Probably days old, it had drooped in its crystal glass vase. It straightened back up as soon as Freya touched it, its petals folding out more.

"How?" Garrett leaned forward, fascinated.

Oops. She didn't realize she'd done it in front of him. It had been almost instinctive. "I draw the water back in. It livens it up a little." It was a small trick kids learnt. Lily and Jon could easily do it, and perhaps add a little more flair.

"Will it live forever?" he asked thoughtfully, picking it up from the vase and studying it.

"No," she answered wistfully. "They live on borrowed

time. I can only add a little bit. But... Even too much water can kill it."

She watched as he dropped it back in the vase with more care than she would've imagined him doing. "It's a balancing act, then," he mused.

She nodded. "A lot of things are, when it comes to our abilities." Freya touched the petals of the other flowers until the brown that tinged their edges melted away.

"Lily and Jon asked me to help teach them earlier," she shared. "They struggle with control, and without it... It can be dangerous."

Garrett turned oddly quiet. Her remark only seemed to make him unhappy as he stewed on something.

"Garrett? Is something wrong?"

"I talked to Serafina."

There it was—was he going to get rid of her now that they couldn't secure a deal with the Lhiannes? She braced herself at his words. She waited, sensing there was more.

"She said the others blamed you for the storm," he said calmly. But she *knew*. He was anything but calm. "You endangered yourself for us, Freya. And yet they say *you* caused it."

She wasn't prepared for that—it came like a stab to her chest. She drew in a deep breath, but even that felt like it got trapped in her lungs. "And you believed them?"

She couldn't look at him, afraid that if she did, it would break her. Still, she lifted her head up. Because if she was going to convince him of the truth, she would have to meet his gaze squarely.

What she saw on his face stopped her.

"You would think that?" he asked, his voice came out strained.

Oh no. She'd misunderstood him. Because she couldn't be more wrong. He wasn't accusing her at all—he was angry for *her* sake. Oh, this Kilrhinn.

His purple eyes met hers, blazing. "I always wondered about you—they said Lhiannes would try to control my mind. That they've got the power to change my thoughts. To *be careful*," he scoffed.

That was what was said about them?

"Ever since you came here, you've done your job. You've never sought for help, never asked for more than what you needed—you only ever gave it.

"Elara told me how long you've spent in the kitchens. You never spoke badly of other Kilrhinns even when I'm sure *they* did, and more. A storm hits, and you dive headfirst into danger without a thought about yourself."

Frustration rolled off him, but all she could think of was how this big, intimidating Kilrhinn cared about what others thought of *her*.

She didn't know what gave her the courage to. Maybe it was the way he was looking at her—the hard look replaced by something tender. He didn't look at her like the others did. But she traced the scar that ran along his cheek. He didn't even blink. He only watched her hand, completely still. Like if he moved, she would stop. Ever since she saw it, she wondered how deep it ran. Wondered what could've been so strong as to cause that kind of permanent damage.

His eyes fell shut, as if battling something with himself, and then he drew back, turning away from her. She wondered why she felt the sharp pang of disappointment. Of course he wouldn't want her touch.

"I knew what I was signing up for when I agreed to this," she admitted. "I knew I wouldn't be trusted as a Lhianne." It was just as well. Their distrust reminded her that her stay here was temporary. For the past several months, she had never really allowed herself to stay anywhere long enough to build roots. It was an ache that she had to deal with alone, unable to confide in anyone.

"It hurts you," he remarked, voice rough with anger.

He'd noticed. Their distrust stung, but this was her life now. Freya touched her forehead. Something was wrong. Her skin felt clammy.

All of a sudden, she wasn't feeling so great. Tiny pinpricks exploded in her stomach. She cried out in pain, clutching her stomach.

"Freya!"

Garrett's touch was cool against her cheek. She blinked. His face blurred in and out of focus. His expression was fierce with worry. He was strength and safety and good. She gripped his arm tight, as if holding him would keep her conscious.

What was happening to her? Her strength was slowly seeping out of her. Her grip on him loosened. She heard Garrett's voice, sharp and urgent, barking out orders to someone. She was lifted up in someone's arms, and then she was gone.

* * *

GARRETT PRIDED himself in being two steps ahead of his foes. Ever since he stepped into the role of leading the Vhenn Bradis Family, the first thing he had to ensure was the protection of his people. He had to consider the possibility that they could endanger those closest to him. Then he made every effort to prevent that from happening. As Freya clung to him, he realized that today, he failed in doing so.

He should've anticipated it. Should've acted with greater caution. It burned in his gut, making him struggle to fight for control. He nearly lost her. *Again.*

She was still alive—it was one small comfort. But every breath that came out of her was ragged, as if even in her unconsciousness, she was in pain. He took her to Jess without delay, but even then, she was restless when he set her down. What was it about her? It seemed like only when she was unconscious did she reach out for him this way, craving the contact. As if part of her found it hard to accept needing him. But unconscious, those walls fell down.

Jess touched Freya's forehead and gasped. "Poison," she breathed out, her brows pulling together. "Who would do such a thing?"

Garrett didn't have an answer.

"We'll take care of her," Jess promised, her expression tight. They'd grown close, he knew. Such a short time, but already Freya drew in those around her. He hadn't mistaken the way his enforcers felt protective of her, too, and not just because he ordered it.

His mind circled back to the possible cause—was it something she'd drank? Something she'd eaten? They hadn't even touched their food yet, when they went outside. She'd said she didn't have dinner yet.

He returned to their table outside, a thought niggling at him. His gaze swept over their plates. His heart stopped cold.

No. He was wrong. He picked up the starbread on Freya's plate. He studied the pastry. So innocuous, but probably laced with something toxic. Xander followed behind him quietly.

Garrett turned to face him, tempering the fury he felt. "Find out what's in this," Garrett commanded, passing on the drink and plate. He would find out who did this, and they would regret it.

"Galen?" he called out. Galen had finished his patrol on the surrounding area and met up with them. The starbreads were made in one place, along with multiple batches, and no one had collapsed like Freya. He couldn't help the growl in his voice as he fought for control. "Find Elara."

CHAPTER 13

"*E*xplain to me the process again," Garrett demanded, his impatience barely concealed.

Elara sat opposite them, her hazel eyes staring up at them in confusion, and, Garrett noted, mirroring his own impatience. They'd called her from her room. He suspected she hadn't had much time to prepare. Where her hair was usually rolled in a tight bun in the kitchens, now, her dark brown hair spilled down, past her shoulders.

She laid her palms flat on the table. "I told you, you knead the bread by hand. You make sure it's smooth and elastic. Then you set it aside to rise. While that's happening, you make the chocolate filling," Elara described. "Would you like me to explain how that works too?"

She turned to Galen. "You've seen us make the starbread." Galen's face remained unreadable. She paused, and as if just occurring to her, she asked carefully, "Is there something wrong with the food?"

"Did anyone have the opportunity to handle the food during the process?" Galen asked.

"Well, I didn't make them all myself. God, that would be a

task. The Roark Family alone must've had three trays. Others would have helped, yes."

Galen's inscrutable expression broke into one of displeasure.

"Freya was poisoned," Garrett revealed, watching her reaction carefully.

Elara's eyes went round. "*P-poisoned?*" she sputtered.

"We suspect it's from the starbread," Garrett added.

She stared at him, as if his words made no sense. "My starbread?" she repeated, when she finally found her voice.

"If you've seen anything at all, it would help," Galen stressed.

Shaken, she ran a hand through her hair in disbelief. "I don't understand. I wouldn't—I've never—oh my God."

Garrett didn't think she could fake her surprise. She'd worked for him for the last four years. He knew it couldn't be her, but he had to make sure.

"Is she okay? How is Freya?" she asked, clearly distraught.

"She survived. Barely," Garrett answered grimly.

"Elara." Garrett tried to call her attention again when she looked as if she'd burst into tears. "Did you find anything suspicious at all in the kitchens while you were there?"

"I handpicked every one of my assistant cooks," Elara said, bristling. She went still, face turning ashen. "Oliver!"

She stood up immediately, beginning to pace. At their confusion, she started, "He was our newest kitchen help."

Garrett and Galen stood to attention.

"I thought it was odd that he was still there. He said the Roark Family wanted another tray of starbread. But he shouldn't have been there. I was just finishing up clean-up. And Izzy told me that there was enough food served there already."

"What did he look like?" Garrett demanded.

"Pale," she answered, a haunted look in her eyes. "Sickly

pale. His lips were dark. Black eyes. The deepest black I've seen in anyone. I didn't have the opportunity to strike a conversation. I should have talked to him more. Asked him questions."

Garrett and Galen shared a look.

"I believe someone had accused Freya of causing the storm earlier," he told Galen. "Bring him to me."

Someone had snuck in the fort. They needed to work fast to catch the intruder, if he was still here. And if the intruder was long gone... They would hunt.

* * *

GARRETT STRODE INTO THE CLINIC, tension coiled tight in him. Freya still hadn't woken, and it set him on edge.

"We got the results back from the clinic," Jess said. From the look on her face, it didn't look good.

"And?" Garrett prompted, bracing himself. He grabbed one of the candies from the glass jar by the entrance.

"We found traces of mirmenthol."

He stopped in the middle of unwrapping the candy. At the blank stare on his face, she said, "When you crush mirmenthol leaves, it can be used as poison. It can cause nausea, stomach cramps, and when you have too much..." The pained look on her face made her stop. "Lucky she didn't eat the whole thing. If she did, she wouldn't be here."

If he hadn't asked Freya to dine with him, who knew what would've happened? He heard a sharp crinkling sound. When he looked at his hand, he realized he'd accidentally crushed the candy, pulverizing the sweet treat. Fuck.

Jess grabbed another candy and tossed it to him. He caught it easily.

"She'll be fine," she tried to soothe him. "She's survived worse."

Damn straight she did. She would pull through. She had to.

* * *

YAEL WAS GROWING IMPATIENT. He stood at the top of the cliff, overlooking his army of the Scourge. His pride. His creation. Blood and tears, and magic. And many, many failed experiments. Years of toiling, coming into hiding, finally coming into fruition.

Beside him, his servant kneeled. Uri had done well. Uri had been serving as his eyes at the fort, in the guise of one of the workers. Maybe they didn't need the Brion anymore, after all. She blended with them, she was powerful, but she was slow. She was soft. He had a suspicion she was growing attached to the Kilrhinns. That couldn't do. Perhaps he just needed to do a little more persuasion.

He told Uri to do the job cleanly.

"It's done. Freya ate it," Uri said triumphantly.

"Is she dead?" Yael asked.

"She—she ate the poisoned bread," Uri stammered. He didn't answer the question. The incompetent fool didn't think to check.

Yael's hand sprang out to grab Uri by the neck and lifted him up on his feet, until he was suspended over the edge of the cliff. Uri's feet dangled, his legs kicking out in fear. "You came here and didn't make sure you saw her corpse." Anger rose within him, turning his hand black. He *was* Scourge after all. He was one of the few who had taken this form. In this form, he could command what was left of their race.

The Kilrhinns didn't yet realize the Scourge wasn't extinguished from the planet. How simpleminded. The Scourge couldn't be wiped out so easily.

"M-master—" Uri's face was turning beet-red.

Yael threw him beside his feet. Uri wheezed, clutching his throat, now rapidly showing marks where Yael's clawed fingers dug in.

"How could you not ensure her body had no pulse?" His voice vibrated with fury. If Uri hadn't gained the gift of speech or sound mind, Yael would have killed him already. Yael's fingers formed a fist. One blow. He needed to have restraint or he could kill Uri.

"We—we still have a chance." Uri crawled towards him, bowing at his feet. Uri began to kiss them reverently. "Their... Their defenses are weak from the storm."

No Kilrhinn could touch them again. Yael was successful in altering himself to gain a Kilrhinn's strength, using a live sacrifice. It was a shame the Kilrhinn he used didn't suffer for too long. After the decades his kind had perished, with their large numbers being wiped from the ferocity of the Kilrhinns' strength, they deserved more suffering. More pain. But Yael's new strength should be enough to ensure their success this time.

Uri had his complete attention. This was the news Yael wanted to hear. Maranthe was the largest city in Arqand and he'd long decided he would conquer it first, weakening the morale of the people, and the other Main Families that came into power. He called forth the short supply of his patience. "Tell me the state of their forces."

CHAPTER 14

"You let her get poisoned under your watch," Serafina hissed. Frost settled in her eyes. The temperature in the room dropped sharply. Garrett had learned the Lhiannes could manifest their emotions through the change in temperature, or through the wind. Not good. "She was supposed to be under your protection."

"Getting lax, Bradis?" Zeke said.

"They poisoned her," Garrett growled. "They didn't set up any attack. It was a calculated move. We are going to find out who did it. She's alive, Serafina."

"I heard she was with you when it happened," Serafina said, the implication clear.

"It's why she survived," Xander added calmly. "If he hadn't met with her, she would have taken enough mirmenthol to kill her. No one's getting into the clinic without proper identification. We have people guarding her as we speak. She's safe."

"Anything we can do to help?" Zeke's sister, Selene, asked. She was always sensitive to everyone's emotions. A rare empath skill inherited from their parents, it was why she was here, as a peacemaker of sorts.

Garrett described their suspect. As much as they knew about him.

"I'll ask my men to have a look," V said, his face grim, deep in thought. As the oldest among them, and as someone who led the Del Fiana Family, his experience meant he'd brought to heel more enemies in his lifetime than anyone else at the table.

Zeke grinned. "Likewise."

"I have to get back to my wards," Serafina said with regret. "They worry about her, too." A stern look came over her face, her eyes steely. "I need to know who did this."

So did he. Having their support made Garrett confident that it wouldn't be long. Those who weren't Kilrhinn often stood out.

* * *

GUILT CLAWED AT KATHERINE. She saw Freya on the bed, her face pallid, and reached out to her.

"I'm sorry, Freya," Katherine choked out. "I'm so, so sorry." Freya wouldn't know just how sorry she was. She felt caged. Unable to help, yet unable to tell anyone. It was slowly shriveling the part of her that dared to hope.

Freya helped save so many lives from the storm, and yet here Katherine was, complicit to the poisoning. She didn't know who did it, but she suspected it was Uri.

Even Freya's hands were cold to the touch. But Freya was alive, and in spite of the fact that Rina's life was on the line, she felt relief. "I don't know what to do. I wish I had met you under different circumstances. It's just not fair." Bleak despair wrapped over her, like a tight fist.

Freya's fingers twitched, the barest hint of conscious

thought. "Freya?" Katherine said. She swiped away the tears, and when Freya didn't stir, she took it as a chance to slip out of the room. She breathed in deep and held it there, before letting it out slowly. She had to go now.

In her hurry to leave, she nearly bumped into Xander. *Great.* What kind of luck did she have to come across him of all people? But she carried on, ignoring his questioning look. She didn't want to explain her tears. And she couldn't get more attached to the people around her. If she could detach herself, maybe this would all be easier.

She was supposed to come up with a plan, but she didn't have any plan. And they poisoned Freya. Dear God, what was going to happen to her sister?

She checked the man whose leg had been crushed underneath a fence. He greeted her with a smile, but she didn't have it in her to return anything but a shaky one. Even her hands shook. *Focus, Katherine.*

"Katherine?" Trixie asked. She was a Kilrhinn who had devoted herself to the medical field instead of training to become a warrior. Katherine admired her for going against the grain, using her strength to help others in a different way.

"I saw you visit Freya," Trixie remarked. "You know, I heard they're looking for the person who poisoned her. They say it's someone who worked here, attempting to disguise himself as kitchen help. Can you imagine?" Trixie shuddered. She tilted her head. "Wait a minute...How long have you been here? Have you taken a break yet?" she asked, a stern look fixed on her face.

"Y-yeah," Katherine lied. "I saw Freya on my break."

Trixie raised a brow. "Go take one," Trixie said. "Now."

Katherine blew out a breath. "Trixie, I'm better off doing the work here. Natalie, Henderson, and Kira—"

"Will be fine even after you take a break. We got this. Go."

It went against every instinct she had. She wanted to bury herself into the work, so she could plan on what she could do, so she could have a reprieve from the guilt that was eating her alive, and the worry for her sister.

She didn't have a choice. She was sick of not having choices. She swallowed the lump in her throat that made her want to burst into tears. She turned on her heel, wishing things were a whole lot different.

* * *

In that haze of unconsciousness, Freya thought she heard someone apologize to her. The voice sounded familiar, but floating in and out of this dark sea, she couldn't identify the speaker. There was pain in it, and so much regret. And although she didn't understand the reason behind it, Freya's heart wanted to reach out and tell her that she understood just how unfair life was. Wanted to ask her how she could help.

"Will she wake up?" Freya heard a timid voice ask, upset. The words crystallized in her mind. It was tempting to let the dark haze pull her back in, but Freya resisted, wanting to comfort that person.

"Of course she will, sweetheart. She's just resting," a woman's gentle voice replied.

"I heard them say that because we came, now Freya's a target," the girl continued.

"Who said that?" This voice sounded irritated. Garrett. Freya immediately recognized his voice. Her pulse jumped. *He's here.*

"A Kilrhinn during dinner," the girl murmured.

"Kane, stop taking all the candy." Freya now recognized that the woman's voice belonged to Jess. "If you take them all, the visitors won't have anything left."

"I'm a visitor."

"That's your fifth," Jess pointed out, exasperated. Freya's lips quirked up at their exchange.

Slowly, Freya's eyes fluttered open. Jess stood almost toe-to-toe with Kane, her arms crossed. Kane only popped the candy in his mouth, regardless of her warning. Jess narrowed her eyes.

Disoriented, Freya realized she was back at the clinic.

"Freya!" Lily cried out. She sprang up, her arms wrapped around Freya's waist. Surprisingly, Jon wasn't here. Both of them seemed to be attached at the hip.

"Freya," Garrett said, stark relief on his face. He brushed a hand over her forehead. "Feeling better?" he asked.

Freya's head ached. She felt weak, her body heavy. She wriggled her toes. Still alive. Somehow. She nodded, trying to recall the last thing she did. Talking to Garrett. Pain. And then blackness.

"Good thing, too. I was almost accused that I gave the wrong antidote." Jess rolled her eyes.

Antidote? "What happened?" Freya asked, lost.

They all looked at each other. What weren't they telling her?

"Freya... Someone poisoned your food," Jess revealed.

Freya sat up immediately. It was a mistake. She felt dizzy, but her hand shot out and found Garrett's. It steadied her. She tried to wrap her head around the news.

"W-what?" Who on earth would do such a thing? And why?

"They laced your starbread with mirmenthol," Garrett explained. They told her what it did to the body and she listened, horrified.

"I don't understand... Why would anyone do that?" *That* was what was wrong with her? Someone laced her starbread with poison? A horrible thought struck her—had Terrence finally found her?

"Isn't that just the question," Kane mused.

"Either someone doesn't want an alliance between us and the Lhiannes..." Garrett concluded, meeting her eyes. "...Or someone holds a grudge towards you."

But that wasn't what Terrence did—he attacked outright. If it was Terrence, he never even showed himself. It didn't make sense. He'd want the pleasure of knowing he caused her that pain. But if it wasn't him... Then this was something else. Something bigger than she could wrap her head around.

"Oh. Freya, I almost forgot," Jess said, something occurring to her. She picked up a small clay pot by the table beside her. "While you were sick, apparently your friend came to drop this off."

Freya reached for it. It was painted a blue pastel color with small beads decorating the sides. She loved it already.

"That is?" Garrett scrutinized it with a watchful eye.

"A new pot for my flowers. The one I got during the Commemoration Feast."

"From Klein?" Why did Garrett say his name like a curse? Just what was his problem with Klein?

"Yes, from Klein," she replied defensively. "He said he'd send me one as a gift."

"Did it even go through security?" Garrett asked suspiciously.

"Why would it need to go through security?" Freya's arms hovered over the pot protectively.

"What if it has something inside? Some explosive."

He had to be joking. "It's a pot!"

"I think it's best if we leave them," Kane said, amused by the nature of their argument. He led Lily outside, Jess following behind him who cackled on the way out.

"You were almost killed, Freya," Garrett snapped, his

patience starting to crack. "And I know someone from the outside did it."

"I know, but *look* at this. Does it look like something you use to kill someone?" She lifted it up, starting to crack up. "Explosives on *this* small thing? Would he be trying death-by-pot by any chance?"

But Garrett wasn't laughing. His fingers tipped her chin up gently. His eyes dipped down to her lips, and she sobered. Caught in his gaze, she forgot to breathe. "I've had to watch you drop on the ground from something so innocuous. From something I missed, because I was careless."

He blamed himself. Her jaw dropped at his admission. His eyes were wild, the ferocity of his temper like a forest fire. So hard to contain, yet he was so careful around her. Ever since he found out that someone had struck her, that she feared his strength could easily hurt her, he made every effort around her. "Yes, it *looks* like a fucking pot. But have you seen how it was made? Do you know what he used to make it, did you see what was put inside it? If not by him, someone with more malicious intent?"

Just what was she supposed to say to that? She knew he must've cared that she lived because she had this job, and it was essential to their future. But this, the intensity of all that was Garrett, swept over her, consuming her.

"I like to bet on many things, Freya," he said, his voice rough and his gaze heated, "but not, I find, when it comes to your safety."

* * *

"FREYA WOKE UP," Kane announced, having returned from the clinic to meet up with Rav and Galen. Hearing the news, they collectively sighed in relief. That was entirely too close. Galen knew Garrett blamed himself for what happened to

Freya, but they all blamed themselves, too, for not being thorough.

The staff had been questioned, and people had seen Oliver, but no one knew who he was or where he came from.

"I remember the server who had the last starbread on the tray," Rav said. "Where the hell is that guy hiding?"

"The last starbread... Almost like they knew what she liked," Kane mused.

He was right, Galen thought, and it bothered him deeply.

"You think it was planned," Rav said. It would make sense —they rounded up everyone who worked in the kitchens, and questioned every single person. They couldn't find the server.

Just in time, Xander walked in the hall with a grim look. "The gardener's gone." From the description they gave, Xander apparently followed a hunch.

"The one that looked like the kitchen help?" Rav asked.

"Like a ghost."

"You think it's the same person," Rav guessed.

"I don't think, I *know* it is. But he'll be back," Xander said, his jaw hard.

"You're so sure how?" Galen asked curiously, wanting to know how Xander's mind worked. No one could connect the dots as easily as he had.

"Because Freya's alive," Kane, sharp as always, answered for him, reaching the same conclusion. Well, no one could, except maybe Kane. Kane didn't talk a lot, but he listened, and he learned.

"You mean he'll be back to finish the job," Galen concluded. That wasn't good. But this time, they would be ready.

Zeke strode towards them from the hallway with the grace of a panther. "His name's Oliver Rodon and he worked here because of his sick dad. Now I suspect it's probably all bullshit, but none of them's seen him again."

"Did you ask about a gardener?" Kane asked carefully.

Zeke's brows drew together. "No. But I asked about a pale-faced scary motherfucker, and hey, it looks like you have several of those. In the gardens, on cleaning duty, and… someone who works with package delivery."

Kane swore. All eyes went to him. "The pot."

CHAPTER 15

"It's impossible. It's not him, Garrett. It can't be."
Freya knew, deep in her gut, it couldn't be Klein.
He was her friend, and in the time she'd known him, the
winds never gave any warning, and he was only ever helpful.
"It has magic, and Klein's a Kilrhinn."

The pot glowed yellow. It was enchanted. Someone cast
magic on it. The Kilrhinns had taken it from her and sealed
it, saying they'd take it into custody. They said they had to
figure out the nature of the magic in it. Considering what
had happened, they concluded it was cast on the pot to cause
her harm.

Garrett uncrossed his arms, sighing. "I know, Freya."

At the question on her face, he continued, "Anything sent
to you needs to go through a security check."

She shifted on her feet. "Really, I don't think that will be
necessary. No one really sends me things, anyway."

Garrett raised a brow. "No friends? Family?"

Her mouth snapped shut. Another thing she didn't mean
to reveal. How did he make her reveal another part of herself
so easily?

She simply shook her head. "No," she confessed.

She knew they were only doing their job, but she didn't get a lot of presents, and she didn't have many friends. So whatever she received, she embraced wholeheartedly.

He saw her face and expelled a breath. "We'll return it, Freya. We just need to make sure it's safe to."

Her eyes were large and expectant. "You will?" she asked, almost afraid he'd tell her otherwise.

He nodded. "It's a promise."

* * *

GET SOME REST, they said. Freya couldn't stand being in enclosed spaces for too long or she'd go mad. Kilrhinns didn't really understand that need, but it felt as if a buzz crawled under her skin, needing to be let out. Her stomach proceeded to made a sound, announcing her hunger. She didn't touch her dinner much earlier, but now her appetite returned with a vengeance. She couldn't stay in this room for much longer. She'd practically been resting the entire day.

She checked the time. Eleven o'clock. They dimmed the lights already. Still, she jumped out of bed, shoving the covers aside. She pushed the door open, glancing outside. No one was guarding her. Odd, but she didn't question her luck.

Using her Kilrhinn reflexes, she sneaked out, light on her feet. The kitchens. She needed to get some food. She knew Elara might be up this time, still. Maybe she'd catch her there. Or Izzy.

Something in the air unsettled her. Freya stopped in her tracks. When the wind tried to tell you something, you listened. Most of the time, it was a warning.

She heard voices outside in the corridors. *This* was the danger she felt. The voices grew louder, and so did the incoming footsteps.

Freya put her back to a large column, concealing herself in time. She squeezed her eyes shut, hoping that whoever they were, they wouldn't find her.

"Do you think that's a good idea?" a male voice hissed. "They have a guard."

They were speaking in Kilrhinn, but she understood every word.

"This will be smooth," another voice answered. His voice was deeper. Familiar, somehow. "They are dangerous. He thinks they're preventing the storms, but it's leading us to destruction."

"We could die, Ignas. Have you seen them?" the second voice argued.

Ignas. The one Serafina had blown away during their banquet when they first arrived.

"We won't. They have magic, but they're slow. We're stronger." She heard something metallic slide from its sheath. "No one will know, and then they'll leave."

Freya's heart pounded in her chest. Her hand flew to her mouth, afraid to make a sound. She could guess at what they were planning.

"It will mean war."

"Nothing good will come out of any kind of partnership. They'll bewitch us, poison our thoughts. Look at Bradis," Ignas said derisively.

"You're right," the other voice agreed. "He's gone crazy."

"When the lights are out, I'll slip into that old Lhianne's room," Ignas declared. "Cover for me. Swear we're together."

"I will." He paused, releasing a ragged breath. "Good luck, brother."

Freya felt sick to her stomach. They planned to kill Serafina, and maybe Lily and Jon. She knew the Lhiannes were misunderstood, but she didn't realize their hatred ran that deep. Even long after the echo of their footsteps faded, she was afraid to move, rooted to the spot.

"I knew you'd do something like this," an angry voice said from behind her.

* * *

FREYA JUMPED IN SURPRISE, whirling around. She pressed a hand to her chest. She was already rattled as it was.

Galen looked imposing as he towered over her. "Why are you here?" he snapped.

He was furious, and she couldn't understand why.

"I leave for *one* minute. One fucking minute, and then you were gone. You'd drive us all to an early death."

"I was hungry." Why was it her fault that he wasn't there when she woke up?

The indent between his brows deepened. He pretended to look around him, and then back to her. "Last I checked, this isn't the kitchen."

It wasn't fair. "The winds gave a warning, and I had to listen."

He looked at her like she'd gone insane. He didn't get it. She wanted to scream in frustration. "You don't have a clue how he sees you, do you? You've nearly been shredded by a storm, poisoned in front of *him* no less, and still you have no idea."

What on earth was he talking about? "Who?"

"Garrett," he answered darkly. "Who else?"

"He needs me for the alliance. Believe me, I'm aware of my value."

He stared at her, dumbfounded.

Why were they even talking about this? This wasn't important. She had to tell him everything she just heard. "Galen, they want to kill the Lhiannes," she said numbly. "I heard them say they wanted to kill Serafina on lights out. We have to stop them."

Now she got his full attention. *"They?* What the hell are you talking about?"

"Ignas and someone. I didn't see. I think they'll—"

"You think Ignas plots to kill the Lhiannes?" His brows pulled together. "That's a serious accusation. Ignas and I have fought many battles together."

He wasn't going to believe her? Her heart sank to the pit of her stomach. "Galen, I heard them."

"You're asking me to choose to listen to *you,* instead of a sworn warrior," he replied warily.

His words slashed through her, as if he'd struck her. He really didn't believe her. She thought that by now, she'd earned their trust. She would never lie about something so important.

She'd known. She'd known they wouldn't listen to a mere Lhianne. But she couldn't just sit by and let it happen.

For months, she'd never let herself depend on anyone. This would be nothing new. He didn't have to believe her. If he wouldn't help her, she would do it alone, like she always had. She'd wait until lights out.

* * *

GALEN ESCORTED Freya back to the clinic. Freya fought the urge to take the easiest route by heading straight to Serafina, and stifled her impatience. Galen would stop her before she took a few steps outside the room if she simply ran for it.

After Galen left her inside, Freya got started. She placed the pillows strategically on the bed, and threw a blanket over it. Serafina's room was a floor above. Could Freya climb outside? She tried to recall where Serafina's room was located. She could enter the wrong room by mistake. Would she chance that risk?

She yanked the window open, and the wind blasted over the curtains, making them whip around in a frenzy. Freya ducked her head outside and looked up, searching for any windows or openings. The wind, icy cold at this time, blew hard, her hair flying around her. She squinted. Layers of gray bricks stretched up, and the faint outline of a window. It would be a climb.

Under any other circumstance, maybe she could have climbed up, but... Could she do that now, dark as it was outside, and still weakened from her poisoning?

"Freya?" It was Katherine. Freya bumped her head on top of the window frame. *Ow.* Freya dipped her head back inside and turned to face Katherine, rubbing the top of her head.

"Are you okay? I've got some food. Galen said you were hungry." Katherine gave her a small smile. She must've been helping those in the clinic the whole day, since she was still here. Admiration swept over Freya. But... Was it her imagination or were there dark circles under Katherine's eyes? Now that Freya had a chance to really look at her, did she lose some weight?

"Oh. Yes. Hungry," Freya answered absentmindedly. Truthfully, she'd forgotten about the food. Her heart squeezing in her chest, carefully, she asked, "Katherine, are you okay?"

The question seemed to take Katherine aback. "Yes, why did you ask?"

"Nothing, I just... I'm here, if you ever need to talk, okay?" Freya understood the value of a listening ear, or a shoulder to lean on. She never really had that.

Katherine nodded quietly, her eyes falling shut. She released a deep breath. "Thank you. I...I have to go," she murmured. There was something there, although Freya couldn't really understand it.

But as Katherine walked to the door, Freya's attention snagged on Katherine's clothes. A gossamer-thin, light blue gown. Her hair held up by a large clip. And then suddenly, Freya had a bright idea. "Katherine, wait..."

* * *

THE PLAN WAS EXECUTED without a hitch. Freya was lucky Galen sent Katherine to bring her the food. Galen didn't even stop to look at her face as she left, carrying the tray back.

Once Freya was a safe distance away from the clinic, she began to walk briskly. She had to work fast. She didn't know when Galen would decide to check up on her. Katherine was so nice that she indulged her request that they swap—Freya owed her one.

The other Kilrhinns on patrol didn't even spare her a glance. Once she reached the floor above, she yanked off Katherine's gown. There. She could move much better. Freya climbed the stairs in twos, using all the speed she could muster. It didn't take long for her to find Serafina's room.

Freya's fist hit the wooden door. "Serafina?" Freya whispered. She blew the wind over to the other side of the door to give Serafina a little nudge.

Moments later, the door opened, the dim light of a lamp spilling outside. Serafina's hair in disarray, she raked a hand through it. She'd been woken from her sleep. Her face pinched with worry, she asked, "Freya? Is something wrong?"

Freya slipped inside the room and shut the door behind her quickly. She looked around frantically and started pushing a cabinet towards the door, in an attempt to barricade it. Maybe her Kilrhinn strength was showing, but she needed Serafina to be safe. She lost her mother a long time ago, but next to her, Serafina was someone she respected and admired. One of the few who understood her and the pains of being a Lhianne.

"What on earth?" Serafina exclaimed, demanding an explanation. She crossed her arms. Freya continued to push the cabinet until it blocked the door completely. Satisfied, Freya's shoulders sagged in relief.

"Freya, what is the meaning of this?" Serafina's voice hardened now, all trace of sleepiness rapidly melting away.

Freya whirled to face her, a haunted look in her eyes. She pushed the fear aside. *If you choose fear, everything will shut down and you'll lose the people you care about.*

She certainly wasn't able to help stop the storm that had claimed her father's life.

"Someone wants you dead," Freya said. "They don't want the alliance to happen." And maybe things weren't heading in that direction, but if anything happened to Serafina, it *definitely* wouldn't be happening. "I'm not letting that happen."

Glancing out the window, Freya saw the torches snuffed from the outside. Her heart hammered in her chest, each beat like a countdown to impending danger. She braced herself.

CHAPTER 16

*K*ane's footsteps light, he leaned his head against the door. No sound from the other side. "Ignas?" he called out. No answer. Not too surprising.

Galen explained to him and Rav what Freya claimed. While Kane understood his friend's doubt, Freya had no reason to lie. And now, instead of spending their time looking for the one who had poisoned her, they were looking for a different person instead. Freya really didn't know the effect she had on Garrett. It was all their heads on the table if he found out. He inserted the key he brought in the keyhole, pushing the door open quietly. It barely creaked.

The room was empty, the bed made.

He would pay each one of Ignas' closest friends a little visit and do some questioning. If Freya was right… This was a whole clusterfuck.

* * *

Stunned, Serafina's mouth hung open. "You can't mean…" She shook her head. "You mean exactly that, don't you? And

164

here I thought the Kilrhinns knew better.' Her lips lifted up in an ominous smile. "Let them come."

They didn't have to wait long. The sound of footsteps outside announced that he was close. Someone knocked on the door. Neither Freya nor Serafina moved, but they exchanged a glance.

Without warning, the doorknob jangled, someone attempting to open it. The movement stopped abruptly. Did he give up?

THUD.

Freya's eyes widened, a hand flying to her chest. Oh God. Someone just rammed himself into the door. This was crazy. When it didn't work, they anticipated the next attempt.

THUD.

Freya's heart slammed against her chest. The door splintered open. It met resistance from the cabinet. With great strength, the door was shoved open, until the cabinet crashed against the wall. Ignas walked in with a frenzied look. They heard the chink of metal. He unsheathed his knife.

Ignas' eyes nearly bulged, seeing Freya.

Not what you expected, huh?

"You—what are you doing here?" Still, he lowered his other hand to another weapon by his thigh. "Doesn't matter."

At the determined look in his eyes, Freya stepped in front of Serafina. "Ignas, don't do this," she pleaded, trying to reason with him.

"It's too late."

She shook her head emphatically. "No, it's not. Walk away now. The Lhiannes are not the enemy."

"Your kind will drive a wedge and tear us apart! Decades of rebuilding again, grieving all the lives we've lost in the war, and you think to disturb our peace."

Serafina knocked Freya aside, hurling Ignas back with the wind, but not before he had a chance to throw a dagger out.

"No!" Freya deflected the dagger with a careful twist from the wind, narrowly missing Serafina. But Freya didn't anticipate that even after he was down, he would continue throwing. He flung another dagger. Another. Freya's reflexes were faster than her control of the wind. She moved. Pain stabbed her shoulder. Her thigh.

He recovered, pushing himself back up and charging for them. *Oh God.* He was relentless. The room turned hot. Serafina bent down, touching the ground, and pushed at the earth. The ground turned uneven and threw him back, knocking him off his feet.

But like a wild boar, he didn't stop, his eyes crazed. He stood up again and lunged towards Serafina. Freya called forth the ground's heat and mingled it with the wind, turning a hot, contained whirlwind of steam towards him.

He cried out, bent over, his skin turning an angry red. His bottom lip curled in disgust. "Lhianne witch!"

It all happened at once. Garrett tore into the room, flinging Ignas away with a hand. Freya thought she heard something crack and winced. Ignas hit the wall with a grunt. Just like that, he'd stopped it.

Garrett took in the sight of Serafina and Freya. When his eyes reached Freya, he scowled. Seeing Serafina was unhurt, he tended to Freya immediately.

"Hi," Freya greeted him with a faint smile.

The corners of his eyes tightened, but slowly, almost cautiously, he lifted his hand, his knuckles grazing her cheek. Freya's eyes fell shut.

"Jess is coming," he said gruffly. But still, he didn't smile back at her.

Galen emerged behind Garrett, lifting Ignas by his shirt. His expression torn, he bit out, "What has gotten into you?"

Ignas stubbornly kept his eyes on the ground. "An alliance will only cause us more grief. You'll see."

Garrett threw him a warning look. "You're wrong. An alliance is exactly what will save us."

* * *

HOURS LATER, after Jess gave Freya some stitches, Galen walked in the clinic.

Freya gave him a small wave, even though he wore a sullen look.

While her whole body ached, she was alive. Serafina, Lily and Jon were, too. They were upset when they met up with her earlier, but she tried to reassure them that she was okay.

Galen proceeded to ask her a few questions about what had transpired tonight. He said he'd just needed to get some answers.

When he was done, she decided she had some questions of her own. "How did you find me? Back there," Freya asked, curious.

He raised a brow, as if the answer should be obvious. "I followed you. I just got held back by some of Ignas' friends." His lips spread thin in displeasure at the memory. "You think we're fool enough not to recognize our charge?"

"Your charge?" she echoed.

No. No way. That was why they were always there. Shadowing her. They were her bodyguards. Did Garrett assign them to her?

He smirked. "Did you think that flimsy gown would disguise you? What the hell were you thinking, bringing Katherine into this?"

Garrett never thought to tell her. It all made sense now. She never even suspected.

"We learned a lesson the last time you gave us the slip. We couldn't let you out of our sight," Galen said.

That cut. That they didn't trust her. That they never told her.

"You didn't believe me," she said, recalling the way he'd so easily dismissed her.

"I didn't," he admitted. "But neither did I leave it to chance. I told Kane to have a look." He pulled in a sigh, reining in his impatience. "Your plan had holes. You were too rash. Kane was joking when he once told us you'd make us age ten years, but I think he was right."

In this, Freya wouldn't back down. "If I'd waited any longer, it would've been too late." Her fingers curled tight, nails digging into her palm. "I could've been there with someone today, but he chose to wait it out," she said quietly. She thought she caught a hint of guilt on his face, but she went on. "Simply because I'm a *Lhianne*. I understand what I had to do, Galen, and I did it. You can't guilt me into making that choice."

And for once, she struck him speechless.

* * *

GARRETT STORMED INSIDE THE ROOM, finding Freya sitting on the bed. *Safe*, he told himself. She was safe. And yet why did he get a feeling he would never be accustomed to that when it came to her?

He missed her—this maddening woman who put herself in danger every time. She slipped into his mind the whole damn day, and he found himself needing to see her.

"Leave us." Just two words, but Galen nodded in acknowledgement. He left without another word.

"Garrett—" Freya started.

"Do you have no sense of self-preservation?" he snarled. "You didn't think to tell us what you were going to do?"

"I told Galen. He didn't believe me. I'm not going to waste time convincing every Kilrhinn when every second counted."

Before he knew it, she'd burrowed under his skin, testing the limits of his control.

"And what plan did you have? You'd just run there and wait for the attacker to kill you?"

"Doing nothing would've been worse. And you had me watched," she accused. "You didn't think to tell me?"

Ah. She finally found out. In this, especially after tonight, he had no regrets. "It was necessary to protect you. It would've worked better if you weren't constantly trying to ditch your guards."

"You're being unfair." She stepped in front of him, toe to toe. Her cheeks turned a shade of pink. "The only time I tried to ditch my guard was when I thought he'd throw me back behind bars. And the second, when I thought someone I care about was in danger, and my *guard* didn't even believe me."

"Exactly, Freya. Because every other time, they were guarding you from the shadows." He'd have a word with Galen. He trusted his enforcers implicitly, but to cast doubt on her would be to cast doubt on him. More than that, her safety was compromised because of it. "Look what happened when you shook them off."

Her brows knit. "You charged me to ensure the alliance goes well. I did my job."

Alliance? Job? He stared at her incredulously. How did she not understand?

"You. Nearly. Died," he bit out. "Not once. Not twice. Three times, under my watch." They were now only a breath apart and absorbing his words, her green eyes widened, startled.

He couldn't take it anymore. Before she could take that chance to back away, he pulled her close, cupped her head, and she gasped into the kiss.

She was sweet. Like sunshine and daisies, and coming home. She fought it for a moment, and then she surrendered into it. Her hand tangled in his hair, urging him closer. He growled, kissing her deeper. She sighed, making a soft sound at the back of her throat. His blood heated. He wanted her. Badly.

It was a need that hadn't diminished—it only grew over time. His other hand dropped to her waist. He savored the feel of her, fitting against him. It was as if the scent of vanilla clung to her, enticing. Vexing, too, in his utter incapability to resist her. They pulled apart only for a breath, and back again, his tongue seeking to conquer, and she welcomed him with equal fervor. Over and over.

"Freya," Rav said, walking in.

They broke free, Freya's cheeks flamed, her lips the color of rose.

Rav's concern dissolved and he froze by the entrance, seeing them. With a ragged sigh, Garrett's patience snapped, thin as a thread. He aimed a glowering look at Rav, intending to chew him out. *What fucking perfect timing.*

Rav's face turned the color of ash. A hand hooked on the back on Rav's vest, where Galen tugged, pulling a stunned Rav out of the room. Galen pulled the door shut, too, without another word. Silence filled the room.

Freya looked down, unable to meet his eyes. For a moment, he wished he could tell what she was thinking. What he'd do to have an empath's abilities right now. "There are things I have to take care of," he told her instead, his voice rough. "Listen to what Jess tells you. It will help you recover faster." He had a feeling it was going to be a while before he could get that kiss out of his mind. He didn't wait for her response.

Because they had some Kilrhinns to grill, and he was going to enjoy every second of it.

CHAPTER 17

"*L*et me ask again—who do you work for?" Garrett asked.

"No—" Before Ignas could even finish his response, blood spurted from his lips. A blow to the stomach. Xander really didn't spare any of his strength. As a half-Kilrhinn who once belonged to the Kasa Altea Family, he was lent the brawn of their wyvern bloodline.

"Did you poison her?" Xander asked conversationally.

"W-what poison?"

"The one you injected in the bread she ate."

"I don't know nothing 'bout any poison!" he screeched.

"Search his belongings," Garrett commanded. Galen immediately left the room.

Ignas muttered a string of curses. "Why are you so focused on a Lhianne witch?" he burst out. "Everyone knows who started the storm. Before they came, it's never been that bad."

The Kilrhinn saw Garrett's face and scrambled backwards until his back hit the wall. On his knees, he crawled to his left, trying to find an escape.

"Say that again," Garrett said, walking forward, in no rush, his voice dangerously soft.

Ignas' face drained of color.

When he didn't answer, a menacing grin touched Garrett's face. "So *you're* one of those who blames her. Just yesterday, poison nearly killed her, and still you speak ill of her." He grabbed the collar of the Kilrhinn's shirt and easily lifted him up with a hand. "Were you responsible for enchanting the pot?"

"P-pot? What are you talking about?" Ignas began to tremble.

"Stop lying," Xander spat. He took out a carving knife from a silver sheath.

Ignas took one look at the light that glinted on metal and he was done. He'd reached his limit. "I don't know! I don't know! Ask Lester. And Reuben. Grisha! Maybe they know. I don't know, swear to God, I don't know."

Fear drove Ignas' actions now. He was a talker, selling out his friends when the pain got too much. Yet, Garrett couldn't help but notice, Ignas didn't once admit to it.

They already knew who Ignas' accomplices were, since they were quick to confess when cornered. Kane held the others now. And considering Kane wasn't done, either it would take them a while to break... Or they didn't know a thing.

But his concern grew. If they didn't poison Freya, then who did?

* * *

"It's just a leaf," Jon expressed his disappointment. He'd picked up a green leaf from the ground and flipped it over, finding nothing interesting about it.

Freya bit the inside of her cheek. He needed to learn a bit more patience.

"The wind dictates the way leaves fall to the ground. If you gain better control of it, you can be more precise when it comes to manipulating direction. It's trickier than you think."

Lily listened intently, staring at her own leaf as if it held secrets.

They sat on a bench in the gardens, under the shade of an acacia tree. It was late afternoon, and Freya had grown tired of staying inside the clinic room. She promised Jess she wouldn't be attempting any strenuous activity at all. Jess eventually relented, after Freya convinced her that fresh air helped Lhiannes relax better.

Out here, people didn't talk. Considering everything that happened to her this week, she was the topic of conversation of the Kilrhinns. People whispered about her behind her back.

Freya held her own leaf in her hand. Small and delicate, but if you pushed it just the right way... The leaf fell to the ground in precise diamond-shaped motions. "Seven times. I want you to do it seven times."

"How did you do that?" Jon asked in awe.

Lily proceeded to give it a try and dropped her own leaf to the ground. The leaf had more angular movement, but it didn't close in a diamond shape—instead, it jerked, creating the shape of a tear instead. *Close.* She had a foot in understanding it, but not quite.

"Good, Lily," Freya observed. "Try again."

Jon stared at his leaf as it fell to the ground in wild circular motions. His frustration grew. "I've been practicing more this week, but... I feel like I'm not getting anywhere."

She realized, after several of his attempts, that in his

desire to gain control of his abilities, he was trying too hard to grasp control of something else instead.

He dropped the leaf again, and instead of a circular motion like last time, the wind fought back, the leaf tossing back in spirals, as if rebelling.

His jaw ticked. *"I don't get it."*

Freya sighed. "You need to stop thinking you can control the wind," she told him softly. "It's not yours to control. Never was, never is. Never will be. You need to guide it. Talk to it, if you must."

He looked puzzled by the mere suggestion. "Talk? To the wind?"

"We're put on this planet, not to control the earth, but become agents of it, in a way." That was what she always believed. That was what her mother told her.

Lily listened, rapt. "Can I give it a name?"

Freya grinned. "Sure."

As she watched them practice, her mind wandered to Garrett, and the devastating kiss he left her with. This was just a job... Right? But it didn't feel like it when he kissed her senseless. It was different from the way anyone ever had. Hungry, untamed, and all-consuming—like it marked her soul.

Beside her, Rav picked up a fallen leaf, examining it closely. He dropped it on the ground, and it swayed from the wind and drifted away. He almost looked disappointed. It looked like they stopped bothering to hide the fact that they were guarding her.

"So you're the one in charge of me now," Freya remarked.

He only grunted in response. He picked up a stick instead, drawing something on the ground. It looked like a face.

Something niggled in the back of her mind. "At the Commemoration Feast—you said you were working." It had been right in front of her this whole time.

"Yeah."

"You meant you were watching *me*."

He pressed his lips together. So she *was* right. And for some reason, it hurt.

"You've been watching me. Thinking I'd escape." She thought they were friends.

He stopped drawing and looked up. "You've done it before." He threw the stick aside and patted the dirt away from his hands.

The face he'd drawn looked familiar. Was that her he drew?

"*Once.* I've only done it once before last night." Of course they didn't trust her. She was just another responsibility. She realized some part of her thought maybe they enjoyed her company, too. Clearly, she was wrong.

The slash of his brows drew close. He threw his arms out. "Why are you mad? We tried to keep you safe. You are his mate, and—" His mouth snapped shut.

"I'm what?" she breathed out. Surely, she heard wrong.

Rav stood up. "I didn't say anything. No one said anything." His face closed off, to her frustration.

"Freya! I did it!" Lily exclaimed. Lily took her hand, pulling Freya beside her. She dropped her leaf. Lily's diamond was shaky, but it was a diamond.

Checking Jon's progress, his leaf moved sluggishly, but eventually, his leaf made a full diamond. He sighed in relief. His eyes, clear and victorious, met hers. "I did it, too!"

She didn't expect them to do it so soon. They were fast learners. Now, they only had to do it six more times. It would be tricky, as one loop could become a circle midway, throwing off the pattern.

When Freya looked back at Rav, his arms were crossed, leaning by the trunk of the tree.

You are his mate.

Just what did he mean by that?

* * *

KATHERINE DIDN'T HAVE much time left. She was acutely aware of the fact that time was ticking, inching closer to danger. To losing her sister. She hadn't slept much, sick with worry. Maybe she could bargain with Yael. Her life for her sister's. She slammed the breaks on that train of thought. He wouldn't honor his promise. She didn't even think he knew what that word meant. She continued to pour her time into helping others at the clinic instead. As if that could help atone for her deception.

She heard what had happened to Freya. Last night, she was surprised when Freya asked to wear her gown. But she indulged her, since Katherine owed her. She thought it would be harmless—it turned out she almost had Freya killed. Her grip on her clipboard tightened. It seemed all she could do was put everyone in danger.

"Katherine," Jess said gently. "Take a lunch break. You'll get sick this way."

Everyone seemed to be telling her to take one. "I don't think—"

Katherine swayed on her feet and found purchase by planting her hand on the wall. With a raised brow, Jess pressed, "You can't help them if you can't take care of yourself. Take the day off."

"Jess—"

Jess pulled the clipboard from her grasp. "Xander. Convince Katherine here to take a break," Jess urged, looking at the Kilrhinn who must've been behind Katherine.

Her body locked up. *He's here.* She didn't even hear him come in. Still, whether it was guilt, or needing to keep her distance from everyone, she found she couldn't look at him.

Jess was right, even though Katherine didn't want to admit it. Reluctantly, she conceded.

"I'm sure Elara's made something, I heard there was some beef pie," Jess called out as Katherine rushed to leave.

But she didn't head to the kitchens for lunch. She didn't even know if she could stomach one right now. Instead, she headed outside, to breathe in the clean air. Instead of veering to the gardens, she headed for the small pond nearby. She sat down on a bench, the rippling sound of the water calming her immediately. She heard the snap of a branch behind her. Xander had followed her.

"You shouldn't have switched with Freya."

So he was here to chew her out. She couldn't argue with him—he was right. Maybe Freya wouldn't have been in danger. But considering Freya had saved the Lhiannes with what she did last night, it was a consolation at least.

He bent down, setting a bar of caffeilate, a bar of sweet cacao goodness with a punch of energy from the caffeine. The unexpectedness of the kind gesture left her dumbstruck.

"My sister died. The storm crushed her underneath the barn, with all the horses."

Her heart felt like it had been ripped from her chest. She covered her mouth with a hand.

This time, she turned to look at him, his pained gaze slipping through the cracks in her armor. She had a feeling it was one she would see in her mind long after, even with her eyes closed.

Slowly, he stood up. "You think you're alone—think again. There are many others like you."

His words cut through the numbness she'd encased herself in. The pain tore through her, threatening to swallow her whole.

After he left, she picked up the bar he set down next to her, her hands trembling. Such a simple gift, freely given, without expectation of anything in return. She unwrapped it, biting into the rich, decadent bar, and through her silent tears, she thought of her sister.

CHAPTER 18

"*I*'ll agree to the alliance proposed, but we have our own terms," Serafina began.

Garrett expected as much. From the start, he knew the Lhiannes had their own agenda.

"We'll hear it," he said.

Serafina leaned forward on the table, arms folded. "We want Freya."

Her words met silence.

"I'm afraid I don't understand," Garrett replied calmly, when he processed her proposal.

"When we leave Maranthe, Freya will come with us."

"No," Garrett replied plainly.

"Garrett," Zeke warned. "Listen to yourself."

"We are here to secure an alliance," V snapped. "Am I wrong?"

But Garrett's eyes never left Serafina's. What the hell was she planning? Take Freya? For what purpose? "Don't you think *Freya* should be deciding that?" Garrett fought to restrain his temper.

"Of course. But I'm almost certain she'll come with us,"

Serafina stated. "Ever since we've arrived, your kind has threatened us, cast doubt on our intentions, and conspired to kill us. Nearly succeeded too. You said you would do all you can to shield us from any harm, but last night, the one who saved my life was a *Lhianne*."

"If she wants to go, there's nothing I can do to stop her." Something creaked. Garrett looked down. It was the armrest of his chair, cracking from his grip. It cost him to say those words. He rested his hands on his lap instead, but they clenched into tight fists. "But if she chooses not to, Serafina, you won't get to force her. I won't allow it."

Unfazed, Serafina's lips curved up. "Very well," she replied easily. "But you'll find that won't be necessary, Garrett. You don't understand her, and won't. Because it's in her nature, she'll bend over backwards to try and please you Kilrhinns, to seek your approval. But she won't get it—I've seen her try. Freya doesn't belong here."

* * *

IT APPEARED that Kilrhinns had a bloody history. After Lily and Jon's training, Freya went to the library. A Kilrhinn book open on the table, she started reading about the Great War. The root of its cause—the murder of the daughter of the Kasa Altea Family Head by the Scourge, who had conspired with the Lhiannes. The war waged on for seven years. The Kilrhinns emerged victorious, but not without suffering great losses. There were several smaller skirmishes after that. The echoes of footsteps from outside pulled Freya from her book.

She closed it, placing a Universal textbook on top, concealing it. So far, she had managed to hide the fact that she was half-Kilrhinn from everyone except Elara. And maybe after last night, Serafina, too. She supposed she was lucky.

She asked Rav if he could stay by the entrance earlier, which he obliged her with, after she bribed him with the pies Izzy gave her from the kitchen.

Her heart skipped a beat when she saw who had entered. "Garrett?"

He didn't smile or greet her. "She needs to talk to you." He gestured to someone behind him, and Freya realized that Serafina was with him. But he didn't spare her another glance. He turned on his heel, and she watched him walk away.

It stung. Didn't he think of the kiss, too? Maybe it was only her who was so affected by it. Her face heated. How embarrassing. She thought maybe he felt something, too. His quick dismissal of her made it all clear.

She knew they were in the middle of their discussions concerning their alliance, but Serafina coming to her now surprised her.

"Freya," Serafina greeted her, the corners of her eyes crinkling in a smile. "If I could have a few moments of your time?"

* * *

GARRETT DIDN'T LOSE control so easily—until it came to Freya. But the mention of her leaving with the Lhiannes frayed the edges of his control. His mind returned to their meeting earlier. That wasn't supposed to happen. Not for something so important for Kilrhinns.

He left Freya with questions, he knew. But he couldn't stay. He pushed the doors to the training room open. Predictably, Xander was behind him, having read his mood.

It was meant to be simple. Negotiate with the Lhiannes so they could form an alliance. Freya complicated everything.

Serafina was right, their distrust cut Freya, even though she tried not to let it show. And while he wouldn't let Freya go easily, her decision would determine how everything played out. He rolled his tight shoulders. The tension coiled in him needed a release, and breaking things did no good.

Xander grinned, picking up one of their training swords. They hadn't done this in a while.

* * *

SERAFINA'S FINGERS brushed over the spine of each book. "I wouldn't have thought that the Kilrhinns would have such a treasure trove in this place."

Freya didn't either, until Garrett brought her here.

"Serafina, is there anything wrong?" Freya asked. Maybe there was something she could help her with. Maybe the Kilrhinns had caused a fuss again about the Lhianne food that was served lately.

Serafina gave her head a small shake. "There's something I'd like to talk to you about." Somehow, it sounded ominous from her lips. Right now, Serafina looked as if she'd aged years, exhaustion in the dark rings under her eyes. Serafina frowned as she looked Freya over. "How are your wounds? I thought you'd be resting."

"I can't stay in bed for too long," Freya admitted. "I get restless."

Serafina slid a book out from a shelf and flicked its pages with a thumb.

Freya waited, having a feeling that whatever was coming was going to be important.

Closing the book, Serafina placed it back on the shelf and

released a sigh. "Let me be blunt—I offered our terms for agreeing to the alliance with the Kilrhinns."

Freya's heart raced. "Okay."

Serafina sank down on the seat opposite her. "We want you, Freya."

Freya blinked. "W-what?"

"What I simply offer is that you come back with us to our village. We understand you better. You could even make it your home."

Is that what Garrett wanted, why he brought Serafina here? So Freya could do her job and secure their alliance? Her heart squeezed in her chest.

"Your offer's very kind," Freya said earnestly. And then because she couldn't lie, she continued, "I'm sorry, but I can't go with you, Serafina."

"You'd rather stay here?" she asked, disbelieving. But then she started to laugh. "You know, I thought you might come with us, but I can't say I'm that surprised. He already treats you like his mate."

Freya gaped at her. "You—you're wrong." Wasn't she?

Serafina rolled her eyes. "Don't tell me you didn't know. I know of no other Kilrhinn here, apart from Bradis himself, who's as heavily guarded as you. And still, somehow you're constantly thrown in danger. He'll have a lot on his hands."

Freya shook her hand. Yes, he worried about her, mainly because he needed her for this job, but his *mate*? "I can't stay here either," she admitted.

Serafina arched a brow, surprised. "Oh? That would be unfortunate."

You could make it your home, Serafina had said. "Homes are for those who have the luxury."

"And you don't," Serafina surmised.

"No." There was a weight of meaning in that one word.

She couldn't have a home anymore, as long as Terrence was still out there, hunting for her.

"He would stop you." Serafina meant Garrett.

A smile touched Freya's lips. "He'd try." He couldn't stop her, anyway. He'd made a blood oath to release her.

Serafina wasn't done. "For a Lhianne, your strength is... unusual." There it was. Freya was waiting for it.

"So I've been told."

Serafina's keen gaze met hers. "Is that why you're staying here for now? Because their blood also calls to yours?"

Freya was caught. There was no point hiding now. "You once told me that Kilrhinns and Lhiannes aren't the same," she began.

Serafina gave a small nod. "I remember."

"I think we are. Not just because I'm both Lhianne and Kilrhinn. But because we both have strengths others don't understand. And we fear those outside of that circle." The Kilrhinns may not understand her as well as the Lhiannes did, but they weren't at all that different. Maybe Garrett wanted her to leave with Serafina, so they could finally secure their alliance. But even if she wanted to help them, she couldn't fulfill her end of it, because to stay in one place for too long would mean putting those close to her in danger when Terrence found her. This was her choice, and they couldn't take that from her.

Serafina studied her. "So that's your answer, then. I won't pry, or force you, like your Kilrhinn believes I'll do. I only wanted you to know you have that choice." Serafina made a move to stand, not waiting for a reply. But before leaving, Serafina turned to look back, smiling faintly. "I used to think you were soft. Easily persuaded. But I was wrong about that too, wasn't I?"

* * *

"WHERE IS HE?" Freya asked Rav, who waited for her outside the library. While she'd never considered herself a violent person, she very much wanted to have a word with Garrett. Well, lots of words. She had so many thoughts bubbling in her mind. So much she needed him to hear.

He must've wanted that alliance so badly that he brought Serafina straight to her. Maybe he even expected her to leave with Serafina to fulfill her end of the oath, getting rid of two birds with one stone. Get the job done, and get rid of the Lhianne.

Rav didn't even ask who she meant. "Sparring."

"I want to see him."

"I don't think he'd—"

She pushed him a little with the wind, and Rav raised a brow.

"Frey—"

The wind swept him off his feet. Literally. He landed on his ass. He blinked in surprise. Before Freya could utter another word, he lifted his hands up in surrender. Because she never complained much, never really fought with her magic, they expected her to yield. She wasn't going to back down. Not when it came to this.

"Hold up—I'll bring you to him. You should know, he's in a mood right now. When he's sparring, things... break." He grimaced at the word. "I won't blame you if you turn back."

"Break?" Freya echoed.

"We have to order new swords and equipment all the time." Rav led the way, past the corridors. Around her, other Kilrhinns watched. She suspected this was an area where few of those who weren't warriors entered. Rav tilted his head slightly, sliding a glance towards her. "You haven't seen him break things yet?" He had an odd look on his face.

What a strange thing to say. Freya tried to recall when

something like that had ever happened, and shook her head. "I've never seen him do that."

"He doesn't mean to, of course," Rav explained. He snorted, as if he thought of something funny. She thought he looked as if he debated whether to tell her or not. He pushed a massive wooden door open with both hands. Freya's eyes went large at how he'd done it with ease. She wondered if she could open the door herself. Her fingers traced the metal frame of the door, and when she saw the chaos inside, her jaw dropped.

Rav grinned at her. "He's careful around you. We're here, by the way."

CHAPTER 19

*X*ander didn't hold back. Garrett enjoyed testing the limits of his own strength, and Xander didn't disappoint. They had done three rounds, and by the end, they both were breathing hard, lying on the ground. Garrett had broken his second damn sword by hitting too hard. Garrett sat up. Spotting his most recent training sword on the floor now broken in half, he dragged it towards him. He picked it up, studying it.

"I thought these were meant to be sturdier," Garrett murmured.

"Will you let her go?" Xander asked. As usual, Xander asked the questions that Garrett had trouble with. Questions he'd been going over in his head since this afternoon, like a vicious cycle that only served to work him up.

She was like an ache in his chest that wouldn't go away. She'd simply taken root there, like the frosted roots of Belpav, and hadn't left. The thought of her leaving drove him mad. And perhaps the greatest wonder of it all, she was utterly unaware of her effect on him. He couldn't decide if it was exasperating or tempting. Perhaps it was both.

Garrett's jaw turned hard. Something cracked. He looked down at his hand. Ah, there went the hilt. "It's not my choice."

"It will be good for us, if she agrees," Xander said. "You've wanted the alliance for a long time." Was he trying to provoke him?

Garrett pulled himself to his feet. He rolled his neck, stretching the stiff joints.

"Another one," Garrett challenged.

He heard the door burst open, announcing their newcomer. Garrett paid no attention—he wanted to fight Xander.

Xander had no such qualms. He swiveled his head, and seeing their new visitor, he only chuckled. He met Garrett's eyes, mirth reflected in them. "Are you sure about that?"

Curiosity getting the better of him, Garrett turned to see what had caught his second's attention. His eyes swept over Freya, drinking her in. Her wavy hair was down now, flowing past her shoulders as she looked him over, green eyes wild like their forests. He thought he caught a hint of desire in her eyes, until she averted her gaze. A faint blush spread over her cheeks. He dropped the sword. "Another time," he announced.

"Thought so," Xander muttered behind him.

Garrett stalked towards her.

From the moment he met her, without even trying, she enthralled him. It wasn't because she was a Lhianne, a Kilrhinn's polar opposite in many ways. It wasn't even because he needed her to secure an alliance. It was simply her. He couldn't get the taste of her from his mind. It infuriated him. It drew him in like a magnet.

"Why are you here?" he asked gruffly. This was a training room. She didn't think to practice here, did she? "You should be resting."

He wondered what Serafina told her. He wondered what Freya chose.

Suddenly, it was as if he hadn't spent the past hour training at all. All the tension returned, drawing his body tight.

But Freya was looking at the mess behind him and her eyes went round. He groaned inwardly. They'd broken the bench. They'd need to replace that.

Considering she came all the way here, he wondered if she came to say goodbye.

Freya closed her eyes and took a steadying breath. When she opened them, fire blazed in her eyes as she met his own. She stood straight, lifting her chin up. "I can't believe you brought Serafina straight to me."

She was mad at him about *that*? He tried to wrap his head around the fact, but she kept going.

"Since she made you that offer, you thought it would make me accept. Is that what you wanted?"

He hurt her. He didn't even realize he had.

"You're not leaving," he guessed, and taking it all in, a weight lifted from his chest.

"Just because I work for you, you think that I'd do whatever it takes to do my job. So you can have your alliance," she burst out. How did she even end up with that conclusion?

He didn't understand this need, this hunger for *her*, but his control, already worn thin, snapped. She was wrong. He only knew of one way to make her understand. He kissed her.

* * *

His mouth came down on hers, stealing all thought. Her hands dropped to the hard muscles of his shoulders in surprise, and all Freya could do was hold on.

His tongue sought entry and she kissed him back, unable to resist it. Unable to resist him. He kissed her once. Twice. Until she lost count, and she didn't know where one kiss ended and one began.

His touch was warm and firm, but not enough to hurt her. He caught her bottom lip and nipped. Her knees turned weak. But through it all, he held her, not letting her fall. And she couldn't help but feel as if his kiss branded her. She shivered from his touch.

He pulled back slightly, breath touching her cheeks. The intensity of his gaze made her heart thud in her chest. She didn't understand him. It felt like he'd been trying to stay away, but to what end?

His eyes shut, as if turning something over in his mind. Without warning, he whirled around, striding towards the exit.

Immediately, with his warmth gone, she felt cold. Still recovering her breath, and willing her heart to steady, she stared at his retreating back.

Why would he kiss her and just... leave?

Only then did she notice everyone watching—those who had stopped sparring, and Xander, and Rav. Her cheeks flushed. She caught the low murmurs, and she aimed a glare at them, daring them to say a word. *Gossiping Kilrhinns*. They looked away, uncomfortable, and proceeded to get back to training.

Freya marched out the door. Predictably, Rav followed behind her. Her steps faltered when she made it back halfway. Tears stung her eyes. She swiped it away with the back of her hand. She sniffed but kept going, her chin up.

She might've driven their progress back with her declining to leave with Serafina. But eventually, one way or another, she was going to leave Maranthe. Why then, did that kiss feel like her undoing?

* * *

YAEL WAS DONE WAITING. His army was ready, and he couldn't chance that the Kilrhinns would form an alliance with the Lhiannes.

Freya survived. The pot they'd paid a caster to enchant didn't reach her. Again, she'd foiled their plans.

Katherine couldn't be trusted. Uri told him he'd found her talking to a Kilrhinn, all alone. She probably told the Kilrhinns all about them. She hadn't made a move to kill Freya. She was useless, after all.

It was a shame that Katherine's sister didn't spill any secrets of importance. Maybe he could use the brat as a sacrifice. But first, he would have to get rid of Katherine. He didn't much enjoy being double-crossed. She knew too much. She might be able to heal herself, but she was no match for his newly gained strength.

"Uri," he called on his servant. "Do what you have to do. Bring Katherine to me."

He could easily crush her lungs until she couldn't breathe. His hand closed into a fist. He could almost imagine her screams, begging him to stop. He would enjoy it. He smiled, thinking that after the lungs, he would rip her stomach apart, and then when he was done, he would feed her to his army. Oh yes, he'd enjoy it very much.

It was time to act. His army was growing restless.

* * *

XANDER FOUND HER.

Freya thought she could hide at the terrace, but it turned out she didn't shake off her guards after all. She wanted to crawl into a hole after everyone saw her and Garrett earlier. She knew everyone would probably be talking about them.

191

To her surprise, Xander carried a familiar clay pot with him. She gasped. "Is that…?"

He passed it to her wordlessly. Garrett honored his promise. She hugged it, a warm feeling settling in her chest, and set it down beside her.

"It has no more magic," Xander said. "It was gone after it nearly made a whole room combust. Luckily, we were able to contain it. No one was harmed."

Her jaw dropped. "You're joking."

He shook his head firmly. "No. I was there, too."

As much as she hated to admit it, Garrett was right about being overly cautious. She didn't know how she felt about that. She was still conflicted about him and how he left after that kiss.

He looked at her curiously. "You're angry at him."

Freya sighed. "I don't understand him."

This time, his lips pulled up in a grin. "You think you're any less of a puzzle to him?"

Her brows rose in disbelief. "He may as well have admitted that he wanted me to leave." Did he feel guilty, so he kissed her?

"It was a declaration, Freya," Xander revealed, all trace of humor gone. "When he decided to risk inciting a war because of you, he made his choice. Yesterday, he dropped all pretenses."

War? What on earth was he talking about?

"Whether you believe it or not, you're his."

"His?" she breathed out.

He smiled, a flash of his teeth showing. "His to protect. His to claim."

* * *

SHE DIDN'T COME to dinner. Garrett didn't find Freya in the hall or the kitchens.

He'd spent the day in the gardens, much to the dismay of everyone he encountered. But the gardeners were patient with him, even alluding to the flowers Freya liked. She'd have them all one way or another, but he already had something in mind for her.

He went to the upper floors, where Kane told him he found her. He found both Xander and Freya at the terrace.

Xander saw him first. His eyes dropped to the plant in Garrett's hand, and they widened a little. Xander knew what it meant.

Xander excused himself and went to him. Fortunately, Freya hadn't noticed. "You're sure?" he asked, his voice low.

Garrett had never been more certain. "Yes."

Xander laid a hand on his shoulder, grimacing. "She's still mad. Work on softening her temper a little." He hesitated for a moment. "You've chosen well. Good luck, brother." Then he left them both.

Garrett watched her. Before she had a chance to react to seeing him, he wanted to see her.

Then he noticed how close she was to the edge of the terrace, and his gut clenched. He'd heard her do this a time or two, too. "You have a habit of frequenting places where you could fall to your death."

Freya, startled, turned to face him. She recovered, an indent forming between her brows. "And you have a habit of sneaking up on people," she muttered. "The wind makes us feel safe." Her eyes dropped to what he held in his hand. She was curious about it, but she didn't pry.

"You're aware how high up we are?" he asked, unable to wrap his mind around what she just revealed.

"It gives me comfort."

A Lhianne oddity, then. Good thing his quarters were in

the upper floors, too. He grinned. "Does it?" he tested, switching to the Kilrhinn language.

"Yes," she answered in Kilrhinn without thought. Realizing what just happened, her mouth snapped shut. Another piece of the puzzle clicked into place. That was something he'd wondered about, and she'd just confirmed it.

"So you speak Kilrhinn."

* * *

HE DID IT SO SMOOTHLY, Freya didn't even notice at first. And for a moment, she'd forgotten to mask her surprise. Damn it. "Yes." She bit her lip. "How did you know?"

His eyes glinted in triumph. "I didn't." His smug smile came slow. "Interesting skill you've learnt."

Her lips sealed shut. She wouldn't tell him any more. How had she been so reckless?

"We interrogated Ignas. I realized he prefers not to use Universal, maybe out of caution since the Lhiannes arrived. So I wondered."

He held out the flowering plant, and cautious at first, she accepted it. At her questioning look, he began, "You seem to understand us and parts of our culture, but I'm wagering you don't know about these."

The flowers were beautiful. Deep purple at the center, turning a lighter pink outwards. She marveled at its vibrant colors.

"They're amaranthine flowers. Maranthe took its name from it. Do you know why?"

She shook her head.

"Our founder found the rare flower in the mountains. Trample on them, but they won't die. In heat or frost, they flourish. They're exceedingly resilient, but few survive when they're replanted. As if they choose their own home. It's a mystery how they grow in the oddest places."

She touched the tip of its petals, soft as a feather.

"Some believe they sprout from the ground where the spirit of our ancestors once laid."

"And do you believe that?" she asked.

"I'm not superstitious, Freya, but one grew from the grave of my grandfather. One day, it simply appeared."

She held the potted flowers close to her. "Why?" she asked quietly. He'd given her something so precious.

"A gift."

Because she once told him that she seldom received gifts, he'd decided to give her one. It made her heart so full, it ached. "Thank you." She didn't know what else to say. Already, she treasured it. Maybe it was even his way of apologizing.

Whether you believe it or not, you're his.

She wasn't sure how Xander came to that conclusion. She was no prize. Anywhere she'd stayed for too long put everyone around her in danger. And around Garrett, her heart was in danger, too. She didn't know when that had happened, only that she knew he had the ability to make her spill her secrets with little effort, and when he looked at her like he did now, the ability to steal all reason. Because if she were to admit it to herself, she desperately wanted to stay. But she couldn't—time was running out.

CHAPTER 20

*K*atherine stared outside the window. Below, the guards were making their rounds like clockwork. Always the same time every day. Still, watching them allowed her to think.

She should've killed Freya. But what kind of monster would that make her? One that wouldn't be able to look herself in the mirror. But then, if that were to make her a monster, what would she be now, unable to do it for her little sister?

"Katherine?"

Katherine jerked in surprise.

It was only Jess. Oh no. Jess wore a look of concern. "Are you okay? Lately you've been a little... jumpy."

Katherine sucked in a deep breath, forcing herself to relax. She didn't sleep a wink the past few nights. It felt like there was a noose around her neck that only grew tighter each day. She pasted a smile on her face. "I'm fine."

It became an automatic response now. What could she tell them, anyway? *I have to kill Freya so my sister can live. In fact, I should've done it ages ago, but I didn't.*

"That's it. You're getting a break," Jess announced. "You're not allowed to work in the clinic for the next three days."

"W-what?" she protested. "But—"

Jess' face tightened. "Make that for the whole week. I don't know what's going on with you, and I wish you'd tell us. But Trixie tells me you've taken all the workload for yourself lately." *Thanks, Trixie.*

What would Katherine do? She needed the work. Conflicted, she decided maybe she needed to go downstairs to go for a walk. Then she remembered the last time Uri had cornered her and stopped cold. She had nowhere to go.

"Jess, please," she begged. She needed to be busy. It drowned out the guilt.

Jess' expression softened, taking Katherine's hands into her own. "Most people would be *asking* for a break. What are you punishing yourself for?"

Was that what she was doing? Punishing herself? Maybe Jess was right.

Katherine shut her eyes instead, feeling the weight of her deception intensely. She didn't deserve to be here. Didn't deserve their kindness or their concern. Or their friendship. Because that's what they'd become in the short time she was here. In a place where she never thought she'd find friends. But she had to keep them all out, or her poison would taint them, too.

"Nothing," she whispered. "I just need the work."

Liar.

She felt Jess' disappointment keenly. "I see. I'll see you next week, then. Get some rest, Katherine."

Katherine couldn't have left any faster. She didn't know where she was going, only that she needed to clear her head. Her frustration mounted. Before she knew it, she was outside, breathing in the fresh air, hoping it would provide a measure of calm.

She headed to the spot by the pond—someone grabbed her, roughly dragging her, a hand over her mouth. Katherine tried to scream, but it came out muffled. She was pulled into a small space between the buildings. She tried to kick and elbow her attacker, struggling to break free. Someone hissed behind her. In the next moment, she was pinned against the wall, a black claw extending from her attacker's hand, pointing at her neck.

"It's been a while, Katherine," Uri said. All fight immediately left her.

He came for her. Instinctively, she knew. She was staring at the eyes of death.

She had to try one more time. "W-we won't need to kill Freya after all. They're—they're having trouble with the alliance now. The negotiations are falling through." She was speaking fast, stumbling over her words.

Uri only smiled. "It's too late."

If they decided they didn't need her, they would still come for Freya. "T-there's no reason to kill them! There won't be an alliance."

"Yael will use your sister as a sacrifice for my greater power. Maybe I'll be able to heal myself, too."

He started to laugh... and then he didn't. Uri's head was sliced off cleanly. Blood exploded, splattering over her face. She stared numbly at Uri's decaying body. That was what the Scourge did—they decayed when they died. But this... This was so grotesque that she emptied what little breakfast she had this morning on the pavement.

To her utter shock, Uri's head remained. "Filthy Kilrhinn!" Uri screamed. "What did you do to me?"

Kane grabbed the head from the ground by the hair. Unexpectedly, he slammed the head in the wall until the shrieks died. Blood spurted from his mouth. Then Uri sobbed. Kane studied the head curiously. Promptly deciding he was done inspecting it, Kane's eyes darted to her.

"I thought something was happening here, so I came to check," Kane said grimly, his expression so calm, it unnerved her. But then he pointed the end of his sword at her. "Katherine Rowes. I didn't know you worked for the enemy."

* * *

KATHERINE SHOULD'VE FELT fear at what she was about to face. The nerves should've rendered her speechless, unable to think or act. But it felt like a thorn, wedged deep into her, had finally been pulled free. It felt like she could finally breathe.

Kane had easily beheaded Uri, who had plagued her nightmares since she arrived at Maranthe. She knew the Kilrhinns here were strong, but until she saw one of them with her eyes, she didn't realize how close she was to giving up. Because now a seed of hope took root.

They would accuse her. She wouldn't even blame them for their mistrust.

Her eyes swept over the room. Garrett and Galen were both here. Did that mean *he* would be coming, too? As if summoned from her thoughts, Xander walked into the room. His eyes searched for hers. She didn't know what he found, but he tore his gaze away, as if he couldn't stand the sight of her. Something twisted painfully in her chest.

"Tell me, how long have you been working for them?" Galen asked her, forcing her attention back to him. "From the start?"

When she didn't make a move to answer, Galen's hand suddenly gripped her chin, tight. "If you don't speak—"

"Easy, Galen," Xander warned.

"From the start," Katherine answered hoarsely. Galen released her.

Garrett stepped forward from the shadows. He had been silently watching all this time, but it looked like he was done.

"She's a traitor, Xander," Galen hurled the words at him, disgusted. His eyes met hers. "You're a shame to your Brion kin."

That wasn't even an insult. She believed it already. She smiled, but it didn't reach her eyes. "Brion blood has been nothing but a curse."

"And so you saw it fit to bestow the curse upon others," Galen shot back. His words were a direct hit. She always knew she tainted everyone she met. Her and her sister, Rina, only relied on each other instead of others. It was a testament to how she survived the roughest of the slums on the outskirts of Maranthe that she didn't even flinch. But still, it cut deep.

"Did you poison Freya?" Garrett asked sharply, his patience snapping.

She shook her head. Somehow, her eyes found Xander's instead of Garrett's when she answered the question. "No." Because they could all doubt her, but she found she didn't want Xander to.

"Do you know who poisoned her?" Garrett pressed. He was gone for Freya, she knew. Even if she told them her side, they wouldn't believe her.

A long pause. "Do you know who poisoned her?" It was Xander who repeated the question.

She had to answer, or she'd lose him. "Yes," she choked her answer out.

Xander's eyes shuttered. She felt him draw away, and it was as if a part of her shriveled. She shared few personal things about herself. Trusted even fewer. She suspected it was the same for him.

"Same person who enchanted the pot?" Galen asked.

"I—I didn't know about the pot. Not until it was too late."

"*Who*? What purpose were you sent here for?" Garrett asked, his frustration tangible.

"All I know is his name's Yael. He doesn't want the alliance to happen. So he... He asked me to kill Freya."

She saw Garrett's hand ball into a fist. She closed her eyes, waiting for it to happen. The hit didn't come. Inwardly, she thought that if he did, it would've matched the bruises on her battered soul. When she opened her eyes again, they all stared at her, appalled. But she made herself look them all in the eye. "You can believe what you want about me, but I didn't try to kill her. I couldn't."

"The vial?" Xander brought up, his jaw hard.

She winced. He had to remember that. "That was for Serafina. To make her a little sick. I didn't want to do it," she said softly. "I thought it would be better than killing anyone."

"Why?" Xander asked, his voice so quiet, she almost didn't hear him. "Why did you do it?"

No one else had asked. Only him. In another lifetime, she wondered what they could've been.

"They have my sister," is all she said, with all the despair that touched her soul.

What she saw in his eyes made her recoil. She didn't know she could mourn what she never had. Hatred burned in his eyes. An anger so strong, she knew nothing could ever overcome it.

And then she knew. She lost him.

* * *

URI WAS CAUGHT.

Yael crushed the goblet in his hand. Such a simple task,

but Uri couldn't even bring him Katherine. He would have to gain the satisfaction of doing it himself later.

Uri served his purpose. He could use the sister instead. He pushed the doors open. The Kilrhinns were all preoccupied with the Brion and Uri. He could use that.

The girl cowered in the corner of the room. She had done this every day, even when he tried to talk to her.

"Will you give me your sweet blood, Brion?" Perhaps he could keep her alive a little longer. To kill her would be a waste, and if he did it so soon, he would need another source of healing quickly.

She was too scared to answer. He grabbed her wrist and sliced her palm and squeezed. She screamed and cried the whole way through. He had to hand it to her—she didn't break. Yet.

Ten minutes later, he headed outside to his wonderful army. He gave one simple order—to kill. And then he released the Scourge into Maranthe.

CHAPTER 21

"*H*e has a whole army of the Scourge," Katherine told them.

"The Scourge is gone," Galen snapped.

How stubborn could they be? "They're not."

"She's not entirely wrong." It was Kane who answered this time. "The talking head's body decayed. Like they've all talked about." His eyes slid to her. "How many more of them are there?"

"I don't know." She hated that she didn't know. "But Yael commands several, that means there has to be m—"

Screams erupted from the outside. *No*. What was happening?

Xander immediately checked the windows. He swore. With his speed, he was next to her when she blinked. "They're *here*. Did you plan this?" he growled.

Garrett checked the windows, too. His body was strung tight.

"They're *here*? In Maranthe?" Katherine blurted out, horrified. They didn't answer. But one by one, they all left.

She tried to rip her arms free from the bands that held her, but she was stuck.

There was nothing she could do.

* * *

Freya heard their screams first.

She was at the balcony with a book when Rav had broken to her the news about Katherine. Freya couldn't believe Katherine had tried do something like that. And if she did, she didn't even succeed. Freya needed to talk to her herself. She was so close to convincing him to bring her to Katherine, too, when chaos erupted.

"What's going on?" Freya asked. She squinted her eyes. She saw the black line on the horizon and a cloud of smoke. What were *those*?

The line drew nearer.

The wind lashed at them, as if urging them to leave. The hair on Freya's skin rose.

A thought came to her, one that she almost refused to believe, but reality was fast creeping up on them—*Scourge*.

Black hides, teeth needle-sharp, half creature and half man. The Scourge bounded towards them. The screams grew louder. There were people out there still. Freya's knees turned weak.

This... This was something she only saw in the books she read. This had to be a nightmare. Except this was real. Rav was tugging her hand. "Freya. We have to go."

Freya didn't realize that she'd been rooted to the spot, frozen in fear. A feeling of impending doom gripped her. She followed behind Rav, but still unable to help looking at the destruction behind her, smoke billowing out from houses and buildings. She slipped her hand from his grasp.

"Freya—"

Lily and Jon had just gone to sleep, and probably Serafina. Then there were Jess and Elara and everyone. "I need to warn the others!" Freya cried out.

Rav took hold of her hand again, dragging her inside. "They'll be taken care of," he said sternly. But what if it would be too late then?

She dug her heels in the ground. She called upon the earth, and dirt and soil wrapped over her feet, holding her in place. "Rav, *please*. We have to help them."

He stopped to look at her incredulously. "You're. My. First. Priority."

So be it. The wind blew dust across his eyes. She blinked in surprise. It seemed like even the wind agreed with her. She broke free and zipped across the hall. If he wouldn't help, then he'd just have to follow behind her.

* * *

THEY WERE BACK. When Garrett first laid his eyes on them, he could hardly believe it.

His fingers itched to touch his weapon. He needed to get rid of the enemy. The Scourge wasn't gone, like they'd all thought. They only went into hiding. The Kilrhinns had explosive weapons prepared for times such as these. He just never imagined they'd be using them on the Scourge themselves.

Garrett barked out orders. He wanted this to be done soon.

That was when Serafina rushed into the room, her face pale. It wasn't a look he was accustomed to seeing on the Lhianne. There was a haunted look in her eyes.

"Serafina," he acknowledged. "Now is not the—"

"I couldn't believe it at first, but then I looked out the window, and I saw with my own eyes. The Scourge is back."

She pushed her hair back with a hand. "It's just as they've said."

He caught the meaning in her words. Fury rose in him, hot and consuming. "You knew this would happen," he gathered. He gritted his teeth. He needed to keep his raging temper in for a little longer—he'd use it to kill the enemy.

Xander, who was beside him, took a step forward, and then he was behind Serafina, the tip of his dagger touching her neck. "One move, Lhianne. One wrong move, and you're gone." The threat in his voice made Serafina freeze.

"Why did you come here?" Garrett demanded. "Did you have any intention of forming an alliance with us?"

Serafina released a shuddering breath. Clearly, she didn't intend to fight back. "I came here to test if we could trust you."

His eyes narrowed. "And yet you didn't tell us any of *this*."

"Would you have believed us?" Serafina shot back. "You Kilrhinn, so set in your ways, you'd rather not believe. You'd rather criticize things you don't understand, because it suits you."

"A test," Garrett repeated flatly. He wanted to hurl something into the wall. "And you thought this test was necessary. For what purpose, Serafina?"

"Another war may come soon. We needed to know if we could trust you. Your words mean nothing by itself, Kilrhinn. We had to know what your actions tell us about you. We need to know if we could count on you when the Scourge came back." She paused. "And see if you'd sell out an ally, when you felt that you could have greater gain elsewhere."

Freya. She used Freya as a tool to test them, using her for the terms of the alliance. "When we welcomed you here, we took a leap of faith," he growled. "You spat on our hospitality and claim you wanted to test our loyalty, when the truth is you were scared to take a leap of your own, too."

Now he felt like he understood them better. Not like before when their intentions were hard to grasp. In the end, she was just as guarded as they were. Keeping her cards close, so she could use them at the right moment.

Serafina looked as though the earth rattled. She thought he didn't understand her, but he did. Perfectly. They were more alike than either of them had ever thought.

"We need you. You need us," Garrett stated. "So let's start over." He grinned, his teeth showing. "My men are out there fighting, and I don't intend to make them wait any longer. Consider this *our* test. Will you join us in this fight?"

Xander released Serafina then. Surprise hit her, and it took her a moment to recover her footing. "We have a chance to change the course of our bloodstained history. You give us a gift, Garrett." A faint smile touched her lips. Her eyes, clear and a deep, unwavering green, met his. "Yes."

That was all the answer he needed.

* * *

HELL RAMPAGED ACROSS THE CITY.

The Scourge carved into the stomachs of the Kilrhinns. The Kilrhinns were strong, but caught by surprise, all their strength and speed couldn't save them. Yael rode on the back of a creature as it sent him to the fort. All around him, blood soaked the walls and the ground. The terrified screams were music to his ears.

Yael tore through the bodies of the guards. Blood spilled, and the wetness touched his cheek. He laughed, enjoying his strength. In the back of his mind, he could feel his kin dying in their bond. Anger boiled his blood. They were fighting back. He'd make them pay.

He needed to do this fast. The surprise attack could only

last so long. No alliance could ever be made if the Lhiannes died on Kilrhinn soil.

Around him, the Scourge crowded to push inside the seemingly impenetrable walls of their fortress. On the ground was the crest of a lion and daggers, ripped and stained. Yael picked it up with disdain. "Vhenn Bradis no more." He shredded it with his claws, roaring victoriously.

Uri was alive. The connection was tenuous, but it was there. Perhaps he could still use Uri. He turned to find the tower behind him. His connection to Uri pointed him in that direction. But peeking out the window in the very same building was a woman with brown and silver curls. How lucky. "Hello, Katherine."

* * *

GARRETT WATCHED as Serafina pushed the Scourge up with the wind, and the creatures before them slammed down on the ground. Bones cracked. In time, Garrett pinned one to the ground with his body, impaling its head with a sword. He roared, thrusting the sword out and stabbing it into another head. The body decayed rapidly. Beside him, Xander pulled out his sword. Two other heads burned to a crisp. Xander wiped the sweat off his brow.

The area was clear now, except for Kane, racing towards them. From the distance, a booming sound pierced the air, followed by the shrieking screams of the Scourge. Their weapons were finally at work.

"Garrett," Kane said, his face etched into a frown as he stepped forward. "I came to check on Freya. Rav said Freya went to help the others."

Garrett counted to three in his head, hoping it would change. "Say that again."

"Freya went to help the others."

Fuck. "She's not in a safe place?"

"Rav is with her. Claims she insisted."

"She insisted," he repeated blankly. The woman made him crazy. He pinched the bridge of his nose. "His job is not to run around and follow her."

"Rav said she was fast," Kane added.

"She's a Lhianne."

Kane gave him a look. "No. Rav said she was *fast.*"

Garrett's brows raised high. No Lhianne would've been able to let a Kilrhinn struggle to keep up. Freya was proving to be full of surprises.

* * *

KATHERINE ESCAPED THE BANDS. She was still part Kilrhinn. They should've known no bands could ever hold one.

This was her doing. She should've warned them from the start.

The door rattled. Hope sprang in her chest. *They came back for her after all!*

"Xander?" Katherine called out. Her heart thudded in her chest as she waited. No response.

The door exploded and Katherine jumped in surprise. Skin inky-black, with milky eyes that stared at her as it tilted its head, the creature released a shrieking cry. With sharp, curved claws and teeth as sharp as a blade, shock made her go numb. Her legs refused to move.

The creature crawled a few steps closer, as if curious about her.

Of course the others wouldn't come for her. Maybe they even thought this would be a fitting end for her, for having betrayed them. Maybe she even deserved it.

Footsteps warned her that someone else was coming. Considering the creature didn't even turn its head, her heart sank. Yael emerged from the doorway. With his hood drawn, now she could see him properly. His features were deformed —with pasty skin, a crooked nose, and lips like they belonged to a corpse, Katherine's breath got stuck in her lungs. But his eyes—there was a cold, calculated look that sat there. A slow, gloating smile made its way to his lips. "Katherine, Katherine. I thought it was time to visit you."

CHAPTER 22

"*H*e's going to kill me," Rav muttered, looking a little pale.

"Garrett won't kill you." Freya patted his back sympathetically. "We're doing the right thing. Katherine's in this building?" she asked, staring at the tower. Freya had insisted Rav bring her to where Katherine was. She'd given him chase, tapping on her Kilrhinn speed. While everyone could escape, Katherine was locked up, unable to defend herself.

"Yes. But she's safe—" Freya didn't even wait for him to finish what he was saying. She ran inside, hurtling past those who were escaping in a panic.

"Scourge!" a woman screamed. Freya threaded past them. She climbed up the steps even quicker.

"Katherine!" Freya called out. When she didn't get an answer, she called her name out again. Where was Katherine?

"Freya," Rav warned, a hand on her arm. He caught up with her. "Katherine doesn't need—"

But Freya spotted the door that had been wrecked open.

Rav's attention flicked to the door, too, and his face transformed into a hard mask.

"Shit," she heard him murmur. Freya tore her arm free and broke into a run.

* * *

KATHERINE WATCHED as the creature moved behind Yael and sat, like a faithful guard.

Yael's claw extended and without warning, he dug it deep into her stomach.

She didn't even have time to respond. He retracted it. With a cry, she fell to her knees. She touched the wound. Blood soaked her fingers as her hand shook. She'd been lucky before, but she didn't know if she would survive this. Maybe by some miracle, she could escape and heal. But the trauma would stay.

He struck Uri with the same claw. "Pathetic," Yael muttered. He retracted it immediately.

Katherine cried out in shock. He wanted to kill Uri too?

But she was wrong. She watched, frozen in horror, as Uri's limbs started to grow, flesh knitting over bone. "You need a Brion's blood to live. How weak," Yael scoffed.

The process took a full minute, his body bent in odd angles as he untwisted, cords of muscle taking shape. Her stomach turned as Uri stood to full height. As if no damage had been done. "Thank you, master." Uri bowed.

Yael used *her* blood to heal Uri. She didn't even know that could happen. How? Katherine was going to be sick.

Yael's focus sharpened to her once more. He clicked his tongue. "I planned to let you live for your blood, but you had to take their side. Your sister will have to do."

No. She kicked and punched in a burst of anger as her

body healed. But Yael struck her again, landing a set of claws in her belly once more, and she gasped in pain.

She wasn't invulnerable. If he tortured her continuously, she could still bleed out. Along with the memories of her sister, a new one took shape, one of the Kilrhinn who had offered her the single bar of candy.

Another stab of pain hit. Spots filled the edges of her vision, her strength rapidly slipping away. *I'm sorry.*

* * *

KATHERINE WAS DYING.

Freya saw the blood spilled on the ground, saw the man whose claws stabbed Katherine, and anger surged through her chest. A burst of wind blasted through the windows of the room. The glass shattered, jagged shards flying in the air. Freya began to cry.

The man bent down to the ground, a hand covering his head, and saw her. His skin was chalky, the rings under his bloodshot eyes almost purple. He pulled his claws free from Katherine and grinned. Who was he? How could he do something so sickening? Still eyeing her, he licked the blood from his claws. Freya's stomach revolted.

The rest of his features were misshapen. The thin slant of a mouth, and a nose that looked as if it had been clumsily carved on his face. Recovering from the shock, he only laughed. He dusted the shards from his lap and pulled himself up. "Freya! This is a surprise," he said, a speculative look on his face. His shoes crunched on the shards of glass. "This makes things a lot easier. Uri, take care of him," he said, nodding towards Rav. Freya squinted her eyes. Uri? He was the server—the one who offered her the starbread.

"H-how do you know my name?" Freya asked, stepping

backwards. Her voice trembled, her eyes flicking to Katherine. She pressed a hand over her mouth, trying to stop a sob from escaping her throat. "Who are you?"

On the other end of the room, Rav had Uri in a headlock. The creature that was guarding the man lunged at Rav. Rav dodged it effortlessly, but as a result, Uri slipped away, taunting him.

"Call me Yael. To think this was all it took to get you to come to me," Yael continued, ignoring the struggle behind him.

"What do you want from me?" Freya's voice came out brittle.

"I heard about you, the Lhianne chosen to help forge an alliance between the two races. That couldn't happen again."

Again? That wasn't in any history book she read. The Lhiannes aligned themselves with the Scourge.

Rav's dagger slipped from his grasp. It landed close to Yael's feet. He didn't even notice, still preoccupied with Freya.

Rav tackled Uri to the ground. She winced. Rav could handle himself. She needed to focus. Freya eyed the dagger. She could distract Yael.

"I don't understand," she said.

To her horror, more of the Scourge had squeezed themselves inside the doorway, lining up before them. They climbed over each other, forming some sort of barrier. They were building a wall?

"The Kilrhinns wouldn't have won if it wasn't for the Lhianne traitors, of course."

Lhianne traitors? It sank in—the Lhiannes had aligned themselves with the Kilrhinns in the past. Then why was she trying to bring an alliance between the Kilrhinns and Lhiannes if they already had one? Why did the history books say otherwise?

Yael walked closer. She pivoted on her heel, pretending to trip, and landed on her ass. Her hand felt for the dagger behind her. Her fingers met cold, hard steel. Her heart raced as the skeleton of a plan crystallized in her mind.

She looked up at him. He was unusually tall for being one of those foul creatures. "It's too late," Freya bluffed. "There's already an alliance in place."

His eyes narrowed to slits. "You're lying."

Now he wasn't smiling anymore. Good. "Garrett's determined to make it work. Even if I die, he'll just find another way to make it work with them."

"It will be too late then. But Uri told me that the Lhiannes and Kilrhinns couldn't make negotiations work. Maranthe is only the first place I'll conquer. My army's already spread to a third of the city. It won't be long now."

No. Garrett flashed in her mind.

Cold, clammy fingers gripped her neck, crushing bone and strangling her. The revolting skin touching hers made her stomach turn.

He was strong. Freya couldn't breathe. But he made the torture slow. His eyes lit up—he enjoyed her struggle.

She struggled harder. She knew she was strong, too. But she never really tested the limits of her strength before, mostly because she relied on her Lhianne abilities like her mother had, and she'd always been in hiding.

They said only the strength of a Kilrhinn could pierce through the Scourge's thick hide. She was Kilrhinn, too. It was time to put how much of the Kilrhinn she had in her to the test.

"You wield the power of the earth, but you don't have control. What a waste," Yael taunted her.

She knew that was one of the weaknesses of Lhiannes—precision. While they lacked in that area, she honed it to the best of her ability. But she didn't have to rely on it alone anymore.

She kicked at him. Her fingers tried to feel for the dagger behind her, but missed. She tried again, until, finally, she gripped the cold hilt of the dagger, and prayed Rav had sharpened it to a point.

With all the strength she could muster, she stabbed it in the side of his neck, piercing flesh and bone. He was paralyzed for a moment, his eyes widening in shock. *That's right.* She remembered now. She had to sever the connection of the head to the body. That was how tales often described how to defeat one. She sliced through, but to her surprise, she saw a glimpse of skin knitting together. He shoved her back. He attempted to pull the dagger out.

A loud roar pierced the night. Garrett tore through each body, like a Kilrhinn gone wild. One by one, the Scourge lunged for him, their bodies covered his as they pinned him to the ground.

"No!" Freya screamed.

Garrett struggled. His eyes found hers.

A sharp whip of the wind slammed the bodies of the Scourge, and they flew away from Garrett. Their bodies skidded to the wall. But the half-beasts shook it off, growling. They crawled towards him again, preparing to lunge.

Then they shrieked in pain. Hands clawing on their own hide. What was going on? The smell of something burning permeated the air. Smoke rose to the air from their bodies, and the Scourge disintegrated to the ground.

She stared in shock as Xander walked towards what was left of their bodies, crushing the ash underneath his heel. She had no idea he could do that. That was one way to kill the Scourge.

"Show off," Kane called out, as he stabbed one of the creatures that had climbed over Garrett.

Garrett headed for Freya. A creature tried to jump at him once more and Freya cried out his name. He rolled out of the way. He kept his eyes on her. Another creature came at him. Why him? And why wasn't he killing them?

Realization struck her—he was coming for *her*. Even as another one jumped at him, he didn't falter. A wave of emotions welled through her.

No. Save yourself. She watched, her heart squeezing in her chest.

But her attention was ripped away from Garrett when Yael pulled the dagger free. He rolled his neck and his nostrils flared. "You've been hiding a weapon." He tossed a look behind him quickly. "They're too late." He examined the dagger. But it slipped from his grasp, as if pulled by some unseen force. It clattered to the floor. Serafina?

No. It was Lily and Jon who'd just entered. Astounded at the sight before them, they recovered as Kane called out their names.

Oh my God. What were they doing here? With a look of intense concentration, Lily and Jon stood behind the other Kilrhinns, and as a creature jumped for Kane, it was flung off immediately. They were working together.

She couldn't waste the opening they gave her. Freya scrambled for the dagger on the ground. She whirled around and tried to plunge it at Yael. He caught her hands in time, crushing her fingers in a tight grip. The pain made her cry out. Then she was on the ground, and it was as if everything happened in slow motion. Garrett lunged for Yael, knocking him off his feet.

Yael fought back, extending his claws, and slashed across Garrett's stomach. Her heart stopped. Garrett hissed in pain, but didn't draw back like she expected.

Yael sneered. "Kilrhinn filth—' Freya heard the sound of

bones crack, and the man's neck snapped in two. She stared at the blank eyes of the man that had tried to kill her.

He's dead. Freya tried to pull in deep breaths.

Garrett was alive. He was okay. She latched onto the fact to keep herself grounded. The man's body decayed in front of her eyes, and she looked away. It didn't help. The image was still burned into her mind.

Garrett helped pull her to her feet, and his forehead touched hers. He was breathing hard, a hand cradling the back of her head gently. His tenderness made her heart ache. For a moment, everything else faded. "Okay?" he asked.

Freya could only nod, unable to respond. She survived, too.

"Are you?" she asked, seeing the gash on his stomach.

"I am now." Lips touched the top of her head. But he wasn't. He was hurt. All because he came for her.

But around them, the Scourge was still everywhere. He let her go, and she felt the loss of his heat immediately. He turned around to help the others.

God. It never seemed to end. She swept a glance around her. *"Katherine."*

No, no, no.

Freya ran to her, bent down to check on her pulse. It was faint, but Katherine was alive.

Freya sobbed, holding her. She didn't know what to do. She didn't know what she *could* do. She wished she was a Brion, so capable and confident in helping others.

Katherine's lashes fluttered open. She lifted up a hand. "Why... Crying..."

"Don't die," Freya whispered hoarsely. She swiped a tear off her cheek.

Katherine's lips moved, trying to tell her something. Freya waited. "Save... sister," she said.

Save her sister?

Freya shook her head. "No. You'll heal, and you can save her. I'll help. Garrett will help."

Katherine shook her head. "Sorry... Freya," she breathed out.

"It was you," Freya murmured. "You came to me at the clinic. I heard your voice." There was so much anguish in Katherine's words that time, but now she understood.

But Katherine's lips only lifted up slightly in answer, and her eyes fell shut.

* * *

THE BATTLE RAGED ON. The Kilrhinns killed, while the Lhiannes flung the Scourge, trapped them in place, until their skin bruised and bled. Until bones ached, and until not a single creature of the Scourge was left.

Uri's head was torn from his neck by an angry Rav. He lifted his arm up in a cry of victory. In time, a black crow made a loud squawking nose, bursting into the room. It flew in circles, and zeroing in on its target, it closed its beak over Uri's hair. The crow lifted the head and flew upwards. Uri laughed as a glimmer of delight shone in his eyes. *He was alive?* How was that possible?

"Fuck!" Rav spat.

Freya chased the crow with a tendril of the wind, but birds were agile masters of flight. With a slash of wind she guessed Serafina directed towards it, it escaped, even with the wind's resistance. Flying towards the window, its figure further sped over the distance and grew smaller. Freya dropped down to the ground, her knees weak.

Uri escaped. It left a hollow feeling in her chest. But he couldn't survive long... Could he?

Outside, it had turned quiet. The Kilrhinns were warriors, capable of protecting their own, too. It seemed most of the Scourge had focused here in this area, to protect its master.

Freya stayed with Katherine until Trixie came. Seeing the grim look on Freya's face, Trixie told her Katherine would need proper care. And while Freya managed to hold back her tears this time, the skies wept.

CHAPTER 23

*X*ander found Katherine in the clinic. And while he was known for keeping his calm, seeing her state, he wished the motherfucker was alive, so he could kill him all over again.

His eyes swept over her, at her injuries, and he fought to maintain his tenuous grip on his temper. He hadn't sensed her deception at all, even though he should have. And when Katherine confessed why she'd done it, he knew not all of what they'd shared had a been a lie after all. He'd kill whoever had done that to her sister. To take an innocent and use her as a pawn, it made him itch to go on a hunt even though he'd already spent the night spilling blood.

"How is she?" he asked Jess. She'd been hard at work, along with the others in the clinic.

She hesitated before she answered. "She's a Brion. One of the few who could… regenerate."

"Regenerate?" he echoed.

"She can heal herself, Xander."

"So why isn't she healed?" Xander snapped. He didn't

know she could heal her injuries. He didn't know many things about her. This woman, who often kept to herself.

"The extent of the damage… I don't know if she can make it." Jess looked visibly upset now, but she went on. "She needs to recover. She lost lots of blood, and—"

He knew very well what the wyvern blood that ran through him did. He didn't even think twice. "Give her mine."

* * *

MARANTHE'S SUNRISE WAS BREATHTAKING. Freya went back to the gardens, unable to stand the walls indoors. The smell of death clung to her skin, and she was unable to get the images of what she'd seen tonight from her mind.

Strong arms wrapped around Freya and held her. The tension in her body immediately left her.

"You're here. I was looking for you," Garrett's voice rumbled in his chest.

She tipped her head up. "Hey." Then she saw the bandage around his torso and she remembered what had caused it. She closed her eyes as she drew in a sigh. "I needed to be here. Feel the wind. The earth." The uncertainty of her future made her feel restless.

"It's done," Garrett announced, and he looked as if a weight had been lifted from him.

She was confused for a moment, and it dawned on her. "You got it. Your alliance," Freya said brightly. "Congratulations."

His eyes warmed when they met hers, and something stirred in her chest.

"All thanks to you."

"Wasn't all me," she replied. "I'm sure you made her see the good in forming a partnership."

"But it was. Did you know Serafina was testing us?" He chuckled. "When she asked you to come with her. She's crafty, I'll give her that. She needs us as much as we need her."

She wondered where she would go now. Her job was done. She was afraid to ask, so she didn't. They didn't need her anymore. Did they still even want her here?

He let her go, and his eyes dropped to the box of candy that sat beside her and raised a brow.

"It's for Katherine," she said simply.

Garrett's brows pulled together. "I don't think visiting her is a good idea," he warned, his voice hard. "She was deceiving us all this time, working for the enemy. I wouldn't believe anything she says."

He wasn't going to tell her who she could or couldn't visit. She rolled her eyes. "She still hasn't woken. If she says she did it because of her sister, I believe her. And why would they try to kill her if she worked for them?"

"She kept all of it secret. We were in that position last night, Freya, because of her."

"She had no choice," Freya retorted. 'You didn't see her, Garrett. She was bleeding to her death, and she told me to save her *sister*. Not herself. She didn't try to justify anything she's done."

"That's because there's no way she could possibly justify it. She probably persuaded you to go into that room."

Now he was just being bullheaded. "I went there myself. No one compelled me to."

But before he spoke, her fingers touched his lips to stop him. "I know you distrust her. But after everything... Don't you think she deserves a chance to start over?"

His eyes darkened. "You don't know what you're asking of me."

"Please," she whispered. Even with his tough exterior, she knew he was kind.

He pulled in a deep breath, clearly exasperated. "What is it about you?" he murmured. At her confusion, he said, "She'll only have this one chance, Freya, and she *will* be watched. Closely."

She moved, both her arms wrapping around him. "Thank you."

"Garrett," Xander called out. The urgency in his tone brought them on high alert and they turned to him. Xander's eyes slid towards Freya. "There's someone at the gates, demanding to speak to Freya."

Freya's blood drained from her face. She knew. *He* was here in Maranthe. Her past had finally caught up to her.

"At this time?" Garrett asked. An indent formed between his brows. "Are there more of the Scourge coming?"

Xander shook his head. "No. He said his name was Terrence. Terrence Gil."

* * *

"Frey—" Terrence stopped short when he saw Garrett enter the room. Garrett could guess what the Lhianne saw—his large frame filling in the space. Terrence was... short. Maybe a hair taller than Freya, if he could guess. He wore tan clothing adorned with what looked like sophisticated stitches and markings. And a single gold pin on his chest, engraved with the symbol of an upturned leaf. Garrett didn't recognize it. It must've been the Lhianne identification of their leadership. But Terrence wasn't in their village. He was on Kilrhinn soil.

The Lhianne looked taken aback upon seeing him.

Terrence had thought he would get to Freya first. It was

just his luck. He was going to have to go through him first. Garrett didn't know who he was, but he would find out.

"I—I expected Freya, but it's an honor to speak to the Head of the Vhenn Bradis Family. Garrett, was it? My name's Terrence Gil."

Garrett didn't like the way Terrence had assumed familiarity with him so easily. Terrence had a pompous air about him. Garrett didn't make a move to sit opposite the Lhianne. He'd enjoy knocking that ego down a couple of notches.

"This is not a good time," Garrett said, clipped. "Come back another time. The Scourge has returned. My people are grieving." He turned to leave.

"The Scourge? Yes, I—wait! I'm an old friend of Freya's," Terrence explained in a rush. "She's a Lhianne. Not one of yours."

Terrence was wrong. But because Garrett was curious, he turned back around. Now this was a discussion worth listening to, if only to glean more information about the Lhianne that had invaded his thoughts, and unexpectedly burrowed her way into his heart.

He sank down on the seat opposite Terrence. "That's interesting. She never mentioned you."

Garrett watched Terrence's smile drop. "She wouldn't. We've had a bit of a… a misunderstanding, before she left. I imagine she didn't want to talk to me then, but if you let me talk to her, I'm sure we could work it all out."

A misunderstanding. One look and Garrett could tell he was lying. But Garrett indulged him, intrigued.

"I'm sure she'd like to go home. She's been gone for so long."

"From her time here, it looks like she's here to stay." This foolish Lhianne was digging himself in a deeper hole, and he didn't even know it.

"That can't be right. Not Freya. We're lovers, you see. Childhood sweethearts. I've missed her."

"Is that so?" Possessiveness slid over him. Like hell she was this Lhianne's lover. He probably told everybody the same lie. Did those people hand her over?

"You wouldn't deny us our reunion, would you?" Terrence continued, cajoling. If he was trying to appeal to Garrett's sympathetic side, he was wasting his time.

But instead, Garrett stood up abruptly. "This was an enlightening conversation," he said calmly. "Was it you?"

Terrence blinked. "W-what?" The Lhianne didn't sound so confident anymore.

"The one who hurt her."

Hearing the warning in Garrett's tone, Terrence began to backtrack. "I'm not sure—"

Garrett waved a hand dismissively. "It doesn't matter. I'm sure it's another lie that will fall out of your lips."

The mask melted away, Terrence's face twisting in outrage. That was better. Now Garrett could see just who had stepped inside his gates.

"You hand her over, Garrett, and I'll give you money. Land. Lhiannes to calm some bad weather. You've had storms, haven't you?"

His blood boiled. He wondered how often Terrence made this offer. If *this* was why Freya hid.

"It's Bradis." Garrett so loathed presumptive people.

"P-pardon?"

"You'll call me Bradis."

"Of—of course," Terrence amended clumsily. "Bradis."

The Lhianne still didn't seem to understand. Garrett sat back down, his face granite. "This is how it's going to go, Terrence. I'll find out which village you came from. I'm sure it can't be hard. And if I find out it was you who hurt Freya, who so much as lifted a hand to her, I'll make it so you can never step on Kilrhinn land again. Freya will speak to you only when she decides to. *If* she decides to."

Terrence stared at him. "D-do you even understand what I offer?" he sputtered.

"I understand perfectly." Garrett's lips curved up in a smirk, but the look in his eyes welcomed bloodshed. "You don't seem to, so let me state it plainly—you don't get to demand to see her just because it suits you."

Freya decided to stay. Not go with Serafina, even though she would've blended in perfectly with the Lhiannes. His people distrusted her, but her faith in them only made him respect her more.

Terrence only listened, dumbstruck. And because he could, Garrett added, "Freya isn't your lover, Lhianne. She entrusted me her heart, and she's all but stolen mine."

* * *

KANE WAITED for him outside the door. From his scowl, Garrett knew something was wrong. His enforcer was supposed to be with Freya, and considering she wasn't here...

"She's not in her room, Garrett," Kane said grimly. "And her things are gone."

CHAPTER 24

Freya left through the underground tunnels. She'd discovered it during the days she wandered the fort. She suspected it was an alternate route for emergencies, or perhaps supplies, but it was a path less used. Down here, they wouldn't find her.

It was dark and damp underground, and she flicked on the small light she brought with her.

Fear propelled her to move faster. She was reckless. She stayed here for too long. Terrence found her. Terrence would push his way through with bribes, and hurt to get what he wanted. And she'd led him right here, in Maranthe.

If he didn't get through Garrett, who would he ask next to find where she was? To get her?

It hit her like a pang. In the short time she'd stayed here, the thought of leaving her friends hurt. She would need to keep moving. Another week, another place to stay. And more emptiness would eat at her. And Garrett... He protected her, but she didn't understand why he went to such lengths.

She turned off her light when she neared the exit. Each step was heavy as she felt for the walls, until her fingers touched cool wood. Through the gaps of the door before her, light spilled through.

She pressed her ear against the door. She heard voices. Guards. Since when were there Kilrhinns guarding the area?

Her heart raced. Slowly, she pushed the door open and peeked behind the door. Two guards stood a short distance away, deep in conversation. Slowly, she slipped through the small crack of the door and tried to sneak past them, when—

"Stop right there."

A snag in her plans so soon. She didn't recognize the Kilrhinns before her. The first man had his arms crossed, dark hair braided, and markings all over his arms. The other had sharp eyes, a pointed nose, and long blond hair. "Pull your hood down," he ordered, warning in his voice.

When she didn't move, "Pull. Your. Hood. Down," he repeated.

Uh-oh. He sounded angry. Freya complied reluctantly.

The blond Kilrhinn observed her with a frown. He walked closer. Recognition sparked in his eyes. "You're the Lhianne everyone's been talking about. You saved Katherine."

What? "You mean Jess?"

"No, they said you gave Rav chase to look for her." His lips twitched in amusement. "What are you doing here?"

"I was just, um, going to buy some things from the markets." It was a terrible excuse. She didn't expect to find anyone here.

The first man stepped closer, eyeing her from head to toe. "Uh-huh," he said dryly. "And why are you leaving through this area?" He seemed so intimidating, she took a few steps backwards.

"I didn't want to bother anyone," she said in a small voice. Well, it was partially true.

"Don't scare her, Henderson," the blond chided.

"If she leaves without any protection, we're fucked," Henderson argued.

Not good. The situation was rapidly deteriorating. It wasn't turning out like she expected at all. She could slip past the guards... Yeah, once she could run past them, they wouldn't expect her speed—were those the patter of someone's footsteps? A heavy body knocked her breath out, and then she was falling.

Oof. When she landed, it wasn't on the rough ground. Her captor had flipped them over so that he cushioned her fall. Her hands found purchase on the hard chest beneath her.

Freya blinked. She stared into the purple eyes of the Kilrhinn who had so easily found her. "Caught you," Garrett declared, a grin casting his face from lethal to dangerously attractive. His arms wrapped around her, effectively holding in her place. Triumph reflected in his eyes, the purple rimmed by a touch of gold. "I won."

And then she realized what he meant. *I'd wager I can do it better than any Kilrhinn, even with your superior eyesight,* she once said about navigating dark places.

"My liege," Henderson said, stunned.

"We'll, ah, patrol the area further outside," the blond Kilrhinn announced. He elbowed Henderson, who grunted in response. She thought both guards looked relieved by Garrett's arrival. She heard their footsteps fade away as they spoke in hushed tones. How long until the story of their encounter would make the rounds of the fort again?

"How...?" Freya asked incredulously. Garrett wasn't supposed to find her here. She was sure she sneaked past Kane.

At the question on her face, he answered, "Someone saw you escape."

"W-what?" She was certain she didn't bump into anyone.

"Lily and Jon," he explained. "They said you looked like you were in a hurry."

Freya bit her lip. They ratted her out.

"You promised," Freya said, her hands curling on his shirt. "You said you'd let me go when it was all over. You swore an oath with your blood."

His hands squeezed her back gently. "Aren't you tired of running?"

She was. She was so weary of it. "I can't stay here," she said softly.

"Can't or won't?"

She didn't answer. "You have to let me go."

"I talked to Terrence," Garrett said.

She squeezed her eyes shut. Tired of struggling against him, she dropped her head down on his chest instead. She could hear his heartbeat. It pounded erratically, just like hers.

"He offered me money. All the Lhiannes I want."

Pain stabbed her chest. This was the same story every town she went to told her. That they were sorry but they couldn't let her stay. As was the case with her former best friend, people around her were offered gold, and sometimes, paltry silver. And it cut her that their loyalty was only worth so much. She struggled against his grip once more. She twisted and kicked, and tired of her movement, he flipped them over so that he was on top. "I didn't know there were Lhiannes that rich. Fertile land, who could resist?"

She trusted him. Let him into her heart. Let him see her for who she was, but now he was bought, too. The worst of it all, she never really believed he could be bought. Not him, who took care of his own people. Who kissed her like he needed her as much as his next breath. Who nearly died trying to save her, even though it meant that the Scourge had ripped through him with their teeth.

The back of his fingers swept over the tears that had

fallen against her cheek, unbidden, and then the gentle humor that touched his face was gone, his brows furrowing.

"Don't take me back to him, please." Her voice cracked.

His jaw locked. "I told him no, Freya," he revealed, his words heavy.

He released her then. For a few heartbeats, she waited for him to retract his statement, but he didn't. She adjusted her clothes, securing her hood, heat spreading across her cheeks. She all but declared that she thought he betrayed her.

"You thought I'd give you to him," he said, his expression dark. "Land. Riches. You think I'd have a care for any of those?" She'd made him angry.

Because everyone else had, so she thought he would too.

She screwed this up. Badly. "I'm sorry, Garrett. I thought of the time with Serafina…"

"I didn't bring Serafina to you because I wanted you to leave with her, Freya. I wanted you to decide for yourself." She stared. "I wasn't going to push what she wanted, just because they were her terms. I needed you to decide for yourself."

She was wrong about that, too. Her heart in her throat, she whispered, "I'm sorry."

"Why would someone travel across towns and villages, intent on taking you?"

Maybe he could use it against her, but this time, she followed her gut. He didn't know her past, or what she was, and still, he never betrayed her trust. It meant more to her than any oath. "Because I'm half, Garrett." A heavy weight eased from chest, her secret finally out.

He was quiet for a moment as he absorbed her words. "You mean half Kilrhinn and half Lhianne." With great wonder, she found he didn't look at her like it was anything to be ashamed of, like most had done.

"Yes." She met his eyes. "Our kind have never gotten along

because of our history. Lhiannes keep to themselves. But in our village, there was a rumor that the mix of our blood creates even more powerful abilities for both." She laid it all out for him. She wondered what he thought of her now.

"Were you lovers?" he asked.

What an odd question. "No. But I've known him since we were kids. Maybe we could've been, but he was too self-absorbed to care for anyone but himself. And then one day he came to our house and told me he wanted to marry me. I told him no, and he..." She paused, the memory of it making it hard for her to continue. "He... struck me and he nearly forced himself on me." She told their village elders, and they didn't believe her. Or maybe they did and they didn't want to inflict any punishment on their heir, born with a silver spoon in his mouth. She never told a soul about it since. Until now.

She saw his eyes blaze, and how he struggled to rein in his fury. He was angry *for* her, and she touched his arm to soothe him. "They never did anything in your village?" he asked.

She shook her head.

"He'll never bother you again," he declared. She didn't know if there were any sweeter words he could've told her in that moment. But she also knew that there was no way that could hold... Was there?

"You can't possibly control that."

He raised a brow, a corner of his lip tilting up. His eyes glinted. "Is that a challenge?"

She knew how he took challenges and fought a smile. "It's one I'll gladly take you up on."

His hand captured hers, entwining. "Stay. Become a liaison for both Kilrhinn and Lhianne. A representative for both."

Could she have a place here? A draft of wind came, gentle and soft, urging Freya forward.

In Rose Tempest, she'd always felt restless. As if the earth itself wanted to push her to find her own self. Some Lhiannes traveled a lot, until they eventually settled on a place they called home. Although she didn't want to admit it at the time, she felt like her search had ended the moment she stepped foot in Maranthe.

"Yes."

CHAPTER 25

"*W*hat is that?" Rav asked, surprising Freya.

Having officially been granted a new position, Freya's quarters had now moved, which she'd recently learned was closer to Garrett's. A week had passed since the battle. In that time, Katherine had woken up, but she kept herself away from everyone except Freya. Still, Freya was hopeful that things would return to before.

Freya was in the process of moving her things to her new room when Rav found her carrying the amaranthines Garrett gave her.

Galen was carrying a stack of books in his hand and moved his head to see what Rav was talking about. Now that her secret was out, Freya took it upon herself to read many more Kilrhinn books from the library. Kane was carrying another stack of books beside him and stared.

"Who gave you that?" Galen asked.

"Garrett."

Galen gaped. "He gave you that? He gave you amaranthines?" What was wrong with them? "And you accepted?" he pressed.

"Of course I accepted." She looked around. They stared at her, dumbstruck. "Why are you all looking at me like that?"

Kane only smirked.

"Freya... You're aware what they mean, right?" Galen asked, his voice strained. "They're a symbol of loyalty. Dedication. Commitment."

He emphasized the last word, and she tried to piece together what he was trying to say. "I'm not sure I follow."

"Freya, those are engagement flowers," Rav pointed out. "And you accepted them. You might as well have told him 'yes'."

* * *

GARRETT WAS DONE WITH MEETINGS. After he'd been through the long, tedious but necessary discussions about their new alliance, he was ready to give it a rest.

He sought Freya. After Xander had informed him where she was, he finally found her outside her quarters staring at the amaranthines she carried. When he'd given them to her, without her even knowing what they stood for, she handled them with such care.

"Freya," Garrett said.

Startled eyes met his, and her mouth opened, but no words came out. Her cheeks flushed, and he didn't know what was going on in her head, but she was someone who internalized and acted on those thoughts. Often, to his frustration, without warning. He hoped she wasn't planning on escaping again. Ever since he had offered her the new position, she had been unusually flighty around him.

Rav, Kane and Galen emerged from her room and their eyes widened when they saw him. Garrett raised a brow and the three promptly decided that moving away from the door was in their best interests. *Good choice.*

"She has enough books to build another wall in the room," Rav said, as if he had trouble comprehending the fact. "Why would anyone want a room full of musty paper?"

"Books are important," Freya declared, eyes daring them to argue further. "They're fuel for the mind." No one said a word. Smart.

Galen's eyes dropped to the amaranthines she held and cleared his throat. "I believe congratulations are in order," he said, clapping a hand on Garrett's shoulder.

So they found out about the amaranthines.

Rav grinned from ear to ear. "Congratulations."

"Congratulations," Kane added. "Although I can't say I'm surprised." The corners of his lips quirked up at Freya's bemusement. "Good luck, brother." Garrett would need it.

"W-where are you guys going?" Freya asked, panicked, when one by one, the three of them left. Garrett watched her pull herself together. It was rather amusing.

Green eyes met his, emotion making their edges flicker to a lavender color. He'd bet she didn't even realize it.

"I'm—I'm going to rest," she said abruptly. She walked in her room, expecting him to go on his own way. He never followed orders well. He gave them himself. He followed her in, too.

She lifted her hands, giving up. "Yes, come in. Make yourself comfortable," she said dryly.

"How are you liking your quarters?"

The question seemed to surprise her. "I like it," she replied earnestly. "But it's huge."

"Is that a bad thing?" He nearly knocked over a stack of books but held it steady in time.

"No, it just seems so…" She looked around. "So…opulent."

"You deserve it." She helped them secure the alliance. The first step to keeping them all safe from the storms, and from the new threat of the Scourge. If he thought he could get away with moving her things in with his, he'd have done it. But as it was, for the first few days, it was as if she had one foot out the door. As if she expected him to retract his offer.

Her eyes settled on the amaranthines she set down now, and he saw the question in her eyes.

"You... You gave me the amaranthines," she began. So she finally figured it out, too. "Rav and Galen told me what they meant." He caught the current of tension in her voice. "Did you know?" She asked the strangest things. Of course he knew. He wanted her to know there was never going to be another woman who could match her wit. Her courage. Her heart.

But it seemed like she wasn't done with her questions. "Why did you give them to me?"

* * *

"I GAVE THEM AS A PROMISE." Freya listened, unsure of what his words meant—and she needed to know. Needed to hear it straight from his lips.

Unfazed, Garrett stepped closer and his eyes, heated, made her pulse quicken. "I wouldn't betray you, Freya. I'd cut my own arm first."

Pinned to the spot, Freya wondered, not for the first time, how he'd read her so easily.

"Everyone else has, haven't they? That's why you ran," he continued, digging his point in further.

Every single one. And while part of her didn't believe he was capable of it, still, she was afraid. Fear had ruled her every decision, and she was so tired.

"Did they take the money? What else did they take in exchange for your head?"

Her throat tightened. "I know they did it out of desperation." Her best friend had a debt, and Terrence offered to pay it.

"And here you are, trying to justify it," he scoffed.

He pulled her close, his palms easing down on her arms. Never too rough when it came to her. Always with deliberate carefulness.

"I've never met a Lhianne like you. So hellbent on planning an escape. On forgiving those who don't deserve you."

"I've never met a Kilrhinn like you, either," Freya shot back. "You assigned me guards without asking. And you... You kiss people and leave them hanging."

His brows furrowed. "How many Kilrhinns have you kissed?"

"Just you," she murmured.

He muttered something under his breath. "There's nowhere to run, Freya. I won't let you." He sounded as if the thought of it drove him to the brink of insanity. It was because he didn't let her go that she was still here.

"I don't want to run," she admitted in earnest.

He seemed so determined to keep her. She'd never imagined she'd matter to anyone, least of all him. Her rock, keeping her steady, even through the doubts and accusations thrown at her. He'd caught her, back when she climbed that wall, only to persuade her to stay. To think that for a moment, she'd thought he would drop her when he was offered riches. Expected it, even.

"Your eyes," he muttered.

What was wrong with them? She turned to the nearest mirror. Her reflection stared back at her. Her eyes had shifted to a purple hue.

"You've neglected the other half," he remarked. "Now it's wanting to come out."

He was right. Her father had initially attempted to train her in combat, but she was more interested in being able to bend the wind and feel the ground ripple under her feet. Occasionally, her senses heightened, and she used the burst of speed to help her move faster. But it was still a part of her she hadn't explored well. "It does that so rarely," she admitted, a little embarrassed that he'd caught it.

His hand dropped to her waist. A light touch, but it felt as if no layers stood between them. "There's much to learn about us. But our eyes shift in color when we're on the hunt... and when we hunger for our mates."

The purple glow faded from her eyes, but her senses were still sharp. She saw desire in his eyes, but it was more. Something far deeper and shattering. A thread of excitement coursed through her.

He was unshakeable and sure, and right. "Is that what I am?" she finally asked. Hopeful. Torn. The uncertainty that ran through her was almost her undoing.

The way he looked at her, possessive and longing, made her heart stutter in her chest. "If you'd let me," he answered.

He'd all but told her he was hers. Wanting to bind himself to her, if she wanted it, too. His admission wrapped all over her.

"I'm not sure I know how," she confessed softly. What a mess she was. She'd never let anyone in before, and she'd landed right in Maranthe, into his hands.

In answer, his lips brushed against hers, as if asking for permission. When she didn't pull back, his lips coaxed hers open, and she surrendered. His tongue sought hers, claiming. After nearly losing him, after she thought she'd never see him again, he was right here.

Drunk on his kiss, she kissed him back with the same desperation that rose within her. She needed to feel his skin against hers.

He pulled her close, her body against his and he groaned in satisfaction. His fingers grazed the sides of her breasts, teasing. His touch alighted her nerves, making her lightheaded.

She tried to pull up his clothes, but failed and he caught her frustrated cry in his lips. She thought she heard something crash. He swore under his breath. Then her back was pressed to the wall, his lips blazing a path down her neck. His hands on her butt, she was flush against him. She moaned, low, at the back of her throat.

He tried to untangle the ties that held her dress together and growled. He ripped them apart in frustration. Freya gasped.

"My dress—"

"I'll get you a new one," he said, the savage look in his eyes making the protest die on her tongue. His eyes ran over her, like a physical touch.

His knuckles slowly ran over her ribs, to her breasts, the pads of his thumbs running circles around her nipples. The slow, agonizing torture was too much to bear. He tugged one and the bite of pain and pleasure that followed made her cry out. He closed his mouth over the other nipple and sucked.

It wasn't enough. It was too much. "Garrett, please," she breathed out.

"Please?" he echoed. The rumble in his chest sent a bolt of heat through her.

"More." This was what he reduced her to. She couldn't say any more.

His eyes darkened. She wanted him to let go with her.

His arm swept aside all the books from her bed. He lifted her and set her down.

Suddenly, she wondered what he thought of her. She never had a particularly curvy figure. Her hips weren't as busty as Katherine's, or even Elara's. His hand touched her chin, lifting it gently. She met his eyes, now darkening with desire.

"Never met a woman more enticing," he murmured. "What you do to me…"

He kissed her again like a man starved. All doubts fled.

She didn't have much of a chance to catch her breath. She didn't want to. She matched his hunger, one she thought would be sated by his touch against hers, but only to be stoked again. Like a flame that only burned hotter.

"Freya…" Fingers grazed the swell of her breasts, tracing a path downwards. She could only watch, her cheeks flushed. His lips brushed against her neck, light and soft, then downwards, kissing her stomach. Her hand tangled against his russet hair, soft to the touch.

He watched her reaction, eyes hooded. His mouth came down on her. She cried out, pleasure so intense, she lost all capacity for thought. His hand laid flat on her stomach, stroking the tender skin and keeping her in place. Her climax hit her, delicious heat curling all over her body. She cried out.

They were both breathing hard when he rose over her.

"I need you." Hearing the urgency in his voice, watching him lose control because of *her* was heady.

She grinned. "Me too."

His eyes turned warm and he chuckled, his hard length pressing against her stomach. He fumbled for the clothes that he'd tossed aside, and slid on protection.

He went back to her, eyes running over her once more.

"Are you sure?" he asked, and she caught a hint of concern in his eyes.

"Yes." Lightly, she touched the bandaged wound over his torso and frowned. "Are *you* sure?" She was only mildly teasing, but she didn't want to make his injuries worse.

He snorted. "I've survived worse, Freya." But the glint in his eyes told her he took it as a challenge.

He thrust inside her, filling her. He was torturously slow.

Careful. She didn't want him to be careful. Not in this. Nails dug into his back and she arched hers. He growled, pulling back and slamming back in with rougher strokes, less controlled this time. Need mounted higher, until his hand found the nub in her center and his thumb rolled over it. She came apart, clenching around him.

Waves of pleasure washed over her. His own release followed as he filled her, wild and untamed. Pleasure crested and went on, and then she couldn't speak. Couldn't think.

Spent, Freya had never felt more relaxed. With a kiss on her shoulder, he positioned them so that she was draped over him. She dropped her head on his chest. She'd went and fallen for this Kilrhinn, terrifying to so many, but not to her.

Her eyes swept over the room, stunned.

Her lamp had fallen over, some books knocked over as if someone had just ran through it. Oh, they made a mess of the room. Laughter spilled from her lips, unbidden.

* * *

FREYA LOOKED AT HIM, affection blooming in her chest.

She lightly ran her finger across the scar along his face. She'd never had the courage to ask. "Will you tell me about it?" she asked, hesitant, and braced herself.

She thought he wouldn't answer.

"My stepbrother tried to overthrow me." His admission made her gasp.

"I woke up to find him holding a knife to my neck, saying I didn't deserve to lead the Vhenn Bradis Family."

Oh God.

"Before he got to slit my throat, Xander saved me." His hand squeezed her hip. "But not before my brother carved a reminder onto my face."

"I'm sorry," she whispered. What was it like, she wondered, to not even be able to trust your own brother?

His face hardened. "Don't be. It's been a long time, Freya. But it continues to remind me to never let my guard down so easily."

He didn't stop her and watched as she kissed the scar lightly, wishing she could take the pain of the memories away.

His hand swept over her back. "Freya," he said. "You tempt me again." His voice had turned rough.

She bit the inside of her cheek to keep from smiling. He did that a lot—made her heart so full, she couldn't contain it.

Fingers touched her face, the scratch on her cheek, and the bruises on her neck that had now started to fade. "Thought I'd lose you then," he said, his face grim at the reminder.

Uri escaped. Freya knew he was working with someone else, too. "I don't think it's over yet," she said. It had been an unspoken fear, but she needed him to understand that it wouldn't be easy with her.

"I'll be here even after." His unwavering trust in her rendered her speechless.

She glanced at the amaranthines again, wondering what it meant for them.

"It means I'm yours, Freya. As much as you'll have me." She didn't even have to ask.

She knew the kind of love her parents had. She used to wonder if she'd ever find it.

His body tensed, and she realized he waited for her response. And because the depth of what she felt for him was too overwhelming to put into words, she didn't know how to properly express them.

"I used to think it was because of the blood oath that you felt you were honor-bound to protect me," she blurted out.

But mates bled and risked everything for each other, and she realized he'd done so from the start.

At the retort on his lips, she placed a hand on his mouth to hush him.

"I know better now. You never cared that I'm a Lhianne. Or that we do things a little different. You only ever saw me." And that mattered to her more than anything.

"I'm yours, too," she declared, the words stamped on her very being.

She watched as triumph flared in his gaze, golden flecks against the deep purple, and his mouth came down on hers once more, stealing her next words.

And while he held her, she didn't know that Rav, Kane and Galen went to tell Jess about the amaranthines. By morning, the whole fort knew.

EPILOGUE

There was nothing but complete darkness.

Without warning, a door creaked open, and a single torch lit the room. Uri trembled, his body now miraculously healed. He didn't get this far without respecting whoever held power. He went on his knees.

The man before him was young, his hair dark. Like Yael, his eyes were the soulless black of the Scourge's. He gripped a staff, but he by no means needed it to walk. He almost held it like it wielded magic of its own. *This* was power. Far greater than Yael's. Far more terrifying.

"Who are you?" Uri found himself asking.

"I am Zed. Where is Yael?" the voice asked smoothly.

He knew about Yael? Uri slumped. "He's gone. The Kilrhinns killed him." They underestimated their strength, especially now, working side by side with the Lhiannes. If only Katherine had done her job... He had a bone to pick with the Brion. She survived, too. After what *he* went through, the Kilrhinns were able to protect her. She was a traitor.

"He became impatient," Zed said. "It's unfortunate that the Lhiannes decided to side with the Kilrhinns."

"It's too late now," Uri replied bitterly.

"Who said it was?" Zed snapped. "There was no need to target Maranthe so soon. You poison the people's minds first, making them lose faith in their leadership."

That kind of plan took time. It also took a calculating mind, sharp as a whip, to execute it. Uri considered him carefully.

"Since I gave you mercy, you'll do one thing for me," Zed continued. He smiled, pointed teeth showing.

Uri swallowed, his throat dry. "A-anything you want, master."

* * *

"FREYA, THIS IS A TERRIBLE IDEA," Rav began. Still, Freya walked briskly. "If he finds out—"

Her steps faltered. "Will he find out from you?" she asked, tilting her head towards him. He was her friend. She knew his loyalty to Garrett was one forged by blood and battle, but in a way, she had also earned his. Besides, this was something she had to do for herself. Garrett had shielded her the first time, and only now had she realized that by doing so, he'd freed her from her worst fear.

"He won't find out from me," Rav said, and he sounded almost wounded. "But he *will* find out. You know how these things go."

Someone always blabbed. There were no hiding secrets around here. Freya pushed the door open to the meeting room.

Terrence Gil sat on a chair, soft leather on ornately carved wood. He stood up when he saw her. He almost did a double-take. She could guess what he saw now—clean clothes, her hair neatly braided to the side. No longer cowering. Freya had started to make some of her own clothes in her spare time and enjoyed it. His eyes ran over her, and a slow smile spread over his lips. Disgust crawled down her spine, but she resisted the urge to show it. "So you've finally decided to surrender yourself," Terrence drawled. "I'm glad you came to your senses."

"Terrence, what are you doing here?" Freya asked. It wouldn't be long until Garrett found out. She didn't have much time.

Her response took him aback for a moment. "I came to see you. To take you back. You don't belong here with these Kilrhinns."

As usual, he appeared to be delusional. "You should go," Freya said in warning. Face cast by the light of the fireplace, she observed Terrence. He wasn't much taller than her, but somehow, he didn't seem quite so big now. Not as tall as the Kilrhinns she spent her time with. Garrett towered over her, and yet he never made her feel small.

"Excellent, the horses should be—"

"No," she cut him off. "I'm not coming with you." She was proud her voice didn't shake.

"No?" Her response clearly baffled him.

She stood straighter. "You don't have power over me anymore." She'd long wanted to say those words to him. Only dreamed of saying them to him.

His smile froze. "Freya, sweetheart—"

"You terrorized me. Hunted me. Hurt my friends. All because I refused to marry you." She found that now, facing him, instead of fear, anger took place. All the anger she never got to throw at him. "You don't get to call me that. I found my mate."

She watched as his eyes widened. "Your *what?*"

She didn't answer him. She didn't owe him a thing.

Terrence's lips thinned in displeasure. "The Kilrhinn," he spat. He crossed the distance between him. His hands gripped her arms, and he shook her.

Immediately, Terrence's attention was caught by something behind Freya. He released her, as if touching her burned him. That was when Freya heard the movement behind her.

Well, it looked like she was caught.

"My liege," Rav said in a hurry, "Freya—"

"—and I will discuss this later," Garrett's dark voice said in warning. He stopped beside her. But his eyes were fixed on Terrence. "I was enjoying the conversation, but you put your hands on her." His eyes glimmered in the light. "It seems you're more of an idiot than I'd realized."

Terrence's mouth moved like a fish's. "I—I beg your pardon?"

One second Garrett was next to her, the next Terrence yelped in pain, his fingers bent out of shape. "I'll count to sixty," Garrett said conversationally. "By the time a full minute is over, you need to be out of the fort."

Terrence only gaped at him.

Garrett wasn't done. "You thought I was kidding before, Lhianne? Right now, my men have disarmed yours. No men, no horses." His lips curled up, smug. "If you leave now, you'll still have them. If you don't, I can't guarantee when you walk out, they'll still be there..." Garrett's eyes dropped to Terrence's hand. "Or that you'll leave with your limbs intact."

Terrence cradled his broken fingers, wide-eyed. "I can't believe this."

"Fifty-nine."

Terrence looked to him, then to Freya. As if she'd help. "You're—you're joking!"

"Fifty-eight."

"Freya, he's insane."

"Fifty-seven."

"Your *mate*? You've gotta be joking me. Come back to Rose Tempest, Freya."

She was done talking to him. "You should go, Terrence. Don't come back."

"Fifty."

There was a cracking sound, then a snap.

"My—my knife! How did you get that?" Terrence shrieked.

Garrett had snapped the weapon in half. Impressive.

Garrett only flashed his teeth at him. "Forty-five."

Terrence scrambled backwards toward the door and tripped over his feet. "You're all crazy." He stood up again and stumbled, but he was already running out.

They watched as Terrence shouted at his men to leave.

Freya threw Garrett a look. "How did you get here so fast? I thought you were teaching Lily and Jon how to tackle."

As part of the Lhiannes' agreement to help the Kilrhinns in the storms, after discussing it at length with Serafina, Lily and Jon had asked to stay, along with other Lhiannes who were going to help the Kilrhinns in Maranthe. Freya was secretly glad.

Garrett simply shrugged. "They're fast learners."

"He can run fast, for a Lhianne," Rav remarked as he watched them ride their horses at breakneck speed. With his forearms, he leaned over the window.

"I'm a Lhianne too," Freya said, rolling her eyes. "I can give you chase."

"But he's bigger," Rav argued.

Garrett rubbed his jaw. "He was properly motivated."

"I gotta go make sure he doesn't come back." Rav smirked as he left them in the room.

With a sidelong glance at him, Freya lifted a brow up. "Did you have to go that far?"

"Yes, I did," he replied without skipping a beat. "Don't tell me you didn't enjoy that."

"I would've handled him."

"You would've, but I wasn't going to watch him put his hands on you," he said gruffly. "He'd done enough damage, Freya."

Touched by his concern, she leaned on him, and he linked his arm with hers. "Thank you."

Garrett's eyes were thoughtful. "Rav kept it a secret. Kane looked the other way. I'd ask what you've done to my men, but you've changed me, too." He didn't sound angry at all. In fact, he looked at her like he'd won a prize. "I believe you just claimed me as your mate."

While she accepted him, she'd just declared her claim on him in front of another, and his on her.

Then he kissed her, her arms around his neck, pulling him close, all thought of Terrence forgotten.

And they told tales of the Lhianne who ran with his tail between his legs. Some said Garrett had burned him simply by looking at him. Some wondered if Xander was involved. Some said Garrett held the Lhianne over the window while he begged for his life. And while more rumors about the Vhenn Bradis Family's leader spread, they never saw the Lhianne again.

ABOUT THE AUTHOR

Mira Gracen writes Romance with strong heroines, unapologetically smitten heroes, and a sprinkle of magic and danger to keep readers guessing. She currently resides in Australia. When not writing, she loves reading Fantasy Romance, Paranormal Romance, and getting lost in her daydreams.

To keep up to date with new releases, snippets and relevant publishing updates, please join my newsletter at: miragracen. com/newsletter.

facebook.com/MiraGracenAuthor

LEGENDS OF KILRHINN (BOOK #2) - BLOOD'S TAINT

Blood's Taint coming soon in 2023.

* * *

To help save her sister, she'd betrayed him. Now she needs his help.

Branded a traitor by the Kilrhinns, Katherine Rowes is determined not to let anyone in. Having been freed from the hands of a powerful enemy, she now works as Maranthe's medic. But when she learns of a clue that may lead to her sister who was taken from her, she gets help from the devastatingly attractive warrior who seems to loathe her... Xander Altea.

He once trusted her.

Wyvern-kin and trusted second of one of their fiercest warlords, Xander is a Kilrhinn warrior who trusts few. But when the woman who once betrayed them reveals her plan to save her sister, he accepts his duty to keep an eye on her. Only Katherine isn't like what he thought at all, and beneath her tough shell is a woman hurting. This time, he'll do everything he can to keep her safe.

But as a new enemy approaches, they must race in time against the evil that threatens to destroy them and dig its roots into their city.

ACKNOWLEDGMENTS

For years I've had the story of Warlord's Oath in my head, and it's so surreal that it's finally here. Real characters. Real worlds.

Thank you Dj, for helping make the book what it is. It's a lot better because of you.

Thank you to my sister for supporting me in everything.

Thank you, reader, for giving this book a chance. If you enjoyed reading Warlord's Oath, please consider leaving a review. For however long you've spent with the world and the characters I love, I appreciate you. :-)